MASTERS OF
VENGEANCE

ALSO BY ALAN G. DAVIS

VENGEANCE OF A DIFFERENT CALIBER
MASTERS OF VENGEANCE
DICKENS BLACK PENNY BOOK STORE

MASTERS OF VENGEANCE

by

Alan G. Davis

iUniverse, Inc.
New York   Bloomington

Masters of Vengeance

iUniverse books may be ordered through booksellers or by contacting:

iUniverse
1663 Liberty Drive
Bloomington, IN 47403
www.iuniverse.com
1-800-Authors (1-800-288-4677)

ISBN: 978-1-4401-1353-6 (pbk)
ISBN: 978-1-4401-1430-4 (ebk)

Printed in the United States of America

iUniverse rev. date: 1/9/2009

For my family: there are no others like them.
Francine, Jim, Jonathan

In Memory:
My Dad, Nate, who loved a good mystery

CONTENTS

"Vengeance started from the primitive notion that a human life is a vulnerable thing, a thing that can be invaded, wounded, violated by another's act in many ways. For this penetration, the only remedy that seems appropriate is a counter invasion, equally deliberate, and equally grave; vengeance to be sure."

-- Niccolò Machiavelli - 1498

FORWORD

Marco Polo wrote in the thirteenth century, that a Singhalese monarch owned a pale colored pink diamond, seven centimeters long, and as thick as a man's thumb. Polo's personal account of this diamond, translated into the English language reads as follows:

> "Kublai Kahn, the immensely powerful and most feared emperor of Yuan China, learning of this prize stone summoned me. At this time, I served in several high-level Government positions for the Empire. Kahn conscripted me to seek out the
> Singhalese King and offer for the gem stone – "the value of any city he chose."
> After many days of preparation, the arduous journey began. Many weeks later having arrived at the gates of the enormous castle, we were met with friendly welcome and invited to camp upon the castle grounds.
> Three days had passed when finally I was beckoned and granted audience before the ruler. I, Marco Polo, along with the General-of-the-Guard and two commanders to bear witness, we met with the Singhalese monarch at which time I personally presented Kublai Kahn's generous offer for the pink diamond.
> The Singhalese ruler seemed amused; he then beckoned his consuls for a private consultation. Many moments later, the monarch called me and my witnesses to come forward, at which time he voiced his refusal.
> On document parchment the king personally hand-wrote: "Great Kahn of the Mongols, your lavish proposition is declined. Furthermore, let it be known, if you placed all the treasures of the world at my feet, I would not part with this jewel." His signature and great seal imprinted in red wax over red silk ribbon attested to the genuineness of the king's document.
> We were then given fresh supplies, and several horses to replace those that had gone lame from the original journey."

-- Marco Polo, 1280

CHAPTER ONE

London, England
October, 2005

In the warmth and luxuriousness of his Ebury Street Flat, Harry Fellows settled comfortably into his leather easy chair and sat motionless; he was thinking about his friend's earlier phone call. To Fritz Barrow, it had been an intuitive assumption even before ringing his own long time friend, that Harry Fellows would take part in the scheme.

Barrow figured that since Fellows had worked the other side for so many years, wouldn't that in itself make the success of his plan even more attainable.

Harry Fellows had also observed closely the downside to many failed get rich opportunities by simple details being overlooked that would have transferred failure into riches – illegal or unlawful as they might have been.

It was apparent that Fritz Barrow understood Harry's expertise fully enough to want to solicit him for the part he was to play and it was the realization of this by Harry that would give him the push to say yes.

Though amused by the notion of taking part in a grand theft, Harry still felt the need to show a bit of resistance. "*Does resistance really matter? Do I need to ponder any reasoning to reject Barrow's offer? In any event,*" he thought, "*it was they who double-crossed me and sent me packing.*"

It was but a few short years ago that Harry Fellows had dreamed of being top man in the fraud, forgery, theft and other criminal-acts section of Lloyd's of London. It was more than just a step-up the ladder that he had looked forward to - the move would have given him what he loved most about his profession – the independence to apply his own theories and conclusions. He would become chief guardian of the most effective insurance investigative unit in all Western Europe. But on a particularly chilly but sunny morning in November his dream-move burst into nothingness, as a rather puzzled Harry Fellows sat before a panel in Lloyd's Windsor executive conference office whose appointed spokesman told him he was to be given an instructor's post, not overseer of the newly created section as previously promised.

"To be straight forward to the point Harry, the plan for the new section has been, forgive the poor choice of word, dumped. Harry old boy, you know that an instructor's post here is important. It's something like spies teaching spies. Give it a whirl old boy."

That was how Miles Jamison, the Board's headman had put it. "We need to train the new bright boys Harry. Think about it. Forget the new section, it never would have worked."

"Miles, I've just thought about it," said Harry as he got up from his chair."

Miles Jamison said, "Harry, you can't bloody walk out on more than twenty years."

"Just watch me Miles."

"Harry, don't be rash. You could use a long holiday. Take a cruise… Mediterranean… Greek Islands. Get involved with a woman again; get married, you're a handsome guy. And Harry, after you've calmed down, and reconsidered the position whenever that might be, please remember, we'll always have a place for you no matter when you might decide to come back."

Almost immediately, an angry Harry Fellows told Miles Jamison and the board to stuff their offer and walked out of the conference room infuriated at their decision. Fellows had wondered then, but had no means of actually finding out whether the scraping of the new section and the promotion was rejected because of personal reasons or possibly because he would be getting too close to the core of power. "*The bastards deceived me, and the motive doesn't matter*," he still felt outrage as the events once more crossed his mind as he sat in his living room.

Now his silent voice was shouting what his friend Fritz Barrow had said on the phone earlier: "This is the one Harry, the grand opportunity. You can now even the score with Miles Jamison."

Harry removed a long thin cigar from a polished malachite humidor, turned it slowly through the yellow-green flame of a matching cigarette lighter, and drew deeply. He enjoyed the luxury of the fine Havana tobacco and sensed a feeling of calm overtake his agitation. He rounded his lips and carefully exhaled the gray smoke upwards into a miniature jet stream. Though the cheery implications of Fritz Barrow's scheme was quick in coming, Fellows fancied letting his brain imagine the slow terrible pain such a conspiracy might bring to those deceptive masters at Windsor Headquarters.

*   *   *

Investigating criminal fraud was Harry Fellows'profession. It was what he loved and knew best, he had never thought about pursuing another career. But when Lloyd's asserted their departing punch that sent him reeling through the exit door, Fellows had no choice but to take hold of his ego, and choose the next best alternative to his selected trade. And so it was, with great resolve and hope, that he merged stiff and alone into London's hazardous sea of private eyes.

He wasn't part of the private eye establishment very long before he inexorably discovered that business firms seeking topnotch investigators like himself, sought only a recognized handful of the well-entrenched. As a result, desirable situations that he sought had become a dwindling commodity. Yet Fellows, who never pretended to be a prima donna, did know by the strength of his own experience what it was he did not want as a private eye: trilby hats pulled down low and dark-colored raincoats - long nights standing in doorways in the cold - extremes of loneliness and self–deprecation, lack of sleep, a fear to relax against lurking hostile opponents. There were plenty of intrigue minded, inconspicuous chaps to handle the lucrative payoffs those gloomy misadventures had to offer. But luckily for Fellows, some of his newly acquired colleagues faced with the same presented dilemma, did kindly and skillfully guide their new constituent into a proper, if non illustrious direction.

Fellows, as unimpressed as he was with what they referred to as "new wave cloak and dagger," had to admit that the nature of the assignments he undertook allowed his emotions to stay intact, plus he slept soundly at night. And as strange as it might seem, he actually became friendly with many of his clients.

A thin drizzle began to fall; the coziness of Fellows' flat seemed to magnify the dreariness that was outside. He pulled down the open sash windows leaving it slightly ajar for the cigar smoke to find its way out. And as he gazed out the window, he pondered the realization that there was a time he actually enjoyed this cheerless weather. *"Go easy old boy,"* he thought and continued to puff the cigar he held between his teeth, mumbling: "Damn weather, bloody British; spend half their lives trying to keep warm and stay dry."

Consoled by the vision of his surroundings, he rubbed his hands together in a gesture that suggested he had just come in from the miserable outside. He then went to the kitchen where he pan grilled four strips of bacon and boiled a four minute egg. He prepared a tray with everything he needed for a leisurely breakfast, and returned to the living room. He carefully placed the tray on top of his desk and lowered himself in his chair with a satisfying sigh as odors of toast, bacon and egg, augmented his hunger.

Fellows inspected his original Victorian desk as he stirred the tea. Nothing lay strewn about - everything fit orderly into drawers and desk accessories that fulfilled their purpose. The new telephone, forest green, was smarter than the white one he turned back to the telephone company; there were two books, a mystery novel he bought at a second-hand book shop in Chelsea, and though old and somewhat beat up, a copy of Dag Hammarskjöld's book 'Markings'. 'Markings' was held upright between two miniature nineteenth century green and white porcelain owls. Contemplatively, Fellows touched the narrow memoir. *"He was a professional, only he forfeit the sanctity of home and family to help make the world a more tolerable place to live- did I forfeit my home and family to the mysteries of human greed? I wonder?"* He had been reading some of his favorite passages in Hammarskjöld's book when Fritz Barrow rang earlier from New York City. Fellows had answered straight away:

"Harry here."

"Hello Harry, it's me, Fritz," the voice from the handset said cautiously.

"Barrow dear boy," Fellows answered with a pleased tone. "Good to hear from you. How goes it? Where the devil are you?"

"I'm here in New York City, Harry. It is extremely important that I speak to you now, is anyone around?"

"It must be past midnight there, if I'm not mistaken. Well then, bloody get on with it," Fellows said with spirit. "There's no one here, who would be here this early anyway? But what's with the covert sounding voice?"

"Harry, there was no way I could get to sleep since deciding to phone you."

"Bloody hell, Fritz, please don't tell me you've got bloody cancer."

"To the contrary, Harry, I haven't felt better in years. So please just listen, and try hard not to say a word until I am finished."

"Sounds a bit serious, I must say, but I agree to be quiet," Fellows said with brows lifted, a semblance of a grin across his lips."

"Harry, several weeks ago I received my quarterly copy of the Jeweler's Keystone. As you know, it's a monthly trade magazine that covers the goings on in the jewelry industry. In it was an article about an important diamond that surfaced out of South America; Argentina to be exact. They call it the Singhalese diamond. The New York jewelry firm of Vanlo and Eugêne are going to manage the eventual sale of this unbelievable stone, brokering for certain persons not revealed in the article. In charge of the sale is a long time employee of Vanlo and Eugêne; his name is Ernst Gormann. Gormann, well-respected in the industry at large, is an important cog in Vanlo and Eugêne's lucrative diamond business. Gormann was quoted in the magazine's article as saying this diamond would easily fetch several million dollars. I contacted the store, and set up a telephone appointment with Gormann. When I did speak to him, I naturally used a fictitious name. Harry, this is how they are going to work the sale-"

"Fritz, please, hold on old boy, I apologize for not remaining silent, but I must interrupt dear friend. My name is Fellows for Christ sake; I'm not one of the Rockefeller boys. Jesus, you know every damn shilling I have in the world is invested in this flat and furnishings. You're not bloody-well suggesting that we buy this ... this, Singhalese diamond, right Fritz?" Fellows sort of laughed aloud. "Because if you are, I am short about ninety nine point nine percent of what it takes to put-"

"Who said anything about buying Harry? Not buy it, old chap, no indeed," Barrow's voice dropped to a dead whisper, barely heard by Harry. "What we are going to do old salt is steal the Singhalese diamond. And yes, you heard me right … steal it"

At that instant, from outside, came the thud of distant thunder. An omen of sorts, thought Harry. And in the play of colors coming from the Tiffany lamp at the back of his desk, Fellows looked older than his years; his grin had vanished too.

"What the hell are you going on about, damn you Fritz?" Fellows held the receiver away from his ear for a moment and stared at it. At which time Barrow seemed about to add something, then change his mind when Harry said, "Believe me Fritz, I would never do anything that would compromise our friendship. But right now I'm at a loss for words." At which point Fritz Barrow knew that Harry Fellows clearly understood he wasn't joking.

Frowning, Fellows said, "Fritz, are you all right? And if you bloody-well are, then cheeribye old boy for a very long time to come, thanks awful for ringing, and mind how you go." Once more there was a disturbed weather rumbling in the background.

"Harry, believe me," Barrow piped in. "Worked out properly, it could be the gem heist of the century; this plan has mathematical certainty; certainty like two plus three makes five. Now listen carefully to me Harry, tonight we leave for London - Kennedy to Gatwick Airport, arriving in the morning. We will take the train to Victoria Station, should arrive in your neighborhood not much past eight." Fritz Barrow paused anticipating Fellows' response.

"We … did I hear we, Fritz?"

"Barrow edged a quiet "yes" through his teeth. "Bonnie and I will meet you in the lobby of the Goring Excelsior Hotel about eight-thirty. This is her first trip to England; I told her about the full English breakfast at the Goring Excelsior, silver service, starched tablecloths, the complete royal treatment."

Harry Fellows knew from years of friendship that Fritz Barrow never discussed the advantages or disadvantages of any business transaction unless it began over a good meal. This was to be no exception, as balmy as it all sounded.

"Bonnie? Bonnie who? Fritz."

"Stop worrying, and take one of your long walks in the park Harry," Barrow said nearly gaily. "Now I must get moving. And Harry, one more item you might think about," -Fellows had been waiting for Fritz's title page to this preposterous sounding scenario - "Do this with me, Harry - you'll even the score with Miles Jamison and whoever else stabbed you in the back."

Fellows had always been impressed by his friend's loyalty, but in all the time since he was deviously sacked, it was the first time Barrow had ever condemned Lloyd's verbally for what they had done. Fellows felt totally mystified.

"Fritz, do you have any notion of the man hours involved to pull off a gem heist of this proportion, forgetting for the moment a whole narrative about criminal trials, prison and prison food. Then there is the small detail that Vanlo and Eugêne has a security set-up that is tighter than a frog's ass. The system is identical to Tiffany and Cartier over there in Yankee land. I know! Lloyd's insures all three."

For Fellows, it was a simple uncomplicated formula that labeled Barrow's plan an equation with the wrong factors in place.

"What I am asking you is very simple, Harry," Barrow insisted, his voice bequeathing respectfulness. "I am asking you to trust me blindly if only out of years of close friendship."

Fellows made a tilting gesture to himself with his outstretched palm. "Mind how you go Fritz. See you tomorrow," said Fellows before replacing the receiver into its cradle. He peered at it steadily again for several seconds.

Thunder became more frequent, the sky had turned dark and a heavy rain began to fall. Fellows walked to the window, pulled it securely closed then looked down to the dismal façades of Ebury Lane.

*   *   *

Standing, looking at the distant skyline from his tenth floor Manhattan condominium apartment, a pleased Fritz Barrow put down the telephone and turned to the woman across the room who sat watching him from deep in the corner of a sofa. She sat as still as a cemetery stone, shoulders high and hands flat on her lap. Bonnie Adele had short blond hair, wore dark rose-tinted glasses that partially hid her eyes, and possessed the pallor of one who avoided the sun.

He smiled warmly and chimed in happily. "Bonnie, you are just going to adore my good friend Harry Fellows."

Bonnie Adele attempted an easy smile, but inside she felt locked up and frightened. "*Lord help me,*" she thought. One look at her expression told Fritz Barrow what she had been thinking.

*   *   *

The next morning.

As usual, Harry Fellows rose a little past daybreak. With energetic interest to what lay ahead, he hurried barefoot from his bedroom to the living room and gaped out the window to the street below. Unlike the lead-gray day before, the sidewalks already began to show huge patches of clear sunshine. Even the chimes from his desk clock echoed a more cheery sound. It was the kind of day Harry would describe as belonging to anyone; which could make it lopsided in terms of himself. He raised the window two or three inches and shivered as the doubly wonderful crisp cold air slipped through the narrow opening.

Making his way to the kitchen persuaded by the chill for something hot, he wondered whether he should greet his old friend Fritz Barrow abnormally friendly, or whether he should be abnormally wicked. Suddenly he laughed at this childish shortcoming whispering aloud, "Nonsense old dear, you're a ruddy loner and you don't like being leaned on or pushed and that's what it s bloody all about."

After taking in the morning paper, Harry began the kettle for a mug of instant coffee and toasted a scone – the cranberry scone he had bought the afternoon before at Marjorie's Sweet Shoppe at the end of Ebury Lane. Leaning on the kitchen counter he let out a disquieted sigh as he thumbed through pages of the London Times not really taking notice of anything in particular, but still managing subliminally to take in what was newsworthy.

Fellows remained strangely excited as he read, and also a bit worried about Barrow's female crony. He felt the familiar warming of his hands that seemed always to precede the unexpected. Harry closed his eyes and frowned severely. He would not play games if he couldn't make proper sense out of why this person with a first name of Bonnie, at least for the time being had been declared in. Then again, making sense out of Fritz Barrow's ideas often proved to be a difficult chore, even so he would still drop out right away. In all the years of friendship there had never been a female with the name of Bonnie tossed about in conversation. Yet with grudging admiration for Fritz, Harry immediately had to rule out sex as the motive. Although Fritz Barrow wasn't exactly shy around women, he just did not bother with them after his wife had died six years before. And except for a few certain one night flings he had offered as confessions to Fellows so as not to give wonder about his sexuality, Fritz Barrow refused to fritter away time on any woman.

After a second cup of instant coffee he pushed away his half-eaten scone which had turned stone-hard and turned to help himself to the pack of open cigarettes lying on the side-bar behind him. Though he had forsworn smoking, he once again faced a stubborn situation that called for an immediate delay of such a resolution. He lit up, inhaled deeply, and decided to ready himself for the day ahead.

For a man who knew the lyrics and melodies to at least a thousand songs, he now pondered why he was standing in the front room. "*Why the hell can't I remember where I put the damn house keys?*" Fortunately, the answer came quickly when he spotted them hanging from the inside front door dead bolt lock. Ten minutes later, Fellows was heading straight for St. James' Park learning early in life that when he felt stressed it was time for a long walk.

He had a deep love for the parks of London, and it was for this reason he had purchased his flat near Buckingham Palace with its several beautiful neighboring parks. And on this especially sunny bright chilly morning as Fellows strode along Birdcage Walk, his usual imperious gait of long determined strides had been unconsciously shortened as if he was wary of walking into a trap - a deep hole with pointed bamboo spears waiting to pierce him through. Further subconscious thoughts of such a remote possibility did at least coincide with his own brand of puzzling Englishness.

A natural observer of human behavior, Fellows often could gaze into the periphery of man's main parts and often find with unimpeachable accuracy lucid explanations. But now as he stepped along the pond bridge, he saw that trying to figure it all out before he heard all the details from Fritz Barrow was like shining a flashlight into sloshing murky water - seeing was too confusing to continue.

As he made his way along, a close inspection of Harry Fellows from a lofty position atop some tree branch would reveal a tired man in contrast to a visibly healthy complexion, and although a slight paunch revealed his middle age appearance, there existed a splendidly well-defined Anglo nose along with straight graying hair parted on the left, all of which gave the well-dressed London private eye a marked bearing of cultured aristocracy.

A cool breeze cut over the pond as he reached the end of the bridge. Something unknown summoned Harry to stop dead in his tracks and it wasn't an impending trap. He stood stiffly in that spot, clenched teeth and a grim expression pervaded his face as he watched a small lad about fifty feet away idly toss a stick at the trunk of a great oak. He would then run, fetch it, run back and toss the stick with deadly accuracy hitting the same spot on the trunk. The slightly built youngster with a red knit cap pulled well-down over his ears, kicked at swirling leaves as he went to retrieve and throw his weapon once again.

Leaves were falling from all the trees; the coming of another chilled autumn was not that far off. A sudden feeling of nostalgia, an unfamiliar emotion to Fellows came banging through his layers of bygones, and he supposed that whatever the sentiment was, it had to be for vanished days of his own youth.

Perhaps he too had thrown a stick at a tree in the park oblivious of the weather, indifferent to who might be watching. Fellows began to walk slowly along, perceiving the past scene for a few thoughtful moments. A dog barked somewhere in the distance followed by chorus of other dogs barking. He remembered himself as a boy being slightly built -

a string bean and graceless; always walking into things and blurting aloud terrible damnation's. His father Jack Fellows, a man of guileless wit, lovingly called Harry, "A runaway beast in a crockery shop."

Fellows stopped - closed his eyes. He waited for his mind to bring visions of his own son; then immediately he tried to step clear of another vision; that of his deceased wife. It was close to this day many years ago that Margaret Fellows after being released from a private asylum for the mentally disturbed had begged Harry if she could delay her return home and live alone in London for a few months.

"Please Harry," she had cried, "I need to be on my own; away from familiarity, the house, friends who intend to be kind and understanding yet are going to look at me cross eyed like I'm some kind of a freak. Please, I'm better Harry. I need to do it my way. Be on my side now." Fellows consulted with her physician who simply stated that the inevitable, whatever it might be, will happen. Three weeks later Margaret had ended her life alone in her London flat. Fully clothed, sitting on the floor of the shower stall, she had slashed her wrists, then carefully wrapped thick absorbent towels to keep the blood in check. The image of her dead in a pool of her own blood made Fellows ache inwardly for a few moments followed by the over familiar rush of anger and pity. *"You're an old fool Harry, move on. There was nothing anyone could do."*

From years of his dead wife bursting into his consciousness, Fellows had learned quickly to dismiss any memories before the senseless brooding set in. He turned once again to watch the boy, glanced at his watch, neatly adjusted the scarf about his neck; it had turned much colder, the chilled breeze was now a cold wind. He thrust his hands into the pockets of his vicuna overcoat, and began to briskly walk away. The meeting with Fritz Barrow and the unknown woman Bonnie was in twenty minutes at the Goring Excelsior Hotel.

It wasn't long before the quiet and serenity of the ancient park with its abundant wild fowl and ornamental lakes gave way to the pollution and harsh sounds of automobile traffic speeding past Buckingham Palace.

"*Where in ruddy hell can they all be going in such a hurry?*" Fellows quizzically asked himself, watching out for cars as he jogged across the Palace roundabout to the safety of the wide sidewalk. Harry had discovered many years before his profound sentimental affection for England. So today, walking along close to the Palace's iron fence, that affection ran deeper than ever.

Sometimes for no other reason then a feeling of tranquility, he would come to Buckingham Palace late at night. The sight of it, the floodlights illuminating the centuries old building, the Queen's Royal Guards standing like frozen wax mannequins and without having to ask himself why, it all made him feel proud. He would then walk again until he found himself in Soho, the center of the London's West End, confident that even during the nasty hours, he would arrive back to his Ebury Lane Flat unmolested and alive. It was another part of his personal introspection that made his country the larger part of family.

But now a slight sickening, cold twinge developed in his stomach; he felt apprehensive; would it be worth taking this kind of chance for sake of revenge; money? It would all be so meaningless. He shuddered to think he could be denied living in his glorious England. It was all he had left. "Damn you, Fritz", he growled, hurrying along with a group of Japanese tourists across busy Beeston Place to the front steps of the Goring Excelsior Hotel. "This bleeding scam had bloody-well be what the yanks call a lead pipe cinch, or I'll 'ave your bloody head."

At precisely 9:15 A.M. in the Goring's lobby, the long time friends enthusiastically greeted each other, exchanged a few words which was immediately followed with hugs and hand clasps of genuine affection. Afterwards, both men allowed themselves a few seconds to settle down. Then Fritz Barrow, feeling exhilarated that the meeting was successful in the first throws, turned to the woman standing slightly behind him and said, "Harry, I would like you to meet Miss Bonnie Adele. It's a great name Harry, is it not? And Bonnie, this is my dearest friend in the entire world, Harry Fellows, also a great name, don't you think?"

The man from New York than took a discreet step backwards to observe the human side of the crucial first meeting between his future star players - there was more at stake then even the players were aware of at this point

The two strangers smiled cordially, shook hands; each demonstrating a hearty grip. They exchanged intense eye contact using their own personal mastery of instinct to look for positive signs, or some immediate hidden miss - mysteriously some thoughts can be read; certain looks interpreted. For the moment, born from the casual meeting, Fritz Barrow felt renewed inspiration for his carefully worked out, complex hoax. He quickly walked away and sought the Maitre'd. In the meantime, the woman stared at Harry. Harry smiled but became a bit uncomfortable as she continued to stare. He finally asked, "Bonnie have we met somewhere? Do we know each other?" Suddenly, Fritz returned, moved in between them, threw his arms around their shoulders, and gently guided them towards the dining room. Barrow was leaving nothing to chance; his special pattern now called for them to enjoy a super breakfast – somehow he had managed to suppress his excitement.

After an unhurried breakfast of perfectly ripe kiwi and pineapple sections, Scottish kippers, thick sliced Scandinavian bacon, mushroom omelets, toast and jelly, blended coffee with chicory, the threesome had a leisurely walk before returning to Fellows' flat.

*   *   *

Now settled comfortably in Fellows' sitting room Bonnie sat militantly straight, silently studying traits of the two men seated across the room. Fellows was complaining of eating too much since he was attempting to keep up a diet and Fritz Barrow was thinking about the reason he had come to England. He said, "Okay Harry we'll skip lunch, how's that?"

Fellows replied, "We don't have to take it to extremes Fritz."

Barrow grinned widely. "Okay then, lunch it is. But for now my friends, time for serious talk. "Here, have a look. Then from his open brief case, he pulled out a magazine and opened it to where a red post-it flag marked the important page. The picture at the top of the page was a cut gemstone held by a tweezers. "This is the Singhalese diamond my friends. Our assignment, our prey. The color of the diamond can best be described as light color kunzite, or pale pink corundum. Do you not agree Harry?"

Fellows reached out his hand and took hold of the jewelry trade journal, contemplated the photograph of the diamond as he puffed on a cigarette - he had already smoked half a pack After tree or four seconds, he replied, "Yes, yes, either one. Light color kunzite or pale pink corundum. So I agree, but you have to realize Fritz, photographs, even today's high-end digital images can have misleading tones of color especially when preciseness is essential as it might be in this situation. Pale pink in a gem stone is different than pale pink lemonade." Fellows stopped. His voice tones officiously asking "do you not agree?"

"Harry, imagine this," Barrow said ignoring the innuendo of a possible color problem.

"Ernst Gormann, the man in charge of moving the diamond for Vanlo and Eugêne, gets the permission of Charles Daisey, the assistant GM, to give the magazine the complete Gemological Federation of America's confidential trade report about the Singhalese diamond, including Harry, this actual size appraisal quality photograph of the diamond, which you are now looking at. Now come on Harry, you know something like that is positively an industry no, no. But why not a *no* this time, Harry?"

Fellows remained silent and threw a knowing glance to the woman seated on the sofa - they both understood the question was purely rhetorical.

"I will tell you why not this time my two darlings, because this diamond, forgive my New York parle vous Francais, is absolutely fucking unique." Fritz said the next words staccato: "No one can bad mouth it. It is one of a kind, a collector's dream that is why. There is not a living soul who can knock it. So with upstairs Board permission, or whatever you want to call it, the magazine goes ahead prints and reproduces the diamond in living color for all persons in the entire trade to go *ooh* and *aah* over, plus they include an article to help Vanlo and Eugêne promote and publicize what is now referred to as the Singhalese diamond bid-off. I mean really, old boy, talk about dim-witted egos and foolish bragging."

"Forgive me, but who is Charles Daisey?" asked Fellows who had now begun to read the main article about the diamond adding, "And are we ignoring our pretty Bonnie lady?"

Bonnie said, "Honestly Harry, I've studied the picture and the article many, many times." She signaled with her hand for Barrow to continue.

"You asked about Charles Daisey, Harry," answered Barrow smiling sardonically: "Let's just say he calls the shots, the point guard if you will of Vanlo and Eugêne." Fritz paused, waiting for Harry to reply as he was now reading with heavy concentration the page that featured the European Gemological Federation's Laboratory Diamond Report. Fellows looked up and took in Fritz Barrow into his line of sight – then at the woman Bonnie Adele. "Wow," was his only comment.

DIAMOND GRADING REPORT
Vanlo and Eugêne, New York, NY
Singhalese Diamond – 90B 11ZV711
'COPY ONLY – NOT ORIGINAL'

SHAPE AND CUT   OVAL BRILLIANT
Measurements ----30.62MM X 17.65MM X 12.66MM DEEP
Weight --------126.43 CARATS
PROPORTIONS
Depth ------50%
Table ------56%
Girdle -----MEDIUM
Culet -------LARGE
FINISH
Polish -------EXCELLENT
Symmetry -----EXCELLENT
CLARITY GRADE -----FLAWLESS UNDER 10X MAGNIFICATION
COLOR GRADE -------FANCY, PINK
FLUORESENCE -------NONE

As Fellows spoke, his voice had an edge of uncertainty. "Fritz no one has to tell us about the European Gemological Federation's Laboratory's accuracy; it's the best in the world. And yes, what they say is non-refutable. But surely you don't really envision pulling a successful switch with a stone like this? It is not exactly your everyday garden variety large diamond. Just the bloody color-"

Barrow clearly cut Fellows off. "Harry, for God sakes, please don't play this very old game with me. I didn't expect you of all people to start yelling in my ear is it a sure thing and bloody safe to steal a diamond worth millions of dollars without any problems attached?"

Seeing Barrow's expression told Fellows that his long time friend had already decided to go through with the theft however he designed it, and nothing was going to deter him. Once again, he caught the woman staring at him.

For the moment, Harry's thoughts turned to Barrow. *"Yes, Fritz is a fussy man; he and his wife childless and as a result they had spoiled each other in an indefinable way. Barrow now expects me, his boyhood friend to stand behind him by virtue of no more than our solid years of camaraderie."* Harry stared at Fritz for several moments; he had been caught off-guard by the reproachful reaction of his friend. He took a loose cigarette and a book of matches from his shirt pocket. He then said, "Fritz and Bonnie, if you would allow me, I'd like to tell a story." Fellows spoke in a calm but resolute voice. He paused to light his cigarette. Harry turned to the woman; she had restlessly moved to another cushion and was resting her chin on her hand staring directly into his eyes. Aside from her constant staring, Fellows had already established in his own mind that for some very good reason, Bonnie Adele had fit perfectly into Fritz Barrow's plan. Why though? He would have to discover all of that later.

The man from New York fell silent, shrugged an okay, and went to the liquor cabinet. He poured brandy into a snifter, filling half the glass.

Fellows pushed himself out of his chair and meandered to the front window. He stood for a few moments looking out - then he began: "When I was a lad, the beginning of summer brought what seemed thousand of toads to the banks of a huge reservoir not far from the village where I lived, perhaps a mile and a half or so away. It was known as the Notts Reservoir. My father, one particular Christmas bought me a pellet pistol, the compressed air type that used small C02 cylinders and fired lead cone-shaped pellets. When school was dismissed the following summer, I would walk all the way to the bank of Notts Reservoir, find a comfortable spot to sit, and shoot toads with that pistol for sport. When I became an adult, I realized those toads did not die in sport, but died in earnest." Fellows turned away from the window, his eyes set on Fritz Barrow.

"Harry listen," said Fritz sounding confiding. "You are a veteran of many campaigns; some tough ones. I know that. But the way I see it now, is that you are now attempting to be safe where there is no safety." -Fellows stayed silent- "Harry, as far as I know, no one has ever been able to prescribe a relief for not being sure, though I will tell you this, what I propose Harry, is something that we can pull off, and on top of it, you will have your own brand of ... of earnest vengeance and a hell of a lot of money. Harry, you owe it to yourself, damnit!" Barrow threw back the last of his brandy.

Fellows turned and once again looked down to the street. He desperately tried mixing up the reality of the present with old dreams; in hopes that Barrow's scheme could be converted into something that he had once longed for - only a few people know that sometimes knowledge is acquired through sin. It was true; Fellows had been the best thief catcher in the entire Lloyd's organization. It was also true that he learned his trade by attentively watching the misses and mistakes others had committed. But was he ready to sacrifice everything he possessed, everything of value in his world just so Fritz Barrow could prove he possessed the knowledge to win some far-fetched idea of stealing a precious diamond?

Harry also wondered about Barrow's unspoken motive; Money? Probably not. He had never been bothered with financial burdens; his small jewelry manufacturing company had always provided him well. Momentarily, Harry's vision was drawn to the people below as they scampered up and down Ebury Lane, some to the right, others to the left; Ebury Lane never seemed to be without activity. Watching their behavior from above bothered him for the moment. As he watched the activity, he began to sense vicariously the real boredom of their lives.

Fellows loved his flat; his acquired small treasures; he loved to travel and dine at the better London restaurants. Fellows had even begun to enjoy his role at being a private eye. He frowned; he thought about his ambivalence at Buckingham Palace earlier that morning. Perhaps it was mixed dreams that made him doubt Fritz Barrow's provocation, when in fact; the truth was that Barrow's plan to steal the Singhalese diamond would actually guarantee all of it for as long as he lived, all the good things that he really cared for. Fellows studied the vision below again. *"Perhaps the vital thing here,"* he thought *"is to get to the other side of my honest nature. Skills are skills for the good or bad of it."* He smiled at his quick turn around philosophy.

It wasn't as if the three of them would be bursting in to a jewelry store wearing Margaret Thatcher and Richard Nixon masks, shooting, wounding and murdering innocent customers and others hard at work. *"This is a cause for honest vengeance where no one but the bad guys gets it up their asses."*

He turned to look at Barrow, and said in a nasal brogue: "I suppose you want to punch me for watering down the curry. I am sorry, old boy; I suppose I had it in my head to resist from the very beginning. I was questioning myself, understand, not you. What I need to know privately, will come in time, won't it Fritz?" Fellows paused and remained silent. He moved his hand gesturing for Barrow to take charge. Fritz's expression softened. He smiled, then walked to Fellows and the two men embraced.

Bonnie Adele, who had sat quietly on the sofa watching and listening, was so struck by the profound mental transposition that had occurred, she had to give herself a moment to remember where she was and what was going on? She looked at the two men approvingly; she had thought this kind of affection passed only between women.

It was not long after that, that everyone began to relax again. Fellows lit another cigarette, and Fritz continued his discourse of what was required of each player and the intricate details that needed to be put into place - Bonnie finally stopped staring, and the two smiled at each other – what Barrow had planned was like something out of a movie. Between Fellows and Adele, there was developing a more than subliminal feeling of good fellowship.

Harry poured Bonnie a long sherry.

"There is only one reason for doing something," Barrow began to speak again. "And that is because you are compelled to want to. Have to? Some would furiously deny it. Afraid? That's just another word for not wanting to do it. We, my friends, cannot falter during this ... this operation. Every item, each internal organ no matter how trivial, must be covered. No detail can be forgotten. We must keep moving and not once delay or stop. For once one stops, one may never start again. It becomes a special kind of fright that can make you feel so outright foolish, especially when the stakes are so big that you walk away content to call the whole thing dumb. And you can believe me, my darlings, the stakes here are enormous. Millions of dollars for our pockets."

"Cheers," said Fellows, then adding "We're in, so bloody get on with more of the details." Barrow laughed; but he knew Harry's words were irreversible.

Fritz said, "To begin with, the diamond is to be sold by sealed bid. Each bid is to be accompanied by a good faith deposit of two hundred thousand dollars. The big price eliminates the street clowns who don't have the jack, or who just want to play the price is right and see the diamond first-hand."

"Makes proper sense to me," said Fellows.

"Only one appointment per interested party and the diamond is shown only then, only once, and to one person only. It all takes place on the third floor at Vanlo and Eugêne's Fifth Avenue store in Manhattan. From my two telephone conversations with Ernst Gormann, the chap in charge, I can tell you in all candor that this Gormann gives a strong dissertation favorable to pushing the bids to go through the roof. He told me that as a matter of courtesy, Vanlo and Eugêne allowed him the time to speak to potential buyers. The question of insurance came up and Gormann said that Lloyd's of London insures the stone up to the time of delivery to the winning buyer, and that it would behoove all bidders to make preliminary arrangement for protection."

Fellows nodded and crushed his cigarette. He had many questions to ask but remained quiet. His expression revealed nothing but a concentration to the facts as they were being brought forth.

Fritz said, "I'm getting ahead of myself a little, but it was once I had the leg work done you might say with a deliberate cause, that I fully understood myself that the plan would hold together. And the roles each of us will play will simply and clearly come into focus.

However, the thing that I had to do quickly was locate a genuine color stone of any size that approached the soft pink color of the Singhalese photograph. I narrowed the available choices down to two stones. Pink sapphire, or pink kunzite as I previously mentioned. But as you know, Harry, finding a natural pink sapphire with the proper color tone and hue would take weeks, maybe months, and involve too many inquiries with possible curious minded stone dealers and by then, the diamond would have been sold anyway. Plus, we are speaking of a fortune of money even for that quality gem stone. Ergo, the lowly kunzite stone was to be the perfect choice."

"No question about it," Harry said as he walked from the window and sat next to Bonnie on the sofa. She wiggled slightly into the cushion and settled back. Their shoulders lightly touched; neither objected by moving away.

Fritz said, "I went to Forty-seventh street," Barrow looked at Bonnie "this as you know is the center of New York's jewelry district-" Bonnie smiled to the affirmative "A few hours later I acquired for cash, a modest but suitable collection of six Brazilian pink kunzites from a few gem stone dealers in various buildings on the street. Incidentally, I think there are as many gem stone dealers in downtown Manhattan as there are in Jaipur, India. But to go on. As you know, natural light is the best way to determine color. So I taxied to Central Park, found a secluded bench, and commenced to compare my newly procured parcel of kunzite stones to the Gemological Federation's photograph of the Singhalese diamond. Darlings, my breathing got heavy. No more trips back to the Indian stone dealers. One stone out of the six, from a Sikh firm, matched the Singhalese color to a T. I quickly got to a telephone and called Vanlo and Eugêne to double-check the exactness of the diamond's color to the magazine photograph. I spoke to Gormann again, and he assured me it was absolutely identical. There is really no reason to doubt what the man said. The truth of the matter is that there are buyers throughout the world looking to own this diamond. He'd have no reason not to be perfectly honest."

Suddenly Fellows began to nod in quick jerks. "Of course. Beautiful. Bloody beautiful Fritz." Fellows then clapped like an elated child waiting to be handed a surprise package - Barrow rose to his feet and in a long sweeping motion, dramatically extended his arm and bowed majestically.

The woman peered at both men. Though she was puzzled by the histrionics, she realized that Fellows knew exactly where events were leading, and that Barrow could not have been happier seeing Harry's response. The heaviness of whatever had transpired previously had now totally disappeared.

"So this is the case, my darlings," Barrow resumed undistracted. "We have a gem stone, a genuine nine carat pink Brazilian kunzite that matches the color of the Singhalese diamond, or, let us say at the very least, close enough to deceive the unsuspecting eye of Mr. Ernst Gormann or anyone else."

Bonnie who had cautiously remained silent throughout all the dialogue, for the first time took the initiative. She spoke with an edge of contrived humor. "But a nine carat pink colored kunzite does not make a one hundred twenty six carat, rare pink six million dollar plus Singhalese diamond."

"You are quite correct my dear Ms. Adele," responded Fritz cheerfully. "And to begin a search for a suitable natural kunzite crystal big enough to recut to exact proportions of the Singhalese and at the same time hope the color would match would be more then insane, foolhardy, and quite impossible to say the least. Not to mention the stupidity of making inquiries even if such a stone were to exist." Barrow cupped his hands around his mouth- "SO MY DARLINGS!" he shouted. "What we are going to do is make our own Singhalese diamond!"

Fellows announced with verbal enthusiasm, "The only place I know who has the ability to create such a duplicate is Idar-Oberstein in West Germany, the precious and semi-precious gem cutting center of the world!"

"Give that man a box of Cuban Cigars," cried Barrow. Everyone began to laugh.

It was after a fresh round of drinks that Fritz got up from the armchair and began to nervously pace. He sipped his drink and went on. He looked directly at Harry. "Time as always is an enemy when precise planning are the catch words."

Fellows said, "If there's an action with more of a meaning then precise, I'd say we would have to invent it."

Barrow said, "With the interest created by the magazine article, Vanlo and Eugêne decided to shorten up on the bidding time. Twelve days was decided on. So anyone outside the twelve days, who isn't on the store's list, is tough out of luck. Twelve days gives potential bidders in Europe time enough to make travel arrangement, make an appointment, and a have the opportunity to look at and hold the stone. As I said previously, appointments allow one person at a time. I'm assuming there will be the same security as if the president were visiting. I expect guards to be stationed in front of Gormann's office with automatic weapons; hidden cameras inside and God know what else. Time limit for viewing is to be no longer than five minutes per session; this sale or auction as Vanlo prefers to call it, is strictly for pros who know what they're doing. And oh yes, deposit checks up front.

Harry, Bonnie, the simple fact is that I must have the bogus stone in my possession when I have my first and only meeting with Gormann, which Harry, is the reason I waited until the last minute to call you. It was only yesterday when I finalized everything with Vanlo and Eugêne and got my appointment. The switch has to take place when it's my turn to actually hold the Singhalese. If I miss, that's it. No second chances. As far as my appointment, I got lucky. I requested that my appointment be on Friday, which is the final day for all appointments; twelve days from tomorrow. They had that time slot opened and I grabbed it". Barrow pensively studied the glass he held. He held it up to the light coming from the window as a glass blower might examine a newly manufactured artistic piece. No one spoke during the long pause. Fellows turned and looked at Bonnie; her eyes were half closed - she was yielding to exhaustion.

Fellows said, "I'm back to thinking you're balmy Fritz. Idar-Oberstein is a long way away."

Even through her being tired, Bonnie managed an audible chuckle. Ignoring Harry's remark, Barrow said, "Now about the events that took place following the buy of that kunzite in New York. This you are going to love Harry. I booked a flight on Air France, and flew to Paris that very night. I slept at a hotel near to the airport, and in the morning flew to Frankfurt-"

Fellows got to his feet, whistled softly and raised his hand for Fritz to stop.

"Come on then," Fellows appealed. "The pubs are just now opening; let's all have a walk, the fresh air will do us some good. Personally I would love a pint of lager. We can talk about all the air-miles you've accumulated."

Bonnie laughed openly.

"Here, here, good idea, Harry," agreed Barrow.

"Gentlemen," said Bonnie wearily, "I think this would be an excellent opportunity for me to rest. I am really beat, and besides Harry, I'm certain you must have some things you would like to discuss privately with Fritz."

Fellows looked as the poised woman wearing rose tinted glasses. With an unreserved tone of intimacy he said: "Bonnie, I am an old bear who has been roaming the big forest for many years. I think I know who can be trusted and who cannot and I felt good about you straight away. However, I must say your honesty and intuition is greatly appreciated; in any event, Fritz can fill me in on lots more detail. Now have yourself a relaxing hot bath and a long nap; there's nothing more refreshing after a long journey. There's a stack of freshly laundered towels … please make yourself at home, and as you yanks like to say to their house guests; my home is your home."

-Humpty Dumpty -- dummy.

CHAPTER TWO

Standing on the sidewalk, Fellows half looked at the sky ahead and suggested the Red Lion, a pub near to the Royal Hospital on Pimlico Road. "It's a short distance, a walk before lunch is like an apple a day."

The sun was now partially shielded by a thick cloud cover. He lit a cigarette and tossed the match away. The two men walked slowly along Ebury Lane for several minutes with no word passing between them. Finally with an audible dismal sigh, Fritz Barrow broke the silence. Fellows knew the signal from the old days; after such a sigh his friend was about to deal out something crazy or at least a remark sure to provoke. Fritz then looked at Fellows for a moment, thinking about not what he was going to say, but how to say it.

Fellows asked, "Something bothering you Fritz?"

"Harry, I have only known Bonnie Adele for about six months."

To Fellows, the words had a blunt cruelty to them.

Barrow assumed there would be a long uncertain silence and a glum look on his friend's face. He was right. Fellows swallowed and pressed his back teeth hard against each other. He wanted to moan aloud as though unexpectedly wounded; he had not anticipated this at all. Their walk has slowed considerably. By the end of the silence that followed, the last of the sun shut down behind clouds, and the once bright morning had transformed itself to bleak gray. Barrow's declaration made Fellows surly and frozen. He was about to ask Fritz to repeat what he had just said, but Fritz spoke first.

"As you can see Harry, she has a minor thyroid problem," Barrow said it quietly, almost politely. "Regrettably it is an inherited family trait, property of her mother. Bonnie tells me that the condition has lessened considerably over the years. She described herself when younger as having a frog like look as the result of slightly bulging eyes. Unfortunately, she says the disease is difficult to control since there is no definitive therapy."

Outwardly showing annoyance, Fellows commented loudly: "It is somewhat noticeable, I suppose, but that is why she wears tinted spectacles, is it not? Nevertheless I find her to be quite attractive, actually pretty. Now what in the fucking hell is all this about anyway, Fritz? Jesus Christ, we have much to discuss, and discussing her eye affliction at this time is absolutely ridiculous."

Barrow stopped; his hands clasped behind him. Ignoring Fellows' demanding tone, he continued. "She claims during her teens it was particularly bad when she smiled. Throughout her school years she was called '*ribbet*' behind her back and sometimes cruelly to her face. R-r-r-bet is the sound frogs supposedly make at night."

"I know that damnit; I've killed enough of those little fuckers to know." Fellows now shook his head, he was near being furious. His chest was burning from anger. "Fritz! tighten your ass muscles damn you! I'm about to kick it."

Barrow resumed walking. He continued talking attempting to keep the control he needed. "Harry, please leave me be and just listen for Christ sake."

Harry mumbled something under his breath.

Fritz sighing soulfully, said, "Bonnie lacking a social life of any worth, partially due to her own sensitivity, which she does not deny, avoided mixing with other students and filled her empty time reading novels, mostly mysteries. Says she wrote frequently to many authors critiquing their work, and not surprisingly, she received many replies; some grateful, some otherwise. What is most interesting, was the surprise she received to have actually gotten a interview offer from a New York publisher to be an assistant editor. Reading was her hobby; she was delighted."

"Cut the bleeding bullshit Fritz, before I throw you in front of a fast moving car!" Fellows then, forcing himself from yelling said, "What the hell does all of this have to do with stealing a fucking diamond worth millions from Vanlo and Eugêne?"

"Hear me out, Harry, please. You'll know everything soon enough."

Fellows heaved a heavy sigh and reluctantly nodded his head.

As they walked side by side, Fellows greeted an elderly couple he knew with a terse hello. At the moment he wasn't in the mood to be friendly to anyone.

Fritz said, "Harry, do you remember that incredible undercover source who once told you where you could locate a Soviet platinum coin collection that had been stolen from a shipment out of Southampton, and when you met him, the bugger tried to drown you in the bilge of the abandoned boat where the coins allegedly were hidden. Tell me seriously Harry, wasn't part of telling what happened a fabrication. It was a rather...shall I say, a bit over the edge kind of story."

"Okay Fritz, what's the bloody point. The guy had me down for the third time; I was almost done for, but had enough strength to bite into one of his nuts. I actually think he passed out from the pain … by the time I hit the surface, he was drowning. And believe me, none of it was a fabrication."

"The point is, Harry, my story is not intended to be deceptive either."

Fellows expressed his disapproval of this weary routine by again mumbling something inaudible. Then he said, "Okay, for Christ sakes go on."

"Adele went to Columbia in New York," Barrow patiently said, his voice tone even. "In her third year, she was recruited by the CIA and trained to be a professional reader, searching out what might be considered subversive or questionable from books and articles or whatever the CIA wanted searched. She also has an aptitude for remembering, thus she was able to reach back to past details and bring them forward to tie into whatever was needed - if you get my drift. She is still under the Security Act, so avoids any references to her past work. Then two years later, she actually discovered that a well known British novelist with whom she had frequently corresponded with during her high school days, but never had met, was instrumental in her being recruited. Several months later she transferred to the FBI and became a major researcher and co-author for certain Bureau related manuals dealing with domestic overt espionage procedures. She obviously is expert at what she does."

Fellows mentally fixed on the words Fritz used to describe Bonnie Adele: *research, domestic and espionage.* Fellows thoughts ran on, "*She's not a field agent – she's behind a desk covered with books and magazines and a computer. She's a bloody federal policeman – she sees to it that thieves are arrested, she doesn't work on their behalf."*

Fritz now took hold of Harry's arm and brought him to a halt. He faced his long time friend straight on, his own heart beat quickening. He said caringly: "Harry, I felt you needed to know her background."

"Why Fritz? What I heard was great for America, but little did it have to do with participating in a serious crime. I think the proper word is felony."

"The reason; it's part of how and why she met Guy – your son."

Fellows' knees buckled slightly. He became aware of pulsating in his temples. A sharp pain emerged in his stomach. He made no reply. From an open window came the sound of music playing and there was laughter. Fellows turned sharply away and looked upward to the open window. He didn't want Fritz to see his twisted face. So Bonnie's prolonged staring when they first met, was now clearly explained; she saw Guy's face.

Barrow knowingly allowed Fellows a few moments to compose himself. Then leading him onward by the arm, resumed telling him the story of how Guy Fellows met Bonnie Adele, fell in love, and eventually how she acquired a good deal of stolen cash that Guy had pirated away preceding his fatal airplane crash.

A windowless blue van went by; the ginger haired driver honked his horn and waved at Harry only to be ignored.

At this point Barrow had a sense that Fellows had accepted the beginning of a particularly vile afternoon and was now prepared for other gut wrenching news – at least Barrow hoped so.

Harry took hold of Fritz's elbow nudging him forward.

Fritz taking the cue, continued, "Bonnie also says, and it is believable, that Guy promised to marry her after Guy's son Tim, your grandson, graduated high school. Guy felt his wife Ellen would not object to a divorce once Tim was enrolled in college. Both he and Ellen had apparently fallen out of love, plus they had little or nothing to do with each other sexually. It was important for me to know if what Bonnie had told me rang of truth, so I called Ellen, now Guy's widow, and she did verify what Bonnie had told me, and added that even before Bonnie had come onto the scene, they had basically lost interest in each other. The relationship in total had taken a complete nose dive. But Ellen added, unfortunately the future for Guy and Bonnie never developed ... the airplane crash."

"Fritz, Guy never told me," said Harry. "Because he knew I was very fond of his wife ... I knew they had their problems; what married couple doesn't. One thing is for certain now, none of it bloody matters a lost ticket, does it?"

"I suppose not," said Barrow.

Before long, they reached the end of Ebury Lane and turned left onto Pimlico Road - Fellows came to a stop.

"Fritz," Fellows said, his throat feeling rather dry. "We have been close friends for many years - blood brothers I'd like to think. I just want you to know how grateful I am that you are telling me the story. But there is a part that's missing. The cash money that Guy pilfered from the Condo. I know relating all this to me has to be rough going for you, and you really didn't have to. Thanks for hanging on, but now I need to know about the money. And what role Bonnie has in it."

"This is how Bonnie related the story to me," replied Fritz. "She could only surmise how certain events led up to the money. Bonnie recalls that a few days prior to the plane crash, Guy called her and sounded a bit edgy. She definitely remembers that he was involved in the installation of telephone surveillance equipment in a luxury condominium on Key Biscayne, not an island, but a small land mass surrounded by water but attached to Miami proper by bridges. President Richard Nixon once had a home on Key Biscayne. She remembers the installation business because Guy told her about it and he rarely spoke of his activities, especially on the telephone. This surprised her. Bonnie feels he discovered, or at least saw the money while installing the equipment and hid it somewhere in that condo or perhaps in the building. When Guy returned to Washington a few days later from this particular assignment, he did not go to his home, but went directly to Bonnie's apartment. He had never done this before, and again, acted uneasy. Once more he got detailed and told her the F.B.I. and the Miami police had made a successful bust. It had to do with stolen negotiable securities from a Philadelphia brokerage firm. She recalls Guy saying that after the arrests of the persons involved, he returned to the apartment and removed the surveillance equipment. Bonnie thinks that's when he took the cash he hid. The stolen securities had already been confiscated. Now, on that very evening, Guy received a call on his cell and told Bonnie he had been assigned to go the Bahamas for a few days. Concerning this up coming operation, he told her nothing which was his usual style. So, there is the story. We'll never really know for sure what actually happened in that Key Biscayne condo."

Harry asked, "Where is the money now Fritz?"

"I'll explain that presently."

Harry said, "One thing is for certain. Having a wife and family and a girl friend, there was no way for Guy to save two hundred grand, not on his salary." Fellows then laughed aloud. "Fritz," he said, "do you know what my dear Margaret use to say when we first were married and things got out of bloody hand, or an argument ensued?"

Smiling, Barrow shook his head. "What?"

"She would say, Harry, someone dropped a turd in the punch, let's ditch it." Fellows laughed "What a silly thing to remember," he said softly to himself. "Fritz old boy," Harry said with perfect posh English accent, his shoulders pushed back, officiously rising to his full height, "typical of proper British deportment, what with all that Bonnie Adele entrusted with you, I am now prepared to brighten up and recreate the English charm that my very good friend from America deserves. What is done is done and I thank you for telling me." Fellows then hummed a few bars to the song, 'Bye Bye Blackbird.'"

Fritz not making even a reasonable connection to the song that he also knew the lyrics to, so in an inspired response turned to Fellows and said: "Blackbird, Bye Bye."

Fellows took hold of Barrow's arm and began to walk briskly. He pointed to the Red Lion across Pimlico Road. Waiting for a green pedestrian light, the men stood in front of a well-dressed flower shop. Through the window Barrow took notice of some hollyhocks planted in a wide wood planked tub. From some place in his mind, a sentimental memory of Paris began to take shape. He felt a warm surge inside, that lapsed into a state of reflection – it had happened during one of his summer holidays away from boarding school.

Near to Fritz's father's Paris apartment on Rue Le Manoir, were two spinster ladies; they owned a superb old small brick courtyard cottage – the zigzag placed pavers were all covered with a very green moss. Slippery when wet. Behind the dove-gray painted wrought-iron gate that protected their home, was a wonderful swinging bench constructed from real cedar wood. Surrounding that bench was a built-up garden containing bright yellow flowers and hollyhocks. Each evening after finishing work at his father's jewelry shop, and before going home for supper, young Fritz would hurry to the spinster's home. They would pay him five francs to pick the multitude of Japanese beetles from the hollyhock leaves; he would plunk them into a rose-colored drinking glass that was partially filled with mineral spirits. Every evening, no matter how long he imprisoned those beetles, there were always hundreds more to contend with.

Once, when in Paris as an adult, he taxied to that cottage only to find the ladies, the cottage, and the garden long gone. Now as he gazed at the hollyhocks in the window of the shop on Pimlico Road, he was positive he detected a faint whiff of cedar and mineral spirits.

"Fritz," said Fellows, breaking his friend's reverie. "A pub has stood at that very place across the way since the eighteenth century." He pointed as they moved quickly across the road towards the pub - "To me it's a fine example of what the true English pub ought to be. It has charm, the menu is traditional, and the atmosphere is plainly cheery."

Fritz smiled broadly; there was triumph in his eyes. He gently pounded Fellows on his back; a gesture that stated everything was going to be straight-out okay until the day of the big diamond switch.

The fire from the huge hearth and the horse-brasses that hung uniformly above the circular bar gave a wonderful look of what Fellows said was a fading part of true British ambiance

"Come on then," Harry said, "I'll get the bloody drinks, you order a table in the dining room from old gravel throat over there." Fellows went to the bar and ordered two pints of lager with lime. Later, standing at the bar, they touched mugs wishing each other 'Cheers.' Harry took a long swallow and placed his glass on a stained cardboard coaster.

"Tell me candidly Fritz, how is all this ... this business about my son Guy and Bonnie Adele, how is it going to play out in the pending scheme of pulling off the biggest single diamond heist of the century. And, as far as Bonnie is concerned, how do you know how she will react under fire; she's been a desk jockey most of her life and what do you suppose is her reason for wanting to join in on such a jewel theft? Are the two of you lovers?"

"Your table is now ready gentlemen," the raspy voice informed the men.

After being seated, Barrow pulled his lips in tight to keep from smiling at Harry's asking if Bonnie and he were lovers. Instead of answering, Fritz remarked how comfortable the pub was, and then stared at the fire for a few thoughtful seconds. He drummed his fingers on the table, stood, removed his jacket, carefully, folded it and placed it on the empty chair next to his. Fellows knew that each of Barrow's gestures had been a deliberate stall. What Fellows did not know was why.

"Okay, bloody hell, old boy," Fellows said simply, "get on with it. You don't think I am going to judge you for bedding down a young attractive girl like Bonnie do you? So she knew Guy. Damn meaningless, what?"

"You have a naughty mind, Harry. No, Bonnie Adele and I are not bedding down. But there is more to the story."

"Really. Could it be possible there's even more," Fellows said sharp-tongued. Then sounding more charitable said, "All right then, go on, I am perfectly willing to listen."

"First, Harry, I think you trust my instincts. I truly believe Guy and Bonnie were very much in love at the time, and that is extremely important to understand or at least believe. The details Harry. The bloody details. I have been over them hundreds of times. You know, Harry you cannot shit an old shitter. And sometimes things are what they actually appear to be. It's like you use to say Harry, evil has a smell of its own. This girl is sin free, and my feelings are that under the gun she will come through like a star."

Barrow pushed back on his chair and watched Fellows with cool determination. Instead of returning the stare, in slow motion, Fellows removed a cigarette from an already crushed pack, lit it with a wood match and flicked it several feet into the fireplace. Fellows had known Barrow since childhood; there had never been much disagreement;

moreover, they mutually liked each other. They had routinely aligned on most subjects and shared openly their most dark intimacies. Each had their own set of how-to-live rules, and never questioned the other's opinion no matter how trivial the point.

Now as he returned the stare, though a few aging wrinkles were beginning to appear on Barrow's handsome face, the face was no different then it was when he was growing up. Barrow's pale jadeite eyes had always attracted women as well as men. His smile still was seemingly sincere, and his sense of reality that unfailingly drove him to success and contentment appeared to be intact. Regardless, Fellows still coldly searched his face for a single tell-tale flaw. The years had revealed much for Harry Fellows the investigator, and he was not about to allow smooth surfaces and polished meanings to betray his one alcove of protection. He wondered if Barrow sensed it. Was there a self revealing expression on his own face that his friend might identify?

The restaurant section of the pub was a busy place with clashing wallpapers and matte finished lampshades. The Georgian table where they were now seated was small but solid. The room imparted a sense of old world hospitality as did Mrs. Green the proprietor's wife who appeared with a basket of soda bread and anchovy paste, and with a terrible northern accent loudly suggested her luncheon specials for the day.

Fellows ordered the Ploughman's with Stilton cheese, Fritz a Shepard's Pie with another round of beers.

"Bonnie knows quite a lot about you, Harry," Fritz said benignly.

"Really?" Fellows questioned, an annoyed look on his face.

"Guy obviously trusted her implicitly. She even related to me accurately the entire episode about you and the Lloyd's tiff."

"You don't say," said Fellows. "Did you have anything to say about it? Something perhaps that Guy omitted?"

"I related nothing, Harry."

"Then do tell me what she knows. I'm curious," asked Fellows, now looking demure.

"Simply stated Harry, she knows that you were the top insurance investigator for Lloyd's dealing exclusively with claims that involved heavyweight loses mostly with jewelry. Certain consortiums that underwrite large risks sometimes find themselves immersed in too many losing claims. It was these consortiums that often insisted you personally take charge of the investigation. According to what Guy told her, you actually saved several of Lloyd's underwriters millions of dollars by sniffing out fraudulent claims as well as successfully negotiating the return of many high-priced collections and estate pieces. Adele knows you're a member of the British Gem Society, have advanced training American style in criminal investigation, and that when it came time for a top drawer promotion, which you had been long promised, you were passed over owing to a miserable son of a bitch named Miles Jamison, a Lloyd's senior executive and master at back stabbing. You took it as more than a rejection and quit the firm out of disgust with a severely damaged ego, which in fact was behavior old Jamison had never anticipated."

"It all came down to the fact that I was bloody sacked," exclaimed Fellows a contemptuous look across his face.

"Your son Guy was extremely upset," Barrow resumed purposely ignoring Fellows protest. "Jamison never figured you would walk out, he figured you'd stick around for at least your retirement party. Twenty years of service deserves at least an engraved gold-filled wrist watch and a Kansas City steak dinner at one of London's better eating joints."

Harry mumbled, "Hmm."

"Guy told Bonnie he would like to have killed Miles Jamison. For whatever reason, the boy felt some personal guilt or at least expressed it that way to Bonnie. An explanation of that guilt could very well be that Guy subliminally felt he influenced you into leaving Lloyd's. Who knows? Plus he wasn't particularly thrilled with you becoming a private eye in a city like London."

"Utter fucking nonsense," Fellows said a bit too loud. He looked around slightly embarrassed. "Maybe so, Harry," Fritz said, "but he also told her he would work out a plan of vengeance to get even with all of them for the hurt and humiliation they caused you. Revenge, or a case for honest vengeance can keep a body at temperature in the nineties for a long time; no refrigeration necessary."

Both men stayed silent for a several moments.

"Christ Almighty," Fellows finally said. "Hopefully I will have an opportunity to sort out this bloody business properly with Bonnie at some future time ... but for now Fritz, please can we move away from all this and get on with the bloody plan. I am beginning to get chest pains from all this rhetoric."

Smiling, Barrow said: "Okay Harry, but believe me, it all fits. Mysteriously perhaps, but still it all fits. However, let me add this. I was the keeper of the money. Guy had mailed it to me straight away – two days before the plane crash. During the time that followed my giving Bonnie Guy's package of cash as instructed by Guy if something happened to him, she and I remained in close contact; mostly speaking on the telephone, occasionally having dinner, depending upon my schedule. I had already upgraded my jewelry-line and had gotten really busy. As we got to know each other, platonically that is… truthfully Harry, I find her to be terrific company. I also find her sad in some respects; I would say she is a lonely person, not many friends, which is an extension of her younger years. I'd bet Guy was the only man she had known sexually and most likely it remains as such."

Fellows longed to be free of this seemingly endless saga, but knew his friend was perfectly right in revealing all details. Both Fritz Barrow and Harry Fellows were self-trained to pay strict attention to details which ultimately led them to being keen observers.

Barrow drained away the last of his beer and said, "On the day I received the copy of the Jeweler's Keystone Circular, Bonnie and I had planned to lunch in Washington; I was driving to Connecticut to show my sample line to an important account as well as a friend, and would delay the trip with the lunch stop in Washington. Figuring I might have to wait a few minutes at the restaurant, I took the magazine with me to reread the article. As she approached the table, she saw the magazine, asked about it, and during lunch I off-handedly told her of an idea I had to avenge the screwing that you, dear Harry, got from Lloyds's of London. All of it a situation of rare coincidence."

Harry said, "That's when the idea came to light? What were you eating? LSD sandwiches?"

Barrow replied, ignoring the comment about LSD sandwiches. "Harry, before the day was over we reasoned out a preliminary working plan. We even drove to New York City, had a fast walk around Vanlo and Eugêne, after which she offered the two hundred thousand dollars to meet any up front expenses. As I said before, it ended up that Vanlo and Eugêne required a two hundred grand good faith deposit to accompany each bid."

Fellows interrupted, "The two hundred thousand dollars that came from the Key Biscayne hit?"

Barrow said, "Right. And if the switch goes rotten and south and we gotta scurry out, well, she's willing to blow the dough. Harry, I'm telling you, she is clever; has a natural ability to think out potential problems. I've never caught her in an exaggeration or found her making excuses. She is an extraordinary woman."

Barrow then took Fellows' hands into his own applying pressure. He looked his old friend directly in the eyes. "Harry, if it works, and if my math is correct, after expenses each of us stand to make over one million dollars; and that my boy is better than a sharp stick in the eye."

Fellows whistled, then mused aloud. "At my bloody age to become a jewel thief." A serious expression visibly followed. He said, "Fritz, but why. Why her? You are not a poor man. When they slam shut those steel bars on us, it could be for many years."

"Harry," answered Fritz, "and I am speaking for Bonnie now, and I sincerely believe this is her point of view, I feel she sees this as the perfect opportunity to act out Guy's revenge. Dead or alive Harry, at this time in her life, Guy's love is still all she has going for her."

Fellows put his forefinger to his lips, signaling a stop in the conversation. "Ah, lunch has finally arrived," he said to the waitress in a cheerful voice.

Barrow ate his Shepherd's Pie with gusto and ordered two more beers. Fellows picked laboriously at his Ploughman's, turning over in his mind any fragments of the story that needed putting together.

During lunch, Fritz kept glancing at Harry, a sardonic smile across his lips.

Pushing back his chair, Fellows got up, left the table and slowly made his way for the men's lavatory through the busy noontime crowd surrounding the bar. By the time he stood in front of the urinal, he had contemplated the ambiguity to reasoning things out; the personal kind of reasoning that moves human forces. To Harry Fellows there was no truth on earth, only that which is believed - there was nothing that was as dependable. Belief could be counted on in its purest form of deduction even when man moved to act out of obsessed zeal. Thinking about it now, Harry realized that it was totally logical that Barrow would want to plan and pursue a theft of such magnitude. Although everything seemed to fall neatly into place, the missing part that had been worrying Fellows in the entire well-contrived ruse, now out of the blue ascended the form of Barrow's deceased wife.

It had promptly become clear that a probable answer to his friend's motive lay in the absence of his beloved Ann Barrow. Fritz had not spoken of her, or made reference to her, happy or sad, for a long time. Fellows curiously suspected that Fritz already discovered for himself that her untimely death had left him obsessed with filling all the hours of the day with work and new projects - solitude was a dirty word. Ann Barrow was the unfortunate victim of a traffic accident in New York City. A drunk driver lost control of his vehicle and smashed head-on into the taxi that Ann sat in. The taxi driver and a female friend of Ann's also perished. The lead in story of the newspaper's account read: "There is always the risk that the unthinkable' will happen as long as drunk drivers take to the streets."

Fellows shrugged, and his thoughts turned to Bonnie Adele. Her own possible motive could have been sympathetically nurtured by Fritz Barrow. Was it not possible that he had cleverly convinced this love-torn woman to unwittingly play a role in this very dangerous scenario? It was obvious that Fritz did like her and trust her. When again would circumstances like these present themselves to build such a perfect opportunity for the kind of gigantic planning it would take to pull off the diamond hoax of the century.

Later when Harry returned to the table, he quietly sat down in the empty chair across Fritz.

Fritz looked up, blinked and smiled; somehow he looked older for the moment with hundreds of tiny wrinkles winking like tiny stars at the corner of each eye.

*   *   *

It was just before two o'clock when they were convincingly asked to leave the restaurant. "Ere now duckies," Mrs. Stiles spoke in her resonant pitch. "D'yu require anything else, if not, we'd like to 'av the bloody table back."

Outside the pub, the two men though far from being dangerously inebriated burst out laughing and made fun of the proprietress, imitating her shrill voice. It wasn't long before they happily settled down and sat on a wooden bench placed between two large empty white urns. They sat quietly with their legs extended, arms folded across their chests. Soon, Harry lit a cigarette.

Fritz broke the silence. "Harry, as I was saying before we were rudely kicked out of your friendly renaissance bar, the afternoon that Bonnie and I met for lunch, somehow in our seven hour get-together, the Singhalese diamond plan advanced into a life of its own; a thinly formulated plot to pull the heist was born. Instead of my going on to Connecticut, and after I drove Bonnie back to D.C., I drove to Long Island, locked my jewelry samples case in the bank vault, and returned to my apartment. I was exhausted as you can well imagine from all that driving and planning. It was the next morning as I explained that I went to Forty-Seventh Street to locate loose kunzite stones to match the magazine's photograph. Early on the following day, I flew to Paris and then on to Frankfurt, Germany. I split the flights just in case. One can't be too careful."

"Good thinking," said Fellows earnestly. "You have the natural skills of a successful M-5 agent, and I mean that."

"Thanks Harry. I might consider taking that as a compliment if I knew what a successful M-5 agent was. Anyway, I hired a car at the Frankfurt airport and drove directly to Idar-Oberstein. I located the busiest tourist hotel I could; The Parke, and at the check-in desk I handed the girl a business card I had made at a fast print place in the city that read the name Andrew Longmeyer with a phony New York address. I told her my passport was in another piece of luggage being delivered shortly and promised to bring it by reception as soon as it arrived. I paid in German marks for three days, and once in my room ordered my evening meal from room service. The following morning

I slipped out of the hotel, drove to the post office, and made all my telephone calls from there."

At once, Fellows said: "I have always preferred venturing out alone."

"Damn right and probably a very good reason why later in the day, I sat in the factory office of Bitterman and Friedrich, a very old established house specializing in the manufacturing and cutting of synthetic gemstones."

"Yes, yes," Fellows said with enthusiasm, "I know that name well. They made all the replica stones for the British Crown Jewels back in the late thirties. Matter of fact no one actually knows if the famous pieces displayed in the Tower of London are the real thing or not."

Barrow laughed devilishly. "I'm not surprised. These people are also well-known for duplicating certain gems for museums as well as private collectors. God knows how many phony colored stone gems are being worn to impress the American's upper bourgeois."

"And might I add, as well as the bloody very British upper-crust, what, eh I say?" Barrow enjoyed hearing Fellows' very British gesture.

Harry glanced at his watch; "Blimey, look at the time. We really ought to get cracking. I am positive Bonnie will be half starved when she wakes. What say we stop by the green grocers and pick up some fruit and cheese?"

A chilled wind came up from nowhere; pewter clouds descended and began to move swiftly. Both men hurried their pace. Sporadically, the headlights of cars began to come on.

"Please go on Fritz, you've gotten my blood driving rapidly through every one of my damn veins."

Fritz said, "In one of the offices, I spoke to Herr Adalfredo Leder the manager and head chemist of the firm. I knew I must be very careful with what I told him. By no coincidence, Herr Adalfredo Leder is the essence, the central core of the entire plan. Without him we're dead in the water. I have no idea if he's familiar with the Singhalese auction in New York or not. So the story I told him went like this. I have a client in Canada who desires to have a synthetic duplicate made of a rare, large, oval cut genuine pink kunzite he inherited. I show him the nine carat kunzite stone that I had bought in New York for the color, along with the finished dimensions of the finished stone required. I round out all the numbers: Thirty-one millimeters by eighteen millimeters by thirteen millimeters deep. So minuscule are the differences from the numbers on the gemological report, no one will notice unless they measure with a micrometer. That is a guarantee. Because synthetic kunzite and genuine kunzite have the same optical properties and the same inherent structure, I told him I didn't care about the finished weight as long as the measurements were there. Gormann isn't going to weigh a diamond that never leaves his possession or office. Herr Leder says matching the color would be no problem. He explained that he would use synthetic pink spinel and suitably colored glass. Says he will be able to make the duplicate by an old, but traditional method called the Vermeuil flame-fusion system. I tell Leder I am familiar with the process, but my instructions are implicit; the color cannot vary more than a quarter-shade of the sample nine carat stone. He says with brassy German authority, 'do not to worry my boy, in all probabilities it will finish a perfect color match.' I follow up with the cost price is no object; but my client is under a severe time constraint. Herr Leder glances at the thousand German marks I push into the top pocket of his jacket, one can't be cheap at this stage, and he promises to have the stone made and cut by his lapidary shop to my exact dimensions in less then one week."

Fellows keeping pace with the slightly younger man mumbled, "Money is like a sixth sense, you can't make use of the other five without it."

"Who said that?" Fritz asked

"Somerset Maugham, the great English author who wrote "Of Human Bondage."

Fritz asked, "Bondage and Money?"

"It's a very sad story about a chap with a club foot who takes up with an undeserving girl… showers his affection and all his money on her. A destructive relationship to be sure. Concern about money is all throughout the story… keeps the poor crippled chap in bondage, ergo, the title of the book."

"Harry, what are you going on about?" Fritz asked.

"The irony Fritz."

"You want to talk about irony and money? Here, what about this. During the war, the Nazi crooks stole this precious stone by blackmail, murder, torture, or other uncivilized means. After the war, the diamond goes to some family in South America who probably had ties with certain German generals who quickly fled Germany before they were captured. The diamond gets passed around. Finally, it comes in from the cold."

"The irony is clear?" said Harry.

"Of course. Bitterman and Friedrich, an old German firm who probably helped the Nazis, are now in the process of remaking the stolen diamond and are making a trio of American crooks a lot of money."

Harry said, "And the bondage. Imagine the bondage it created with the guardians of such a diamond?"

Fritz replied, "Ah, I see said the blind man"

Harry laughed aloud.

Barrow, wanting to depart from this intellectual pause dealing with bondage said, "To go on. As I mentioned, my appointment with Gormann is in one week, on a Friday. Tomorrow I fly back to Frankfurt, rent a car, drive back to Idar and as soon as the stone is in my hot little hands, I'll drive back to the airport and do my best to get back to New York *vite, vite*. If all goes well, we'll have at least three days grace to practice our roles before the appointed day."

Fellows stopped to light another cigarette. He cupped his hand around the flame and gazed upward to the steel-gray sky. He said with a frown, "That's the day we pray like hell you can make a successful switch."

"Amen, Brother Harry, and we'll also pray like crazy that Ernst Gormann discovers he's been fucked before he locks the Singhalese away in the store's vault."

"Very important that he does," added Fellows. The two men then turned to contemplate each other. With crossed fingers they raised their hands; just like they did as boys. There was a roll of thunder; it began to rain.

*   *   *

When the men returned to Fellows' Ebury Lane Flat with the food, they found Bonnie in tailored black slacks, a purple furry sweater, comfortably slumped in Fellows' easy chair reading the book MARKINGS. From the radio came the sound of classical piano. Pleasant greetings were exchanged by all - both men approached Bonnie to kiss her on the cheek. She had lit the small gas fire and the room was warm and cozy. Barrow humming comically walked to the liquor cabinet and poured out three glasses of Barbadillo Oloroso Sherry.

"One thing about Harry Fellows," Fritz said, "he has excellent taste when it comes to sherry."

"You'll find this deplorable weather," said Fellows gazing earnestly at Bonnie straight away, "cuts off sunshine for many prolonged periods, yet despite how awful it looks to you now, you will be amazed to find in just an hour or two, this front that is passing through, will leave washed clear skies."

"Good old, Harry," Barrow said cheerfully. "Always polished, always duty bound to the motherland. God forbid anyone should find something wrong with this island that sits under a huge rain cloud." Bonnie was too polite to join in with Barrow's laughter, instead, she alluded to Dag Hammarskjöld's book and said, "You know, Harry, the U.S. State Department has little doubt that the Russians planted a bomb on the plane that Hammarskjöld was flying in; everyone aboard was killed. Guy told me this book is among your favorites and how much you admired the man."

Fellows gave a rather sentimental smile. He had been about to make a comment concerning the book, but the instant she mentioned Guy's name, he could feel the undisguised love she must have felt for his son simply by the way she expressed his name."

"Yes Bonnie, Fritz has enlightened me as to your relationship with Guy."

Harry clenched his teeth, then hurriedly walked to where she sat and leaned down to kiss her cheek once again. He took her hands into his saying, "Bonnie, I'm very glad that you and Guy knew each other." She got to her feet, and they hugged.

Fellows knew right away the sensation he felt from her body was more than just embracing a young, shapely and attractive woman. The storm that emerged from deep inside was also more than normal male arousal. His hands began to shake slightly and his heart raced. He backed away though it was second too late; Bonnie had felt the rise of his erection against her thigh.

"Now my dear," he said attempting to keep his voice natural sounding, though there was an imperceptible crack to the words: "It is English tea time. I'm certain you must be ravenous."

With no pretense, Bonnie looked into Harry's eyes. "I can honestly say I've never been hungrier." From the radio came a loud and lengthy crescendo.

Installing himself in the kitchen, Fellows began to prepare Adele's snack. He chitchatted while Fritz lazed comfortably in a chair, sipped his second Sherry, snacking on salted almonds Harry had put out. He tapped his fingers in time which was now an orchestrated selection from the Broadway show Fiddler on a Roof.

"About the book, MARKINGS," said Bonnie "Don't you find it intriguing to think a man like Hammarskjöld, so equipped with ability, would forfeit the sanctity of home and family to want to make such a screwed up planet as ours a more tolerable place to live especially for the likes of those who despised him so deeply." Fellows stopped what he was doing, and stared blankly; he scowled as he considered his own private thoughts: *"I bloody well surrendered my home and family to the mysteries of human greed."* He downed his own second Sherry and went to pour himself another. Bonnie signaled she was happy with what she had.

Five minutes later, Bonnie ate hungrily and listened to Barrow's slightly slurred words as he began once again to discuss the plan. Shortly she let out a sorrowful sigh. Both men had dozed off from the effects of the potent Sherry.

*   *   *

Having no interest in listening to the pair snore away, she carried her dish and glass to the kitchen having decided to take a long invigorating stroll. She had slept long and hard and was beginning to feel cooped up. She left a note by the telephone saying if she happened to get lost, she had plenty of pound notes to return Ebury Lane by taxi. .

London: of all the European cities, Bonnie just knew she would love this one the best. One: It was English speaking. Two: It was probably the most civilized country on the map - people still queued rather than push their way into transports and the like. Three: Without King Henry the Eighth and English law, where would the free world be?

For years she had read about its grand history, noble leaders, perplexing intrigue, and a fascinating odd blend of architecture that it offered. The sky, though still overcast had cleared slightly; a light misty drizzle fell. She felt stimulated as she slowly walked along unfamiliar neighborhood streets of the towery city that displayed its inhabitants wearing so many styles of dress. Probably for that reason did she recall the tall visiting Cambridge University professor who specialized in construction design. Years before in the presence of Mr. Webster, the FBI's Director, that same professor had questioned her about a certain book on foreign Embassy surveillance in certain European terrorist-prone zones.

The book had been written by an American architect, Cornell Stephens. Stephens who had been employed almost regularly by the State Department as a consultant on Embassy buildings their design and construction had disappeared mysteriously while in Athens; there had been rumors about a possible defection to the Soviets.

The Cambridge professor who was introduced only as "the professor" was a counter-intelligence operative given the task of maligning Cornell Stephens within certain London circles where Stephens was well-known. The reasoning was that certain Soviet plants would then pass along to the Kremlin the invented negative information of Stephens supplied by the Professor. Sometimes it worked, sometimes it didn't, but it always left burning question marks as to its effectiveness.

The English professor's interest in Bonnie was that she had met with Stephens a year prior at a private debriefing in Washington with other Bureau agents to discuss a possible security leak in the American Embassy in Athens - the possibility of a mole. It concerned hiring locals for secretarial positions. What the Professor was looking for were any impressions or uncertainties she might have felt about the author at the time they met and might possibly recall.

Bonnie could still picture the professor sitting uncomfortably in a heavy wool suit. They were in the middle of a Washington heat wave and the air-conditioning system had been overworked - room temperatures were close to eighty degrees.

He had stubbornly declined numerous suggestions that he would be more comfortable in shirt sleeves though he eventually gave in.

He had also ordered tea with lemon and was brought a pitcher of ice tea expecting a pot of steeped hot tea. He drank ice tea for the first time in his life and had a good laugh at himself. "*That is what makes the British so charming,*" Bonnie thought. "*They don't mind making fun of their silly unimportant shortcomings.*"

Continuing in a direction to Soho mapped out on a small tourist guide she had purchased from a book store, she suddenly hesitated in front of a corner pub - The Barking Cat. It was all Tudor with horse-brasses placed everywhere; a friendly looking place to be sure. She peeked in. It was filled to capacity with well-dressed young men and woman; Bonnie immediately sensed a certain decorum; the ladies were relaxed and sure of themselves, definitely not flashy. "*So different,*" she thought, from the usual bars and clubs in Washington, DC that had become hangouts for isolated lonely singles. Turning to leave, she took notice of several couples across the narrow boulevard slowly meandering along the edge of Green Park. She sighed deeply. Having always envying anyone that was lucky enough to have someone near and not be alone; she suddenly felt vaguely remote. Her thoughts turned to Guy. She missed him terribly. So much in fact, that during the first few days following his death, she thought she might die herself from the sheer pain that constantly tore through her heart. They had kept the affair secret as the Bureau frowned heavily on such indiscretions that involved outside affairs while the participants were married. Another problem that added to the small dark lines under her eyes was there was no one to confide in about Guy's death. Her section supervisor beseeched her to seek medical attention as she was rapidly losing weight and looked "awful"- so it seemed everyone was saying.

Now, desiring to be closer to the beauty of trees and flowers, Bonnie crossed the boulevard to the park side. "Oh, Guy, please come back to me my darling," she anguished aloud as she walked along. Bonnie thought about the first night they had spent together. She had never been with a man until that wonderful evening. First Guy had removed her shoes and gently massaged the bottom of her feet. He undressed her, and as he did, caressed each part of her nakedness. She held onto his arms and agonized to the times she so imagined this ravishing pleasure. It all happened so beautiful and slow. He carried her into the bedroom, gently removed her glasses then kissed her passionately.

"Where, God. Where is my lover?" she cried softly to herself. Tears were suddenly running down her cheeks. He had touched and kissed her everywhere - he made consuming love. She gave herself permission to be satisfied; she remembered her own absurd screams of her first orgasm.

"We were lovers, real lovers in the true sense of the meaning," she cried shamelessly recalling the note he had left on her dresser:

"Dearest Bonnie,
I was never as happy as I was yesterday evening.
I hated to leave you this morning. Hopefully we
can see each other all the time.
Your sole mate,"
Guy

Bonnie could barely see her way along the sidewalk. A narrow foot path provided escape to a vacant park bench. She pictured herself on those terrible long lonely nights after his death. She continued to weep like a child - a passing stranger noticing her, asked with kindness if he could be of help. Bonnie shrugged saying "No thank you, I'm fine." Embarrassed by the image she was creating to passerby's; she wanted to get up and run but instead got up and walked slowly away. "Emotionally, I'm on the tipping edge;" she said softly aloud, "close to falling off - I have to work through it; I must."

Minutes later she passed under a giant archway. Unexpectedly her thoughts turned to Harry and Fritz and the plan to switch the Singhalese diamond. Stopping for a moment and seeming to realize her irrationality, she silently recited the nursery rhyme:

Humpty Dumpty sat on a wall.

Humpty Dumpty had a great fall.
All the king's horses and all the king's men
Couldn't put Humpty together again.

"Guy, Houdini and Jack Kennedy are not coming back." She forced a laugh at the thought. She knew that Guy believed deeply that destiny had to be understood when certain moments existed where predetermined future events, even though heavily disguised to try and side-track us, could actually be understood and acted upon. *"Maybe all of it does matter, this quest for revenge and wanting to recreate lost loves. Why not, damn it? At least I learned we know ourselves best through love and not knowledge - and am I not happier now than I've ever been, at least since my beloved Guy died."* Her eyes were beginning to clear of tears - *"Time to shed the tragique. There was a reason for the money he found. I'm involved, that's the important thing. Miss Goodie Goodie, flesh and blood FBI lady turned conspirator, perpetrator, villain and accomplice to a multi-million dollar diamond rip-off. I love it. By God I absolutely love it!"*

One hour later she returned to Harry Fellows' flat by taxi feeling confident and determined. To her chagrin, both men were still snoring away.

*   *   *

It was after 7:00 that Fellows had gotten up and plodded into the kitchen for a glass of cold water. Fritz Barrow was no where to be seen. Bonnie was busy in the kitchen making a fresh pot of coffee. The telephone rang: Fellows answered; said "yes" three times before hanging up. "My brief conversation," he informed Bonnie, "is to do with dinner reservations this evening at one of my favorite Italian restaurant; Rossini's."

CHAPTER THREE

At 8:15 Fellows entered the living room. Taking a position of standing straight; upright. He unquestionably looked distinguished. His linen shirt was white and expensive; a twin letter script monogram HF in silver thread was stitched on the lower right cuff. Bonnie could smell his cologne; "*Jesus Christ, the same that Guy wore.*" Fellows gray hair was full and sensibly combed back.

Bonnie stared into Harry's eyes. There passed across her face a look of painful recognition as if Guy had just entered the room; there was a remarkable likeness; then there was the scent of the cologne. With tortuous emotion she fought to keep her composure. She wanted to rush to him, put her arms around him and remain there forever how long she had to. Fellows stared back for an instant and pushed his hand into his trousers pocket to remove an almost crushed pack of cigarettes.

"You really ought to quit smoking," Bonnie said. She quickly considered the statement and was sorry she said it; it sounded too familiar. Then with feminine motion, she picked up the cigarette lighter from the desk and went to where Fellows stood. He gave an agreeable smile, removed a cigarette from the pack for her to light.

There was a loud knock and the front door opened. It was Fritz. "Good evening," he said. "Forgive me for complaining, Harry, but it has turned goddamn cold and rainy." He dropped the evening newspaper on the front table and stuck his umbrella into a ceramic elephant's foot. "*Anyone* who complains about New York weather being unpredictable should come to this godforsaken island for a few days."

Fellows laughed and had a fleeting vision of Fritz as a young man; glib, always wanting perfection, pretending to be no different than anyone else, but always managing to be a leader. The first drops of rain thumped lazily against the panes. A chilled bottle of Moët and Chandon champagne appeared from a parcel Barrow carried. "A before dinner celebration," he said.

*   *   *

Harry had reserved a table at a small Italian restaurant he frequented in London's Soho section. The restaurant was owned by a unsavory, but likeable character known only as Rossini. For years Angelo Rossini had been a known fence for stolen jewelry primarily from London's middle-class neighborhoods. Fellows had first encountered Rossini during an investigation of a potentially large claim involving an art and jewelry theft from the home of Arthur Finney, a well known London antique dealer. Aside from a sizable loss of valuables, the unfortunate victim had died from a massive coronary while trying to defend his collection of treasures. Lloyd's had been requested by the broker early on to oversee the investigation of this particularly noxious crime.

The underwriters, a fledgling syndicate, had been hit with a series of cargo thefts at various European ports and one more costly payoff would result in the group having to drop out of the Lloyd's consortiums. Lord Sheldon Cord-Kissel, a highly ethical man with the old Lloyd's organization, knowing full-well that taking risks was the nightmarish name of the game, came uncharacteristically from a place of sheer forbearance knowing that a few good premiums would help get the consortium back on the right road. He personally contacted Harry Fellows and beseeched him to save their bloody asses; find the culprits and rescue the stolen goods. Fellows agreed, and after a few phone calls, found there was talk that a certain restaurant owner in Soho had dealt with the deceased dealer on more than one occasion. Although it was veil thin information, and one that the police had already investigated, Fellows had a private theory that any lead was a good one, and if acted upon, a whole stream of incidents would issue forth from that decision and all sorts of things would occur to assist.

Not being naïve at all, Harry also knew from being near to the criminal system that many so-called legitimate dealers themselves did occasionally deal in stolen goods - there could be a connection. Also, if Rossini did have dealings with the now dead Arthur Finney, just possibly the Italian chef might have had him set up. With no proof but a far-fetched idea, Fellows decided to chance it and visit the restaurant owner.

Later that evening, Fellows did receive information that Finney and Rossini did know each other. Fellows walked slowly along the pavement towards the restaurant. He carried in his pocket a list that New Scotland Yard had furnished Lloyd's describing the dead man's own personal jewelry, which included a platinum ring set with ten small rubies and ten diamonds, as well as the other missing property.

If the dining room was busy enough, Fellows knew it would be madness for the owner to get unreasonable. He also knew that for him to lose control in a public place, though not a indication of a guilt, it could open the flood gates for one to speculate such criminal activities. With a cover story that was quite flimsy, and a disposition that could be seen as wicked, Fellows entered Rossini's Ristorante. Three hours later after Rossini said good night to his final customer, did the bulldogged Fellows manage to corner the man who knew the deceased dealer. The greedy restaurant owner was wearing the missing ruby and diamond ring, Rossini protested. "Finney sold me this ring off his finger. I paid him cash money."

"You're a liar Rossini. Know what English juries think about criminals who wear the jewelry of victims who die trying to protect their valuables."

"No. How would I know? I ain't ever been on a jury."

Grimacing, Harry said, "More than likely you were never selected. Know why? Because you're a fucking dummy. Can you prove the buy from Arthur Finney? Can you come up with the date and time this transaction took place? Is there anyone who witnessed the sale? Jesus, Rossini, I'm looking at the dead man's ring on your finger. Here, look, it's described in this list from New Scotland Yard. Look at it. You know the law Rossini. The perps can be charged with homicide, at least first degree manslaughter… simply because Finney croaked… even if they never laid a finger on him. Anyway, can I use your telephone? I'm going to inform the Yard of the ring."

Rossini yielded. He was one who respected the London underworld code 'don't rat anyone out' and would sooner cut his throat than deal with the police, so he allowed himself to trust the insurance investigator Harry Fellows.

At the end of two days, New Scotland Yard apprehended the evil-doers led by a second-story man named Juan Tomas. Tomas eventually revealed the names of the persons to whom he sold the balance of the swag making it easy for Fellows and the police to recover all of the stolen merchandise. Rossini received the lightest sentence possible; eighteen months in prison for receiving stolen property in a behind-the-scenes plea bargain, rather than a likely ten for complicity to a homicide. The Lloyd's syndicate lads in their appreciation paid Harry a handsome cash fee under-the-table.

Rossini hated prison like a cripple man hates dancing. He hated the steel bars that kept him from his kitchen and food smells that were so entrenched in his sensory recall. He hated the people around him because they were afraid and that made them dangerous. He also fought a relentless struggle not to permit himself to think about roving free on the streets of Soho, seeing happy and unhappy pleasure seekers. He longed for the early morning yellow fog and the surges of street noise and traffic that steadily cried like insane sentinels protecting the inhabitants of his Soho.

Finally there came a blessed day twelve months later when he appeared before a parole committee who allowed him to leave his confinement at a somewhat early date. Rossini knew full well that Fellows had personally participated in the formal board hearing by submitting a letter indicating the now reformed man no longer represented a threat to law-abiding London citizenry. Still, there was a lingering thought that he would never forgive the man who put him away. One day, he would even the score. However, upon his conditional release, Rossini immediately set out to revive his once successful restaurant business.

Fellows liked eating in Rossini's, often stopping in for an evening meal. When he did, the owner would frequently show Fellows a piece of jewelry and ask his opinion to its quality and worth. Fellows would look him square in the eye and the overweight Italian would cross himself twice and swear on his dead mother's picture that hung over the steam table, that the item Fellows held in hand was absolutely Kosher. Both men would laugh congenially and ended up sharing a bottle of Rossini's best red table wine. Though, still lingered Rossini's thought about his revenge.

On this particular evening Harry, Fritz and Bonnie arrived at the restaurant just after 9:30. The trio was personally escorted to a special table by the owner himself. The sociable Angelo Rossini looked at the trio oddly then informed Fellows that he would personally choose the food and give particular attention to its preparation. Tonight for some reason, Rossini appeared a queer, lonely figure to Fellows. Fellows thanked him, and then signaled he was not to be disturbed any more. Rossini acknowledged that he understood and that he would instruct his waiters as such.

After comfortably settling down, wine and thick crusted Italian bread was brought to the table. Fellows poured - they raised their glasses; Barrow toasted: "Here's to our tacit Mr. Ernst Gormann, hopefully our invisible fourth gang member."

Bonnie adding, "Pour, Oh, Pour the Pirate Sherry." Fellows and Barrow looked at each other curiously, Fritz Barrow adding: "Here, here, to what ever in bloody hell pouring Pirate Sherry means."

Everyone laughed openly and tasted the wine. Fellows lit a cigarette.

Barrow said, "To make sense of what I have to tell you now, is to understand that the entire episode before us is based on approaching a man who has no worldly idea we intend to rewrite his future. But at least for the better." Sliding his chair and himself closer to the table's edge, Barrow spoke in the patient monologue tone of one who was about to provide a complicated answer to a complicated question. "To our advantage was also the magazine's article about the man from Vanlo and Eugêne, the previously mentioned Mr. Ernst Gormann. He is an opera buff; a widower for fifteen years; lives by himself in a luxurious Park Avenue apartment; has always rented; is said to have an adequate social life; wears expensive clothing. His first job thirty-five years ago was as an assistant to Remy Frostman, Vanlo and Eugêne's head diamond buyer. Gormann's entrée to such a desired position was probably due to the fact that Gormann's father owned a small but prestigious supply house. His father Siegfried Gormann, almost exclusively furnished the New York diamond market with all the necessary supplies of the trade: loupes, scales, sifts, sorting trays, gauges, diamond papers, tweezers, plus whatever else was needed. What is important is relatives of Gormann and Frostman date back to the same small town of Sittnow in Germany. Reading between the lines, what I gathered from the article was that apparently, grandfathers of both men were boyhood friends. Remy Frostman, unlike Gormann, he dropped the second letter 'n' from his last name, was a brilliant mathematician and a top diamond expert."

Fellows coughed and stubbed out his cigarette. Bonnie turned to look at him, clearly again seeing Guy's face. She recoiled against a smarting spasm in her chest, exhaling heavily. Her dead lover had reappeared for a fleeting moment once more; she inhaled with two quick huffs.

Fellows laughed behind one hand and patted Bonnie's arm with the other – all the negative sensations had disappeared,

"Actually," continued Fritz unaware that Bonnie had paled and felt light headed, "most diamond dealers, I learned on the street, utterly despised this Remy Frostman. Conversely, those attitudes were mixed with a rather weighty respect for his knowledge and fairness in treating all sides alike. Frostman was goy; a non Jew. Worse than that! - He was German. And the Jewish diamond brokers never would forgive God for the terrible blunder of making Frostman the point man. On top of all that, here comes Frostman's protégé; another German goy, Ernst Gormann." she felt better, the worst had passed.

"But the truth was," Barrow went on to say, "Vanlo and Eugêne would buy more diamonds in a month, than some of the big name houses would buy in six months, plus they paid their bills right away. You can imagine what a cushy piece of action it was for the New York diamond dealers to be part of Remy Frostman's circle of approved dealers. Whether for the good or bad of it, Frostman had no particular favorite diamond dealers as he was little interested in personalities. He represented the true definition of what a devoted company man ought to be. He sought only top quality merchandise at fair market price, and Gormann shared the same mind set."

Barrow paused to sip from his glass. Fellows lit another cigarette. A waiter gingerly walked by, taking a sideway glance at the group who had extricated themselves from a staff so well known for excellent service.

"I also found out that no one would dare try to *schmeer* the palm of either one of these men," Fritz said suddenly with mild protest in his voice, "which is routine in some of the other retail jewelry houses. In fact it was tantamount to treason to offer either Ernst or Remy a sandwich and a bowl of soup let alone money under the table. Their integrity was sacrosanct and intact. When a diamond dealer did sell them, and I am speaking of small sizes, specifically melee, there better not be more than five percent rejection in any one diamond parcel; there were no second chances with these two characters. Eventually Gormann took full responsibility in buying diamonds up to two carat sizes, and like his mentor, if the asking price was out of line, Gormann would simply say sorry; pass. The deal was finito. No offers, no discussions. This made the Jews absolutely fucking crazy; it is just not the American way not to bargain and haggle. They couldn't handle it at first."

All three joined in laughing. Adele took the wine bottle and topped off the glasses.

"It seems that years later when Frostman retired, Gormann was given all his duties including the buying of important size diamonds and that was with the unanimous approval of the Vanlo and Eugêne's Board, that most likely included Nestor Brunnell, the store's GM and the assistant GM, Charles Daisey."

Barrow ceased to speak on Fellows' signal when Rossini appeared with a basket of garlic bread-sticks. Rossini was quick and remained silent. He winked at Fellows as he retreated to the kitchen.

Bonnie was quick to raise her glass signifying another toast. She hunched herself forward, her chin practically touching the table and in a hushed voice said: "To the Singhalese diamond switch." The three touched glasses and the men responded in low voices: "To the Singhalese diamond switch." They all drank to the toast.

From behind swinging doors to the kitchen, Rossini watched Fellows' table with increasing interest. He was thinking, *"I'll take a short trip past their table."*

Barrow commented favorably about the vintage Chianti, and passed the basket of bread. Putting her glass down, Bonnie bit the end from a bread stick and at the same instant caught Harry's eye. Fellows wasn't certain if he misunderstood her meaning, then thinking, *"I'm just a horny old man."* Bonnie realizing biting the bread and looking at Harry, Harry might have taken it for something suggestive and sensuous.

Reacting quickly to that possibility, Bonnie said, "A spokesman for the Bureau once put out a memo that said that an obscure nineteen thirties FBI manual recommended Chianti as the wine special agents ought to drink if they found themselves in an uncompromising situation; in other words, if they were compelled to drink. It seems Chianti is the only red wine that never leaves you with a hangover or headache. I hope you remember that Harry, when you retire."

Barrow and Fellows immediately spluttered agreement pretending to be drunk and Bonnie grinned widely at their antics thinking it all perfectly wonderful that they were together even if there was the possibility of a rotten ending.

Suddenly, Fritz flung himself back into the conversation. He began by saying, "Our future benefactor Ernst Gormann *had an eye*, as the expression goes in the diamond business. Frostman would brag that Ernst Gormann could spot a piqué in a diamond quicker than most dealers could focus their loupes. And it apparently was not an exaggeration; as a result, the smart boys on the street trusted Gormann. Ernst Gormann could determine color and clarity with such a high degree of accuracy that the biggest dealers in New York came to Vanlo and Eugêne to ask Gormann his opinion. And indeed his opinion settled many a dispute between disagreeing dealers." Barrow summoned up a heavy sigh. "Age dear friends, it is age that rots wood or the iron hull – for the Ophthalmologist surgeon, it becomes shaky hands; for the diamond man like Gormann it was the eye. Fortunately, his own nature wouldn't allow egotism or self-importance to become an issue as was with our friend Harry's dismissal from Lloyd's. The worse part of the decline to his near perfect vision simply removed part of Gormann's own imposed sensitivity.

Bonnie blinked steadily; she did not quite get it. She looked to Fellows. He had removed another cigarette from the pack that lay on the table wedging it between his lips. He lit it never taking his eyes off Barrow's face. Why did Harry look so serious? She was about to raise the question.

"There in good people lies the story," Barrow continued. "Though the cataract surgery went perfectly, Charles Daisey ordered that Gormann would no longer buy diamonds for the firm. Maybe Daisey was just nervous, I don't know. As a replacement Gormann recommended an instructor, Gregory Kenland from the Gemological Institute of America to Vanlo and Eugene's Board. The Board respected Gormann's opinion, and Gormann knowing Kenland personally did vouch for his expertise and heartily approved the appointment. Charles Daisey kept Gormann on; one would suppose out of loyalty, though it is common knowledge that it's not one of Charley Daisey's strong suits to be considerate and kindly, so it must be partly due to Nestor Brunnell's close ties to Gormann."

Seeing uncertainty in Bonnie's eyes, Barrow took hold of her hand. "This is the reason why I'm so sure Gormann, in the aftermath of the switch, will bite the hook, line and sinker to join us in our ill-contrived guise. Similar to dear Harry's dilemma, Gormann felt he should have gone upstairs to Board level. After all, thirty years of devotion and talent isn't exactly spit. Add to that he probably feels he saved the company a fortune as a result of his conscientiousness, same as in Harry's association with Lloyd's. However, Charles Daisey boy told Nestor Brunnell no to top management. You can be certain Gormann in his not so secret heart feels he got screwed up his well-bred ass. So unbeknownst to Ernst Gormann, we are going to give him his redemption, vengeance if you prefer, plus one hell of a retirement bonus."

"That's right,' said Fellows cheerfully, pushing the bread basket away. "Honest revenge and one hell of a retirement bonus."

Fritz said, "Harry, it's up to you to find Gormann's button; the button that could ensure he'll work with us. If not, then we'll deal with the aftermath in another way."

*   *   *

It was five-thirty the following morning when Fellows stood over Barrow, gently pulling his arm. Fritz opened his eyes, stretched luxuriously and yawned. "You are going to tell me that you must be on your way; that you ordered me a taxi and there is a pot of coffee and some scones waiting for me in the kitchen."

"Clever boy," said Fellows. "The taxi will be in front of the building at six-fifteen. Right now it's five-thirty, so you should get your ass in gear as you Americans like to say, though the words are meaningless, and I must be on my way if I'm to make my train. Drive careful on that dreadful German autobahn Fritz. See you in New York tomorrow." Barrow got up from the sofa, shook Fellows' hand, hugged him and said, "And you take care too old boy."

Fellows left the flat quickly to a waiting tax. Two hours later, while Bonnie completed her own packing in Harry's guest room, Fritz Barrow boarded a British Airways 747 at Heathrow Airport bound for Frankfurt, Germany. Upon arrival, he would once again hire a car and drive two hours to Idar Oberstein, use the post-office telephone to arrange with Herr Adalfredo Leder the delivery of the synthetic kunzite – his fingers crossed as to its final appearance.

Fellows in the meantime had already taken a train from Charing Cross Station to the city of Guilford. Outside the Guilford train station, Harry questioned three taxi drivers before hiring a chap named Otto. Otto was to drive Harry north on the A31 to a major crossroads called Sandy Lane. At Sandy Lane, as instructed, Otto turned right and continued for one mile, passing through the village of Littleton. Just past Littleton at a T-junction, the taxi turned west and drove directly to the village of Compton-on-Green. At the town center, Fellows directed Otto to Compton's Episcopal Church car park. Harry handed the driver a fifty-pound note; he then tore a hundred pound note in half giving the Otto one half of it. "When I return you get the other half", Fellows said with authority. "I'll be gone a good hour at least." The cabbie nodded acknowledgement thinking this was the most peculiar fare he had had in fifteen years of being a taxi driver.

With quick and long strides, Fellows walked to the opposite side of the church, out of sight of the taxi, walked past a small cemetery, and down a steep path onto a narrow gravel road called Penny Lane. He hurried another quarter mile to an unpretentious cottage - a lacquered board hanging beneath the mailbox identified the cottage as Trippet. At the front gate a barking yellow Labrador and an elderly man, very tall, greeted Harry Fellows.

"Dear me," said Ossie Graves, looking at his wrist watch, "ten minutes late. What has ever happened to my Harry?" Both men laughed and shook hands. "Welcome to Trippet Cottage. It's been a long time Harry Fellows. Come, come into my humble abode. I know you are in a hurry, but we will have a short chat about old times, both good and bad over a cup of strong Russian tea and a few bites of homemade shortbread cookies."

"So Gravy," asked Harry, "how does a retired electronics engineer get along in this modern society of electronic marvels?"

"Well Harry, let me put it this way. As per our correspondence, I'm ready to install a tiny, state of the art transmitter onto the back of an eighteen karat belt buckle of yours, and mount a matching receiver to a lady's silver tortoises shell hair comb that you've brought along. And though I love you dearly, it's still going to cost you a pretty penny. It took quite awhile to find the right components and put them together."

"Can't scare me old boy."

Fellows liked Gravy's small workshop. He liked the way his old friend fussed about it being well-kept and immaculately clean. Harry admired people who looked after things and finished what they began; a condition of his personal desire for accuracy and thoroughness. Fellows had always sermonized newly recruited investigators at Lloyd's, that habits, whether good or bad are difficult to break …"so why not develop good habits." To which he would add one of his favorite sayings, "Habit is like a cable to which we add a strand each day, until at last we cannot break it."

Fellows watched with pleasure as Graves carefully soldered the housing of the minute transmitter to the buckle. Graves was a man who proved himself to be supremely proficient - who during the Falklands' campaign, was decorated by Mrs. Margaret Thatcher personally for developing a communication system that somewhere during the course of engagement, did help defeat the terrible enemy. There were pictures taken of the ceremony, a glass encased medal, newspaper articles and yet, nothing in his shop indicated the genius behind any of it.

There was no conversation during the installation. Fellows walked to the other side of the work table where he stared pensively through the window admiring his friend's rose garden. There wasn't a house on

Penny Lane that didn't have rose bushes featured in their tiny gardens. The only garden Harry had ever been part of was at his parents' bungalow in Saxony. Harry was twelve years old when his father Jack Fellows, had been killed in a spectacular auto accident that included the death of the local Duke and the Duke's mistress at a village seven miles from his home. As a result of testimony at the coroner's inquest, there arose a problem for Mrs. Fellows in collecting the proceeds of an insurance policy. Harry had learned years later that his father and the Duke had a confrontation in the Black Raven Inn. Each other argued vociferously over recent rent increases at the town's center; shops the Duke's family owned, and where Harry's father Jack Fellows owned a clock repair shop.

From accounts of some pub patrons, it appeared that the elder Fellows left the Inn quite drunk, waited for the Duke to leave, than shortly thereafter, intentionally tried to force the royal landowner off the road. Seemingly, their bumpers locked, both drivers lost control, the Duke's Bentley slammed into a utility pole, Jack Fellow's Ford had rear-ended the Bentley – an explosion followed and three persons in two cars burned to death in a blaze that could be seen, some say, for several miles around.

The insurance company refused to pay the proceeds on a technicality and although Mrs. Fellows engaged legal assistance, she ran out of finances and was unable to remain in the bungalow awaiting the courts final disposition. She and young Harry moved to the City of Nottingham where they set up home in a large, cooperative development. There Mrs. Fellows attempted to keep African violets on a small glass coffee table close to the largest window in their fourth-floor tiny flat. Harry smiled, remembering how she would baby those plants.

"Done Harry." Gravy's unexpected voice violated Fellows' daydream. "Come along old boy, have a look then."

After the demonstration and words of encouragement, Fellows pulled out a brown envelope containing cash from inside his jacket pocket and dropped it on the work table.

"Harry, these bloomin' babies are strictly on the cheap two-bit Woolworth specials," Gravy added. "Their range is short, the signal weak. So anyone monitoring for electronic device signals will probably dismiss the signal as a stray radar bleep. But they should be jolly perfect for whatever it is you wish to use them for." The men looked at each other and grinned.

After a quick embrace and soft words of good-bye, Fellows hurried back to the waiting taxi.

Later that same morning at noon, Fellows entered a small jewelry store in the Paddington section of London and had delivered to him a fourteen karat, yellow gold, one inch disc that hung from a sixteen inch thin gold chain. Soldered on front of the disc was a red enamel 'Medical Alert' emblem. Engraved on the back of the disc were the words:

"In Case of Emergency Contact: Harold Frank, M. D. (212) 598-5142"

Fellows said with a straight face, "Bloody perfect Jake. No one could possibly miss that red caduceus. My third cousin once removed, a mysterious chap, will be most grateful."

"Always happy to accommodate a relative of a good friend," said Jake, his face as serious as he could make it, though he was dying to say something sarcastic about Fellow's mysterious relative and the real purpose of the disc. Although these two had been brothers-in-arms Artie Jacobs knew Fellows well enough that he needed to remain on the sensible side of asking no questions.

Artie Jacobs had been delighted that he could be of service to his long time past associate and friend. Jacobs, a retired Lloyd's claims man, had worked closely with Fellows for years in the fraud section. He and his wife Bess had purchased the small retail store when retirement had lost its appeal, and the cost of living had exceeded his pension check.

"It was a bloody travesty, Harry, what Miles Jamison done to you Harry," Artie Jacobs said. "Me and Bess still talks about it."

"As you know Artie," said Fellows, "the good Lord often works in mysterious ways." Suddenly Fellows yelped aloud after glancing at his watch. "Artie, I bloody-well have to be getting on my way. It was bully of you to do all this for me at such short notice." Fellows pulled an envelope from his jacket pocket.

"No way, Harry. This one is on me. Let's just call it a favor long deferred, mate."

The men shook hands; but Jake held on to Fellows' hand in a hard grip. "Take care, Harry," the words were warm and forewarning.

Fellows smiled. "Thanks Jake, be sure to remember me to Bess." He walked out of the shop quickly managing to slide the envelope so it dropped behind the counter; a wave of emotion had caught Fellows off guard. He hailed a taxi, and then waved a final goodbye to Artie Jacobs who now stood outside his shop.

*   *   *

Bonnie opened the door for Harry smiling ear to ear. She had been standing at the window for the past hour anxiously waiting for the taxi that would drop him off.

They hugged and held each other tightly, then stood apart looking deeply into each other's eyes in silence as though a message of sorts were to be readable. What could only be described as a comfortable air of completeness settled over them both. "I missed you Harry," She then kissed him lightly on his lips.

"I'm packed and ready Harry and I might add that you are a very tidy chap. I enjoyed putting together your list. Nothing more that I could think of, you might have omitted something, but then, I haven't had the occasion to pack for a man. Jesus, Harry. I was worried about you. I had thought you would phone at least once." Her voice was comforting and caring.

"Sorry   about   that   Bonnie…   I   should   have." Irresistibly, Fellows longed to embrace her once again. It had been years since a woman had uttered that kind of concern. He made a move towards her – she moved to him and they embraced. "Thank you for that Bonnie,' he said. Then out of disconcertedness he removed a pack of cigarettes from the overcoat draped over his shoulder.

"I have a drink for you," she said easily, walking towards the kitchen. "Just need to add some ice. Our flight seems to be on schedule departing at three. How did everything go?" A few moments later she stood before him holding a glass of whiskey. A wide grin beamed across Fellows' face; he simply patted the small parcel inside his jacket pocket. "Everything went bloody perfect, and we have got to get cracking.

We are only just running on schedule. Security check takes forever at Heathrow.

She lit his cigarette.

Just as quickly as he could, Fellows readied himself for the trip to New York City. The warmly dressed couple left Fellow's flat each carrying their own suitcase. After locking the door Fellows hesitated briefly. Bonnie had already begun to walk down the corridor and took no notice of his pause. Fellows had an over-familiar notion, and the reflex thought came cutting into his imagination. It was the same train of thought he had had in the old days when getting close to winding up a particularly difficult case. He mumbled one of his time worn lines: "Take it easy old boy, if you go to the races indifferent, the odds of winning increase." He frowned. *"This time however, I can't afford to be indifferent. Too much at stake… everyone's reward and maybe all of our necks."* He did not want to consider the rotten-apple theory.

They left the building and walked six blocks at a brisk pace which brought them to a sidewalk Airbus pickup stop next to a small pedestrian park. "You might think a taxi would get us to Heathrow quicker, but believe me with uncongested bus lanes, it's much better than a taxi especially when we get into the thick of air port auto traffic."

They boarded the Heathrow Express, climbed steps to the upper deck then seated themselves. With arms interlocked, they huddled closely without embarrassment; it had turned extremely cold and they kept each other warm. Ten minutes later the bus pulled away. It was 1:30 P.M.

As the traditional red double-decker transport slowly rolled into the busy afternoon traffic, Fellows began to relax and talk about the city of London pointing to places of historical interest. Although the bus was filled with noisy tourists pointing and shouting, it was obvious that Fellows was enjoying being Bonnie's self-appointed personal tour guide. She watched and listened carefully, knowing full-well that little would be said concerning the great upcoming New York diamond heist, or not until they were at least airborne.

Fellows happily continued his discourse about the open spaces the city provided its inhabitants and visitors, as well as its many glorious royal parks - London's museums were amongst the best in Europe and in the United States, shopping Knightsbridge at Harrods and Harvey Nichols, Oxford Street's Marks and Spencer, Fortnum and Mason in Piccadilly brought the wealthiest from around the world, "though I must admit that even if our culinary treats have improved, more important Bonnie is the British pub and our fish and chips, and they are the best on earth if eaten off a page from yesterday's newspaper." Bonnie laughed and Harry paused momentarily closing his eyes as the bus moved onto the motor way – seconds later did the weary speaker peacefully doze off.

CHAPTER FOUR

Bonnie looked kind-heartedly at the man who fathered the only person she had ever romantically loved. Her thoughts wandered to Fellows' deceased wife. During their short lived affair, her intermittent inquiries concerning Guy's mother always proved distressing to Guy, therefore the subject was avoided. Bonnie recalled what Fritz Barrow had told her on the flight coming to London. He began by saying, "Margaret Fellows was fastidious to a point of bug house lunacy." -Adele had chuckled at Fritz's droll description- "It wasn't until Harry had actually decided to have Margaret institutionalized, that he would come to realize what so many already knew - her obsession for cleaning seemed to be the only thing to fill her mind and life. Harry had pleaded and begged her to try and combat this compulsive disorder. She refused medication but agreed to allow him to bring in daily help. But she soon discharged each of them for reasons only she knew. Her level of anxiety increased. Margaret agreed to hypnosis, but that failed. Electroshock therapy was physician recommended, but Margaret declined. Eventually, Harry stayed away, spending very little time at home. This absence actually enhanced his career as an investigator at Lloyd's.

Bonnie had asked Fritz if Margaret Fellows had been the same when they first married.

"An interesting question," Barrow responded. "I think so. The truth is Harry was proud of her at the beginning. He would brag to his friends how she kept everything so immaculate and orderly. After all, everyone knows Harry likes orderliness. At that time they lived just outside London in a marvelously large flat; one can imagine each day for her must have been like an uninterrupted cleaning party."

Bonnie smiled thinking how she had laughed at Fritz's dry humor.

"But as time passed Harry could see this phobia about cleaning, transform into advanced psychosis." Barrow had paused, trying to recall a name- "Harry told me it was a chap named Nicky Wheat, another Lloyd's investigator who initially tipped him off about a group of friends and acquaintances being uncomfortable when they visited his home."

Bonnie had tried to avoid the subject, but couldn't. "What about Guy?" She asked softly. Fritz replied that "Guy somehow appeared by accident, at least that's what Harry says. Whatever the word accident means."

Bonnie inquired, "Did her being pregnant change her focus?"

"Margaret's pregnancy did little to change things" Fritz explained. "The cleaning malady lingered on. She gave birth all right, but unfortunately couldn't cope with her new baby boy; actually ignoring him. That of course became the final straw for Harry."

The bus rumbled along in the fast lane; Bonnie pressed her hands against her face recalling the sadness she had felt at the moment that Fritz had cleared up the subject.

"The seriousness of this neglect," Barrow continued, "is what finally drove Harry over the rails to where he had no choice but turn to the courts. The court acted quickly and soon she was institutionalized. The only decent part to the whole episode occurred when a British couple employed by Lloyd's, a couple Harry knew quite well were being transferred to the United States to manage a claims office in Los Angeles. They were childless, and being familiar with Harry's hardship asked for the opportunity to take charge of Guy. Let's face it, Harry wasn't equipped, and hated the traditional business of nanny rearing. He agonized over the decision for weeks; there were really few choices. Harry wanted what was best for the child, so he agreed – it was a very tough decision.

Margaret was released from the hospital two years later, but it was too late; she was still, forgive the expression, a fucking great whack. She visited Guy a few times, and that was at the pleading of her case officer. I think Guy was so angry over his mother's stinging rejection of him, and though Harry was in constant touch with Guy, I think Guy never really came close at all to appreciating his foster family – though to my knowledge he never spoke disparagingly of them."

Bonnie said, "Guy only briefly mentioned them, though always with polite words."

The buses gear-box wailed a grinding high-pitched screech when the bus driver clumsily down shifted to exit the motor way.

Fellows began to stir; Bonnie turned to him and lovingly pressed her cheek against his shoulder. It was 2:30 when the bus came to a stop at the entrance to British Airways Terminal Building.

* * *

As the giant silver 747 soared homeward for Bonnie at an altitude of thirty thousand feet, she tried, but was unable to drift into sleep. Unlike her drowsy counterpart who slept easily, her adrenaline level was a calibration mark too high to relax knowing that in a few days the unholy alliance, a name she privately adopted for the group, would pull one of the most daring and illegal confidence strategies in history. This thought was followed by a series of quick short breaths; she felt dizzy. "Absurd" she murmured, shaking her head in disgust. She had not experienced any of that breathing shortness since her days in high school. *"What is going on here?"* She repeated the words softly aloud: "What is going on here?" She made two fists remembering well the stuttered breathing was never really from a single emotion, but from a whole mess of things that hovered over her until she was able to retreat and bury herself in one if those exciting pretend mysteries piled on shelves in her bedroom. Then it was good riddance to the huffs and puffs.

"My God, it was so pathetic," she said in a whisper, thinking how miserable it had all been before going with the FBI. But here it was again. Leaning forward in her seat, she reached for the flight magazine in the pocket directly in front of her; it would be filled with travel articles and mail order specialties. She suddenly withdrew her hand. She was furious with herself; her final coming out ceremony had now arrived; it was graduation day from what could be no more than a pseudo illness. The realization of never having to burrow for peace of mind in some book or magazine pushed combatively through her brain. The story next to her was a real one and there were no guarantees that the ending episode would not be awful. "But damnit, so what?"

Bonnie turned to look at the sleeping man; for his sake at least, she had to come through a winner. She no longer had to be frightened; it was time to jump into the frosty water and begin to consider her own skills. Skills she seldom admitted to. Risk was the domain Bonnie knew about most. She half closed her eyes and pressed the recline button pushing back the seat, her hands folded loosely, relaxed. Though the plans would be discussed thoroughly many more times in the next two days, still, she would remain apprehensive. Apprehensive because she knew from her experience with the FBI, that the most shrewd and highly intelligent provocateurs were often revealed to be the greatest potential risks. In most cases of failure, always did the grand flaw lie in what took place after the big ploy. But it was apparent these two men did not feel any real concern about this negative aspect of the operation; furthermore, Barrow felt confident it would all end like a Graham Greene story – the right ending.

Bonnie personally, had covered herself well. She had taken her annual extended leave, a formality the FBI required of all think-tank people. Barrow appeared to be covered sufficiently. He was a self-employed jewelry manufacturer who traveled with his own line of precious stone, diamond and gold jewelry. All his business orders had been completed and delivered. Plus he contacted each customer informing them he would be taking a short holiday and would be in touch with them as soon as he returned. As for Harry, he lived abroad in London, was a licensed private eye and received a pension from Lloyd's of London. When not working he was relatively inactive, living quietly; a solitary' person to those few who knew him. Moreover, he would be returning to London in four days and had advised his building security the same. Often, he would be gone days at a time; nothing to arouse any curiousness. At this juncture, for Bonnie, there were no weaknesses pertaining to the cast of characters.

Tomorrow she and Harry would go to a hospital supply shop, a theater supply shop, and Bergdorf Goodman to purchase their disguise items after which they would go to the Morgan Bank where Bonnie would remove the two hundred thousand dollars from her safety deposit box

- the money that Vanlo and Eugêne required as a deposit from Fritz Barrow.

Her thoughts were momentarily interrupted when Fellows moaned softly in his sleep - she looked at him briefly and wanted to touch him. For a moment she was once again filled with apprehension. She wished she knew a little more about him and how much of that pretentiousness was assumed. For the first time she felt afraid about her feelings towards him; she knew she was vulnerable and did not want to make a fool of herself. Bonnie also admitted to herself that she was more nervous than she would like to be knowing from experience the long-ways and side-ways that each event needed to be chained together - no weak links.

The two men had also adopted the same stern attitude which brought into scope the one big uncertainty for all three of the players. *"Critical to the success of the plan even after a successful switch, would be, Lloyd's contacting Fellows as predicted by the two male stars of the show? The men felt no profuse concern about this aspect of the operation as there was always Plan B to fall back on."*

However, Fritz Barrow was particularly confident in his feelings about Lloyd's contacting Harry. *"What the hell-fire is the difference,"* she thought. We'll have the Singhalese diamond neatly tucked away in some old shoe."

The flight continued to be smooth. Fellows awakened feeling revitalized, and a short time later the two heartily ate dinner. After coffee and a brandy, Bonnie went into her own dreamy sleep: "Do you like daisies?" asked Harry gruffly, seizing hold of her nipple between his thumb and forefinger; he held tightly. He grabbed her buttock from behind with his left hand, and against her will pushed her onto the grass. Bright yellow daisies were everywhere; they both were naked. Fellows forcibly turned her on to her stomach, her arms were stretched forward. Bonnie felt his hands spreading her buttocks; she wanted to get up and run away but couldn't. He held the outside of her thighs and lifted her ... she gasped, then screamed out in pain as he forced himself inside her. She cried out feeling the pulsating in and out jolts of his erection ... "Oh God, please fuck me Harry, please fuck me my love ..." Her face was covered in perspiration suddenly awakening to her orgasm.

* * *

'Fasten Your Seat Belt' light flashed on signaling the plane's final approach to New York's Kennedy Airport. They smiled happily at each other and tightly held hands. Fellows began to laugh loudly. It was the first time since meeting him that Bonnie actually heard him laugh hard-and-fast.

She grinned and asked: "Now what's that all about, sir?" She pressed her thighs together, she was still wet.

"When this all over," -Fellows laughed again- "I'm going to Vanlo and Eugêne and buy you the most beautiful piece of cut-glass you ever saw."

Imagining the scene she was going to create in the fancy store on that big day, Bonnie retorted: "And it had better not be chipped or broken." The passengers nearby smiled at the couple in row six; they were laughing so hard it became infectious.

At 8:30 Bonnie Adele and Harry Fellows stood outside the airline terminal building. "My gawd, it's as bleeding cold as bloody England," joked Fellows.

"Quite," said Bonnie taking Harry's hand. "'ere now, old chap, at least its bloodyclear." She tried her best to imitate a British accent. Fellows laughed.

"Look here, Harry," Bonnie said speaking seriously. "I must be on my way. The shuttle leaves every hour and I need a good night's sleep. If I leave now I should be home before eleven. Tomorrow we will meet at ten in the lobby of the Plaza, and have brunch-"

Fellows interrupted not really certain what he wanted to say.

"'It will be ...'" - he put down the suitcase and took hold of her wrists - "I wish…" He kissed her lightly on the lips. She kissed him back, they're tongues met – she turned and hurried away.

-Everybody, its dress rehearsal time.

CHAPTER FIVE

A grunt of disapproval followed Fellows switching on the lights; the room was freezing. With his foot, he shoved the suitcase into Barrow's foyer, closed the door, reset the ADT Telesonic security alarm and fixed the thermostat to seventy-eight degrees.

A glance at his watch revealed one hour had passed since kissing Bonnie good night at the airport. He mentally wished he knew more about her private life; he was falling in love with her and at his age he did not want to take a chance of making a complete ass of himself.

He looked around Barrow's living room - nothing had changed significantly since his last visit to New York City.

Fellows happily never felt out of bounds being alone in his friend's flat, though it tickled him that these surroundings were well out of the money range for most of his London acquaintances.

Fritz Barrow's personality unless one actually knew the man closely for years, would think frankly that he had no passion whatsoever for possessing works of beauty. Barrow not only did not believe in showing off outside of his own domain, he rather enjoyed playing a discipline game of displaying contempt for that which would manifest such feelings to any extent. Yet, unlike Harry's own flat, having an under-look of elegance, Barrow's tenth floor suite was tastily embellished. It pealed out with museum attraction. Pedestals of various composition glorified erotic bronze sculptures; masses of shelving exalted the spiritual and worldly; and tops of everything else honored that which was simply art form.

Harry studied the room for several minutes, taking particular notice of newly-acquired Southwest bronzes which were the current rage in collecting. In addition, there were two large African ivory carvings of old men - unmistakably beautiful. Aside from admiring Barrow's taste, Fellows had always been impressed with his ability to display each piece to full advantage. Fritz had always possessed a magic touch for arrangement and lighting.

Harry picked up his bag and headed for the guest bedroom. He knew sleep was out of the question for at least a couple of hours, so for the present he would take a long hot bath; "*Bloody American's shower, we the civilized British bath.*" Afterwards he'd select some jazz CD's from Barrow's giant collection, and scan a few art magazines.

Walkiing past Fritz's bedroom, the light from the hall spilled on a blue-enameled picture frame sitting on the dresser. Fellows without any hesitation entered the room. It was a picture he definitely had never seen. It showed Fritz's father as a young man rigidly sitting on a park bench, the Eiffel Tower in the background. Kneeling by the senior Barrow's feet on the grass, wide eyed and forcing a smile was young Fritz at about age fourteen.

Fellows reached out and picked up the picture. His fingers touched paper. Taped to the back of the frame was a small pink envelope addressed to Fritz. The address read:

Master Fritz Keith Barrow
Grisson Boys Boarding School,
Devon, EX02 5NY, UK.

Fellows reminiscently recalled that many years before, Barrow had shown him this same letter; it was written by his mother for Fritz in an attempt to explain, as Fritz had succinctly put it, "father's own special idiosyncrasies."

Staring at the picture, a mélange of long-forgotten memories came surging forth. Fellows thought back about a youthful sensitive smooth-cheeked Fritz swinging a beer mug back and forth in a Champs Elysee bistro telling stories about a father he never really knew. He recalled Fritz's voice always squeaked when he began to speak of Monte Barrow.

The father, Monte, had been practically reared in the jewelry trade. At age ten the elder Barrow was sweeping floors, cleaning jewelry work benches and running errands for the famed Parisian artist-jeweler Raymond Templier. It was with Templier's firm that Fritz's father learned his craft; in later years Monte Barrow had become one of the most brilliant sought-after goldsmiths in Western Europe.

Fritz once described his father to a boarding school teacher as, "a bespectacled, odd, strange, withdrawn man who couldn't smile with sincerity even if someone paid him to, worse, even if he wanted to." The then famous jeweler divorced Fritz's mother it being common knowledge that his full devotion to work, transcended any marriage bond. Carefully removing the letter from the flimsy envelope, Fellows returned the frame to its exact position on the dresser. He sat on the edge of Fritz's bed and let his eyes scan the letter for the excerpt he *would always remember and admire:*

"... *and so Fritz, my darling boy, art by no means has a hold on the ability to arouse peculiarity in a man. Each creative trade shares queer traits and it continuously shapes a man's characteristics which distinguish him differently from all others. Each occupation also has its own particular mood: cheerful, gloomy, loving, humble, and so on. But Fritz, the effort of the goldsmith and jeweler is to produce the most peculiar man of all.*

No trade binds him down to such detailed attention of small things, or offers so limited an area for displaying his talent. He always works in miniature, always a jeweler's magnifying loupe to his eye. For the painter or sculptor immortality is always possible. Not so for the fine jeweler. Sooner or later his work is dispersed through greed of man..."

Fellows stopped reading. He carefully refolded the letter and replaced it in the envelope.

Harry looked deep into the picture, seeking, trying to grasp something that he knew was untouchable. Because now, he wondered if the complexity of Fritz Barrow's primary motive to steal the Singhalese diamond was not somehow connected to both his dead wife Ann and his father. Using his handkerchief he carefully wiped the edges of the frame. Back in his room, waiting for sleep, Fellows thought about Bonnie.

Later during the night when deep slumber finally came, Fellows had an orgasm dreaming about Bonnie - he tried to prevent it but Bonnie had stayed attached to him, her legs powerfully locked around his buttocks, her hands pressing his face into her breasts. He made loud licking noises as he lustfully sucked on her hard bright-red nipple.

Fellows' brain awakened to the ringing of the telephone; his eyes opened; there wasn't the usual faint thin border of light surrounding the closed blinds. The room was night-time black. "Jesus Christ," he said aloud, "how embarrassing – a wet dream at my age." Subconsciously attempting to recreate the scene as he groped about the night stand next to his bed, he finally managed to find the small fold-up phone.

"Yes, hello," he said, and then began searching for the lamp switch.

A brusque voice unmistakably German, told Fellows to hold for a call from Herr Fritz "Yes, operator, I'll hold. Ja, mein guter Mann."

"Harry, is that you old boy? How are you?" Barrow was practically shouting. Is everything to your liking?

"Yes it's me Fritz ... your flat is great. Is everything all right? Where are you?" Fellows' head had worked itself clear of sleep.

"Everything is perfect Harry. I am in the Frankfurt Airport; I'll be flying out of here in about one hour. That would make it about eight-thirty New York time"

"What about the candy?" Asked Harry. "Is it the right flavor?"

"The right flavor yes, and unbelievably delicious Harry. Like Rex Harrison used to say on the TV commercial, 'unbee-leevable.' As soon as I arrived, I called Herr Leder. The candy had been cut; sugar coated and was ready for delivery. I asked if it was possible to have it sent to the Eisenmeister Cafe on Haupt Strasse, as I had a meeting there with some business associates, and if so, it would greatly be appreciated."

"Good. Very good Fritz."

"Leder agreed. I asked what the final bill was and it came to the original estimate. One hour later, I paid a young delivery boy in German marks and gave him a very large tip. Plus he delivered back to Herr Leder a token bonus in a small envelope. Harry, the bottom line is that the candy is absolutely perfect; matches the photograph to a T. Honestly, it gives me the chills just to hold it."

"Thank God for the krauts. Are you getting nervous, Fritz?"

"Damn right I am."

"Good. So am I. And I think Bonnie is too."

"Then everything is normal. Harry, I must say ta-ta. They just began to play my song ... the Frankfurt-to-New York flight-boarding melody. Can't wait to see you and Bonnie. Later amigo."

Fritz Barrow hung up first.

Fellows quickly got out of bed and began rushing around to ready himself for the day ahead – then it dawned on him: "*What the devil is my hurry! Slow it old boy; you'll give yourself a heart attack. She'll be there, not to worry."*

*   *   *

They spotted each other at the same moment. Bonnie looking like a little girl seemed as though she was waiting for her birthday party to begin. She was sitting in the lobby in the center of a large leather couch, her shoulders were hunched forward, the right leg crossed over the left, slowly swinging it back and forth. She waved with enthusiasm, then immediately rushed over to greet Fellows. They hugged like good friends running into each other after a long absence. Then after staring at each other for several moments, they joined hands, and slowly walked to the dining room.

The hostess showed them to a table; Fellows happily repeated the conversation he had with Barrow four hours earlier; Bonnie was ecstatic. Ten minutes later they were enjoying eggs benedict, extra Canadian bacon on the side and chicory-flavored Colombian coffee.

"Fritz has always been rigid about detail," Fellows said in a quiet voice. "I reckon as a result of his spending quality time as a child with his father. He had an extremely fortunate childhood, not withstanding of course the business of his parent's divorce. As a boy he spent a good part of his school holidays assisting his father in his Paris jewelry shop."

"Undoubtedly the reason why he is a successful one man operation," said Bonnie, then adding, "But Harry, to digress just for a moment, answer me this about diamonds and precious jewelry. What is it that makes people from all corners of society so adamant in wanting to possess these ... these items, these articles of gold and stones? Does it have to do with the riches once possessed by kings and rulers? Am I being naïve?"

"I don't know Bonnie that I exactly have an answer. I suppose from one point of view, it could be said that the goldsmith and his work is the summation of centuries of inherited skill. By and large however, the pieces made by these men actually belong to a relatively small segment of society; once Kings and rulers as you suggested. Today, it amounts to a personal logo; a very weak statement of one's worth, at least the way the person thinks others observe him or her. Then there is a bunch of crap that is commercially produced for the masses. Given that explanation, one can suppose that I am not a very staunch admirer of the profession." Fellows stared blankly for a moment. Bonnie had hit a delicate spot in Fellows' psyche. Sensing something amiss, Bonnie stayed silent and sipped her coffee; it was hot and strong – just the way she like it.

Harry said, "You must first understand that my job at Lloyd's as an insurance investigator included false claims, phony thefts, real thefts from within homes and companies, the entire gamut known as fraud. And that fraud existed in all walks of life. Unfortunately, these precious metals and dazzling gems and the desire to own them can cause such a high level of insolence and arrogance, that in many cases it creates a total disregard for the law. Often times it destroys people." Fellows stopped. He looked into Bonnie's eyes and smiled; he took hold of her hand. "I am afraid I did not answer your question very well; at least you discovered I am a cynic at heart."

"Well, Harry," she said, "whether the three of us are goodies or baddies doesn't really matter does it? What matters however, is that I think I am falling in love with you." She then quickly excused herself, and moved away from the table towards the ladies' powder room.

Fellows, his brain numb from Bonnie's words, nodded for the waitress to refill the coffee cups. Now, that a mutual love existed and even though he had been remiss in saying so aloud, he asked himself, "Is it not appropriate to say something like let's get married? Harry you are an asshole! She said *I think* I'm falling love."

When Bonnie returned to the table, her coffee was cold - Fellows barely recognized her. She was heavily made up, her hair tucked back under a boy's old fashioned bill-cap. She wore sport-styled dark sunglasses that covered a good deal of her face, and she carried an old Air Bahamas canvas tote bag half filled with soft-covered pocket books.

"Jesus. Where in the devil ... oh goodness." Fellows belched loudly. He covered his mouth with his napkin and embarrassingly excused himself to the people closeby. Both Harry and Bonnie somewhat amused at what was occurring began to laugh quietly. Bonnie took her seat. Harry still laughing said, "I began to ask you where the devil you came up with that outfit?"

Bonnie said, "I had left this canvas bag and my suitcase with the baggage room attendant. I told him a friend would pick up the suitcase later and give a very large tip." Fellows began to laugh again. Bonnie handed Fellows the claim check. "I am ready Harry," she said, "Let us get on with it."

"Okay," Fellows replied, "first stop, theater supply shop."

It was about 11:00 when Bonnie Adele and Harry Fellows arrived by taxi at the Whiteway Theater Supply and Wig Outlet.

Once inside, Bonnie wandered about the aisles; she had removed her bill-cap and was taking her time putting on and taking off hair- pieces from the bountiful choices. She scrutinized her new look in several mirrors standing at various distances trying the effect of different wigs with different sunglasses. It didn't take long for the selection process to be completed; the choices being two natural colored hair wigs. The first was a moderately long, straight hair strawberry blond wig, the second a dark reddish color which would also successfully conceal her own medium length light colored hair. Harry also had Bonnie try on a pair of see-through lace gloves. They fit perfectly and most of all, looked quite natural. Fellows did not care for the choice of sunglasses; he rather opted for designer sunglasses to compliment the wigs.

As soon as Bonnie completed her task, Harry chose for himself a wig of natural salt and pepper hair all curly and short with no part.

A taxi ride to a Sunglass Hut in a close by shopping center followed. For Bonnie, Harry selected a pair of tortoise-shell frames and square cut apricot tinted lenses by Bvlgari. For himself, men's Ferragamo with heavy black frames and medium dark lenses.

Once outside the store, Bonnie stopped and took Harry by the arm. She said, "Almost three thousand dollars is a bit much for sunglasses, isn't it Harry?"

"Not if we walk away with the prize. If not, we'll sell them on eBay. Bonnie darling, for you, we are creating a disguise – a look of someone with eccentric taste - a person that would shop in Vanlo and Eugêne. Not only do the lace gloves look fantastic, they'll remove any off chance of fingerprints even with your knowledge of knowing how to avoid that situation."

"Harry, each day you make me feel more secure concerning the you know what."

Later, at a Physicians Supply store, Fellows chose for himself a Doctor's knee length, light-blue office smock with a large caduceus patch sewn on the left breast-pocket. In addition, he purchased one stethoscope and one black physician's house-calling bag. He selected quickly without conversing with any of the sales clerks; paid the bill with cash, giving a phony name and address. Bonnie had waited out front in the taxi.

During the cab ride to Bergdorf Goodman at 58th Street and 5th Avenue, Fellows chatted in whispers about the plans and strategy. "Since you will be in Vanlo and Eugêne's on two consecutive days, it would be best not to repeat any particular movements from the previous day. Also, Bergdorf's security people are top notch; they have in-ceiling TV cameras being monitored at all times. Management has also installed an excellent in-store security program; any employee, who is instrumental in the capture of a shop lifter, gets a cash bonus on the spot. Not that you are going to try and steal anything, we just don't want some over zealous salesperson getting in our way by following you. You never know what will stick in a salesperson's mind."

"Check, double check," she agreeably acknowledged.

Once inside Bergdorf, they checked their packages at the service desk then went directly to cosmetics where Bonnie spent some time in choosing makeup – she decided on cosmetics made by Bobby Brown. Knowing exactly the finished look she wanted to portray, she purchased moisturizer, an ivory-beige foundation, plus ivory color blush, and a medium textured face powder. Thinking while paying cash for the items, "*If these cosmetics don't make me gaunt, ghostly, ghastly, and gory, and unrecognizable, then nothing will.*"

Next came a short break on the Seventh Floor Restaurant where Bonnie had coffee and a slice of apple pie. Harry ordered a pot of Earl Grey tea and three shortbread biscuits. Both ate and drank in silence. Afterwards as they made their way to the faux jewelry section. Peering into one of the counters, Fellows said in a whisper, "Bonnie, I have a serious request to ask of you." He looked around. "I know you didn't see the check, but what do you think the price our coffee and tea and small refreshment came to?"

"Okay, I'll give a serious answer since you asked. I'd say, about fifty bucks including the tip."

"Thank you dear," Harry said.

"Well, aren't you going to tell me?"

Harry said, "I'll wait until my heartburn passes."

At one of the several fashion jewelry showcases, Fellows selected large costume earrings, and several large size bangle style bracelets some interspersed with turquoise beads. Bonnie kept a distance from Harry, avoided conversation with sales people, and paid cash for the items.

With the main shopping chores complete, Bonnie followed Harry up escalators to the fourth floor where he led her to a line of five public telephone booths - the booths were adjacent to the store's customer's lounge. Keeping his hand down, Harry pointed, put something into Bonnie's hand. He whispered in her ear, turned on his heal, and walked to the elevators where he took one of the vacant seats. He pretended to read a newspaper that was left by a customer.

Bonnie opened the door to the center telephone booth, entered, and pushed the door closed. She observed the phone number as instructed by Harry. It was identical to the number engraved on the Medical Alert Disc she now held in her left hand - the disc that Harry had specially ordered in London; the disc and chain she would be wearing around her neck in two days. Returning the chain and disc to her handbag, she smiled at Fellows through the glass, and moving her lips, told him: "You are a genius, and I love you."

Thirty minutes later, in the Morgan Trust bank, Bonnie Adele presented herself at the safety deposit box department using the pseudo name Eva Branch. Moments later in the vault room, she removed the package left to her by Guy Fellows; the package that contained two hundred thousand dollars in cash.

On the mezzanine level, Bonnie handed Harry the overstuffed brown paper bag. He looked at it, and announced in a cockney accent, "All rightie dearie, next stop the old Fifth Avenue Sweet Shop."

Bonnie mumbled, not smiling, "Oh my God, please no, not already?"

The huge overhead clock bearing the name Audemars Piquet, showed the time to be 3:30.

It was the first time that she was in the ritzy Fifth Avenue store of Vanlo and Eugêne. She walked slowly to the rear of the store, taking the elevator to the third floor. As previously instructed by Fritz Barrow, she focused her attention to the three executive offices at the rear of the floor that faced outward onto the showroom.

Standing guard at the entrance to the small office on the left was a uniformed New York City policeman. He had sergeant stripes sewn at the top of each sleeve, a familiar looking black Glock automatic was strapped into its holster - a familiar sight on all New York City policemen. Centered between two offices, recessed at the back of a short hall way, was a private elevator. Stationed directly at the entrance to the private elevator, stood two well-dressed man wearing blue business suits. Bulges over the heart area under their jackets were obviously guns. An ear receiver and transmitter were also part of the dress code of Vanlo security guards. The entire area was cordoned off by thick blue-velvet ropes held in place by seven highly polished brass posts. Bonnie made a mental note of the tables containing glass displays – she counted fifteen – five rows of three. At the moment, there were twenty retail customers, and four sales persons.

Her attention now zeroed in on three enormous glass display tables that made up the front row, closest to the offices. She slowly walked around each display table admiring all of the beautiful glass. Each table was covered with brightly colored glass forms and figurines from countries like Italy, France, Germany and famous European cities where glass making was considered a collectable form of art. There was more Waterford glass than she imagined could exist; there were hundreds of pieces of Baccarat crystal and Lalique plus dozens of names she had never heard of previously. Elegant place settings were also displayed, revealing a side of society that one only imagined could possibly exist. She thought, *"Who would want to wash a single dish that cost five-hundred dollars?"* Slowly, Bonnie made her way back to the center table - several small display signs on the table read:

PLEASE DO NOT TOUCH
KINDLY REQUEST ASSISTANCE

As Bonnie approached a table, a short, elderly sales woman appeared from nowhere and asked if she could assist in selecting a piece. "A gift perhaps, something elegant for your home?"

"Thank you, no," Bonnie said. "I am just browsing. Possibly choosing a present for myself. Hopefully, my husband will be in next week to purchase it. He's in the military, a full colonel." The saleslady smiled, thought the woman somewhat peculiar, but handed Bonnie her business card bearing the name Agnes White - she remained close by.

Not allowing her gaze to wander, Bonnie attentively continued to survey the classic designs and contemporary forms of the exquisite glass that was everywhere. Ignoring the presence of the short woman, Bonnie painstakingly studied the elaborate arrangements which in themselves were artful; then finally, she visually sighted what would be her target; the bull's-eye. Yes indeed, her searched had ended; she then slowly circled many of the tables, nodded to the sales lady, then made her way back to the main elevator – not wanting to hurry in case eyes were upon her. She thought a stop at the ladies room would in itself be quite normal. Inside, she studied herself in a mirror and seeing that all was in its proper place, smiled at herself lecherously. It was now time to leave the store. Minutes later she walked out of the store onto Fifth Avenue.

Walking away from the store, her stomach now felt as if it were full of icicles; she took deep breaths. She thought, *"That goddamn sales lady, how annoying to have her on my heels. I'll have a lot more respect for the undercover FBI guys after this episode."*

Bonnie could not remember crossing to the other side of the street. Stopping, she looked at her reflection in a Barnes and Noble's bookstore window. She spoke aloud to herself: "Relax, you did great. I must call Harry." Bonnie entered the bookstore and walked slowly, deliberately taking her time. Casually, she took notice of the best-seller display; then unexpectedly, even to herself, she turned to see if she had been followed by the short saleslady. All she could do was smile at her own misgivings: "*Jesus,*" she thought, "*all I did was to go shopping.*"

At the rear of the store was a public telephone. Bonnie spoke each of the memorized numbers silently as she pressed the square numerical digits; she heard Harry's voice after the phone rang twice.

"Dr. Frank's office."

"Is Dr. Frank in? This is an emergency!" Bonnie said the words distinctly and slowly, still slightly wrought from the Bergdorf trial run.

"This is Dr. Frank."

"Oh, Harry, I think it's perfect. I cannot hear any background noise at all."

"How did it go with you, Bonnie?"

"I am a bit shaken, but I know precisely what I have to do."

"Good. See you at the Plaza in a bit."

Before heading back to the hotel, Bonnie stopped at a stationary store, purchased a tablet of graph paper, then taking the time necessary, Bonnie put together a rough draft of all that she had observed on the third floor making use of mental pictures she had learned while working for the CIA. Satisfied with her rendition, she would take the time later in the day to create a properly finished copy.

By the time she arrived at the hotel, Fellows had claimed her belongings from the baggage room porter.

Outside the hotel's glass doors, they stood silently holding hands while the doorman blew his whistle for a taxi.

As soon as they had walked into Barrow's apartment, Bonnie kicked off her shoes and flopped heavily into the cushions of the big sofa. She swung her body around lifting her feet, stretching herself out fully; she lay on back, her left arm dangled lifelessly over the edge of the sofa. "My God Harry, I still cannot believe all of this is happening."

Harry nodded, raised his eye brows, pressed his lips together then after a few seconds had passed, said, "I will tell you what else is happening, Bonnie," -his pulse pounds loudly in his temples- "I... I can fully understand why Guy ... why Guy fell in love with you. Perhaps for the same reasons that I have fallen in love with you."

Bonnie held out both arms. Harry quickly crossed the room dropping to his knees next to her; he pressed his face in her neck. She took his head in her hands and kissed him passionately on the mouth. A sensuous groan came sounded from deep inside him.

"Harry, we have to get this out of the way, now. I want you too, darling. Why put it off?" Soon they were locked in an embrace, covering each other with frenzied kisses.

Afterwards, in the bedroom, the full weight of his body still on hers, he kissed her gently on both eyes; he spoke kindly. "Thank you my sweet." Bonnie pulled him tighter against her. "You are welcome, my eternal darling, and Harry, we can't let our personal affair interfere with switching the Singhalese diamond."

It was 6:00 p.m. when Fritz Barrow noisily unlocked and opened the door to his apartment. Bonnie was in the kitchen preparing a plate of assorted cheese, dried Cuban sausage, sliced green apples and water crackers. Fellows was watching the beginning of an evening TV news program. At the sound of the door, both of them rushed to greet him. The three of them just stood grinning at each other. A moment later they were hugging and kissing. Barrow let his jacket drop to the floor next to his suitcase. "Now my darlings," he shouted, "please follow me!"

The three of them traipsed into the living room where Fritz placed a piece of folded chamois he had removed from his shirt pocket onto the center of the glass coffee table.

Fritz said, "The moment has arrived. Bonnie, please turn on all the lights. Lights. We must have light at least for this occasion. Okay, Harry old boy, now will you do us the honors of removing the stone from its safe house." Fellows looked at Fritz, then Bonnie. He began ceremoniously to unfold the soft leather cover.

Almost shouting, Harry exclaimed, "Jesus S. Christ Fritz! Just look at it! I do not believe it." Bonnie gasped ... "Jesus ... it's unbelievable." Picking the stone up by its edges, Fellows brought it closer to his eyes. He examined it, turning it, studying its facet surfaces from all angles.

From his jacket on the floor, Barrow retrieved an envelope from which he removed the original picture of the stone to be auctioned at

Vanlo and Eugêne; it was enclosed in a clear protective plastic window. He laid it flat on the tables. Fellows then place the newly acquired replica next to the picture. Bonnie excitedly exclaimed, "Oh my God … look at it! It truly is a perfect match to the photograph."

"Well my darlings," Barrow said, "we will all know just how perfect on Friday, won't we? And Bonnie, how did your dress rehearsal go?"

Bonnie left the room for a few moments – when she returned she held a sheet of graph paper which she handed to Fritz. "When you exit the elevator Fritz, this is what you will observe if you can take the time to look."

"This is fabulous Bonnie. At least I'll know where to look for you. Good job. Here Harry, have a look at a pro's handiwork." She handed Harry her drawing of the third floor.

"She put the final touches on it about an hour ago." He looked at her and smiled. "She is the best."

CHAPTER SIX

3rd floor plan – Vanlo & Eugêne

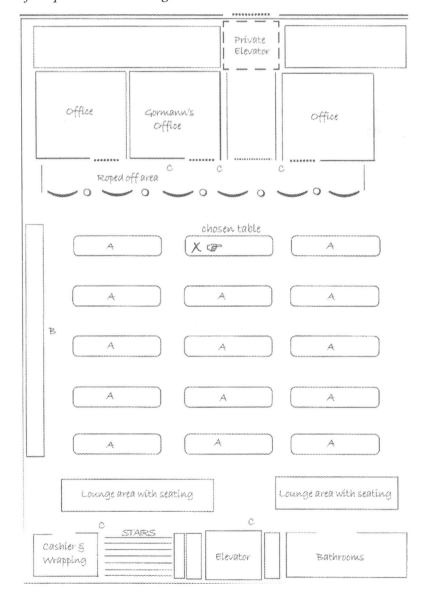

Bonnie Adele was standing close to the third floor elevator when she looked carefully at her watch. It was 11:15. Fritz Barrow, Ernst Gormann and two armed guards departed from Vanlo and Eugêne's private elevator. They turned to the right, one guard returned to the open elevator doors; Gormann and one guard entered the office where the same policeman from the previous Wednesday stood guard. Bonnie was now midway into the showroom – between rows two and three. Following the men's departure into Gormann's office, she sauntered over to one of the glass covered wall cases that housed extremely fragile hand-blown replicas of musical instruments - she remained studying the contents for several moments.

Inside the office Gormann seated himself behind an oval shape mahogany desk – he faced looking out to the show room; though the vertical blinds on the window that looked out to the showroom were fully closed. Gormann pointed to a chair, and Barrow sat down on the opposite side of the desk facing Gormann, his back to the door. Gormann said, "Mr. Longmeyer, your five minutes will begin momentarily." Fritz thought that Gormann had the appearance of a thoroughly tired man. His eyes were droopy, perhaps from a bit too much alcohol which did not bother Barrow in the least. It had to be a tenuous week for a man his age. Then with an eye signal from Mr. Gormann, the armed guard that had accompanied the men into the office spun the dial to a wall safe, opened the safe door, and removed a small white suede box that he handed to Gormann.

Gormann in turn began to hand the box to the masquerading Andrew Longmeyer but stopped when Fritz got up to remove his jacket - hanging it on the back of his chair. During the activity of removing his jacket, Barrow sighted the single security camera on the ceiling to the right of them. The camera was positioned to cover the entire office area. Barrow then picked up his briefcase and laid it flat on the desk.

"If you don't mind, Mr. Longmeyer, I would prefer that nothing of a coarse nature be on this desk. I treat it as one might treat a newborn." Gormann gently smoothed his hand across the surface. "Particularly anything that might mar its surface such as your beautiful leather brief case. Here, let me put it on the floor next to me. The money is quite safe, I assure you." Gormann pursed his lips, then said, "A check drawn on any bank in the city of New York would have eliminated any of this brief case business, but then there are always those who prefer cash. Be that as it may," he patted the white suede box in front of him and smiled, "now if you would, please observe the Singhalese diamond."

Gormann opened the box and placed the loose diamond on a three inch square of a gray velvety fabric. "It's a little too big for a diamond tweezers, wouldn't you agree Mr. Longmeyer?" Gormann smiled. "You are welcome to hold it with your fingers and examine it."

Barrow said nothing, and let the diamond remain on the fabric.

Gormann then said, "As important as this magnificent diamond is from an investment aspect, the story that has developed about it and its participants will certainly test your imagination." Gormann spoke softly with a firm edge to his voice. "Although time dictates that I be brief, be assured a detailed record will be made to the successful bidder, or buyer, which ever category you prefer." He showed a sardonic grin, imperceptibly glancing at the diamond, then turning it by its edge with the forefinger of his right hand.

Barrow frowned, leaned back and with his left thumb, pressed Ossie Graves' tiny transmitter contact concealed behind his gold belt buckle. The initial signal was transmitted to Bonnie. Then with what might be termed as religious deportment, Gormann folded his hands as though preparing to pray. Making eye contact with Barrow, Gormann now spoke in a silky, higher pitched voice. Barrow now picked up the diamond with his right hand and held it between his thumb and forefinger.

"To begin with," Gormann said, "the Roman naturalist, Pliny the Elder, was the first person we know of to write selectively of gemstones. In 80 A. D. he recorded and described a pink diamond, that to quote his writings stated, 'it was a gem of such quality that it would only be known to Kings.' Later in the thirteenth century, Marco Polo wrote that a Singhalese monarch owned a light colored pink stone, equivalent in size to the first joint of a man's thumb and just as thick. Kublai Kahn, the emperor of China, learning of this prize stone, offered the King the value of any city he chose. The Singhalese King refused and responded, 'If all the treasures of the world were laid at my feet, I would not part with this jewel.' Quite a value to turn down; no? Mr. Longmeyer?"

"Depends what you mean by value."

Gormann ignored the man's response, feeling it was ill advised. Nevertheless, he continued to recite information about the pink diamond in a scholarly, historical sequence. Gormann spoke lively with authority and sincerity. It was as though he had actually witnessed each historical event as it had occurred.

"In 1535, Benvenito Cellini wrote of the pink diamond in his autobiography, declaring that he had once fashioned and set a magnificent diamond of pink hue into a pure gold ring for the Holy Emperor, Charles the Fifth. Records show us that in 1660, a renowned seventeenth-century lapidary named Vincent Penzi had recut the diamond into a 126-carat oval shape and shortly thereafter it ended up in the possession of a French cardinal named Jules Mazarin. In 1792, it reappeared again and was pledged for money that helped no other than, Napoleon Bonaparte in his rise to power." All the while that Barrow held the diamond, Gormann never removed his eyes from Fritz's hand. Gormann paused, looked up at Barrow as if trying to get a sense of what was going on behind the man's neutral gaze – even though he held it, Barrow had given the diamond no more than a cursory glance. Barrow, aware of Gormann's relative displeasure, purposely suppressed a yawn, and then continued to stare blankly devoid of any expression. Gormann continued saying "Later, when Napoleon went into exile, Marie Louise, his second wife, took possession of the diamond and smuggled it out of France. Shortly thereafter, her father, the emperor of Austria, decided for reasons unknown to return it to France and there it remained hidden, or at least out of circulation until World War II.

In 1940, when the Germans marched into Paris, someone or some group turned it over to the Nazis in exchange for an arrangement of sorts. Very important sorts I imagine. After the war, the diamond surfaced in Berlin, then made its way to Venezuela, South America; final ownership to a wealthy, titled family. Vanlo and Eugêne now represent that family in the sale of the Singhalese diamond, and of course, for obvious reasons, their identity will remain anonymous. So, there we are Mr. Longmeyer. Two thousand years in two minutes." Gormann laughed, amused at his own candor. "The conditions of the sale you know from our previous conversation, but I will repeat them just for clarity purposes. The diamond will sold to the person making the highest offer. It will be determined by seal bid, not auction, as we are not auctioneers. Before going, I will hand you an envelope that details everything, I suggest you read it thoroughly. In the envelope is the form for the bid amount. Each bid must be accompanied by a good faith deposit of two hundred thousand dollars," Gormann glanced at Barrow's briefcase. "No offer will be accepted under six million dollars. Unfortunately, as today is the final day for observing the diamond, and you are the last appointment, your bid must be in my hands by six o'clock this evening; the store closes at eight. Naturally, the earnest money will be returned to the unsuccessful bidders, and the purchaser, should he or she be so inclined, can remain unidentified. Do you have any questions Mr. Longmeyer?"

Barrow leaned forward, turning his body ever so slightly away from the ceiling camera, his left hand once again activating the tiny transmitter. The second signal reached Bonnie as she continued to browse the glassware. Her heart beat accelerated, a pulse in her right temple vibrated. "On your mark," she moaned secretly - then with cautious nonchalance began to make her way slowly to her target area. As she did, she passed the short saleslady that had approached her two days before. Bonnie had no way of knowing if she was recognized or not.

Fritz said, "Yes indeed, I do have a question, Mr. Gormann ... actually, it is a comment." Barrow spoke unhurriedly, giving Bonnie ample time to position herself. "Buying and selling diamonds is essentially my livelihood, and I am candidly speaking, a diamond historian. Until reading about the Singhalese, and I must be frank, it was known, by let us say, the diamond fraternity, that the Queen Elizabeth diamond was the most important pink diamond to be in existence. It appears-"

Gormann brusquely waved his hand to interrupt Barrow, conspicuously trying to conceal his agitation behind a false smile. "Mr. Longmeyer, you are referring to the Williamson diamond that was discovered in the Williamson diamond mine in Tanganyika. Diamonds too are my profession, and I am familiar with the stone you allude to. That diamond weighed fifty four carats and was given in its original rough form as a gift to Princess Elizabeth on the occasion of her marriage in 1947. In 1948, the Queen had the London diamond cutting firm of

Briefel and Lemer recut the rough crystal. The stone finished out to a magnificent twenty-three carat round brilliant cut of true rose hue. It was destined to be set in one of England's ceremonial crowns; however, the Queen decided to have it mounted into a brooch-"

Matching Gormann's hand wave motion with his own, Barrow now interrupted Gormann; he spoke slowly. "Yes, all of what you say is correct, Mr. Gor-mann." Barrow deliberately separated the syllables. "The Queen's brooch, incidentally, was styled in the shape of an Alpine rose with five gem quality round-cut diamonds set into each of the petals. But, be that as it may. What I started to say is this Mr. Gormann. The Queen's diamond is only valued at about three million dollars, and-"

"Mr. Longmeyer! Please be sure that I do not want to break in your legitimate inquiry or discourse, but Queen Elizabeth's diamond is not for sale, this one is. As we are under somewhat of a time constraint, please have a final look at the diamond." Gormann was inwardly and outwardly livid. All the others who had appointments prior to this man had been wealthy and knowledgeable; and still, he had held them in the palm of his hand. *"A disgrace that this unshaven idiot with his stupid ill-fitting wig and ugly bronze tinted spectacles is in a position to purchase such an important diamond."* All the others were agreeable, and even gleaned smiles throughout Gormann's dissertation. They were especially high spirited and excited when the time came for them to examine the diamond.

Barrow now transmitted the third signal.

Bonnie on receiving the 'get ready command' moved immediately to her spot at the display table. "God protect me please," she mumbled aloud.

Barrow began the motion of handing the diamond back to Gormann.

GO! The final feint beep reached her ear. Bonnie quickly removed the hair comb with the receiver, placing it in her pocket. Like a flash of lightning, she thrust her left arm outward; her chilling scream pierced the air throughout the entire third floor. Everyone nearby froze. Bonnie grabbed at her chest with her right hand; she shouted, "Someone, please help me!" She began to fall. Her extended left arm began to sweep across the table covered in cut glass; she grabbed blindly at piece after piece of the larger sizes of fine crystal, as if attempting to keep her balance. Crystal kept crashing to the floor; others broke on the table as they toppled like falling dominoes. Two female customers screamed. Everyone turned towards the place of commotion.

Commotion begets commotion.

Hearing the unusually loud disturbance, Gormann and the guard raised their heads and eyes for an instant to look at the showroom monitor. The guard then opened the blinds to see out Barrow stood; he did not turn– the phony kunzite stone dropped out of his cuff into the hand that held the diamond and at that same instant, he turned his body slightly left towards the loud noise that had drawn everyone's attention - he raised his arm slightly allowing the diamond to fall back under the cuff of his sleeve. The synthetic kunzite remained between his thumb and forefinger. Gormann's gaze quickly returned to the desk; his eyes immediately making contact with the pink stone in Barrow's hand – Gormann glared now seeing Fritz lovingly rubbing the stone. "Excuse me, Mr. Longmeyer," Gormann spoke harshly. "Sounds as if there is some major problem." Barrow looked at Gormann directly in the eyes. "I like it," he said, "it's mine." He then preceded to hand back the stone.

Gormann took hold of it, wiped the stone clean with a small yellow cloth, gave it a cursory glance, and placed it back into the white suede box. He then extended his hand to the guard who returned the box back into the safe; closed the door, pulled the locking lever downwards, then spun the combination dial. After watching the entire procedure, Gormann then picked up the wall telephone from behind him. "What is going on?" His only response to the information given him was one word. "Shit."

After replacing the telephone, he said to Barrow, "It seems Mr. Longmeyer, a customer has had an attack and fell into one of our display tables. An unfortunate incident to be sure. I am afraid we will have to conclude this meeting temporarily as there is quite a bit of commotion, plus police and an ambulance have been summoned. I will be needed to help with the chaos. I'm sure you understand what with all that is happening we need to secure the office." Gormann pressed a button beneath the desk and the guard unlocked the front door – another security man entered the room. Gormann signaled that everything was in order. He said, "Matthew, when the visiting gentleman here leaves, I'll open the safe and will give you a white box that is to be taken to the vault room immediately. I'll call for a team of security men to accompany you. Morris Hopkins in the vault room will be expecting you. He'll take care of securing it. After you leave, please lock my office up.

"Here is your envelope for the bid Mr. Longmeyer; we have a wonderful private lounge one floor up where you are most welcome to go and relax. Just tell the receptionist, her name is Helen, that I said it was perfectly okay to admit you."

Fritz said, "If you don't mind Mr. Gormann, I'll just hold onto my briefcase." Barrow's voice tones distinctly revealing his own annoyance. "I will be back in maybe an hour or so. Maybe we can get on with the business at hand. I have a few important questions." He slowly removed his jacket from his chair. Gormann hated this man Andrew Longmeyer - he handed Barrow his brief case. "Yes, do that Mr. Longmeyer." The guard stepped to the side allowing Barrow to exit – Fritz's heart froze seeing Bonnie being attended to. Suddenly her eyes made contact with his; knowing his concern she blurted out to someone, "I'm fine." Another guard then appeared to escort Barrow onto the elevator.

Outside, Barrow turned right, and walked down Fifth Avenue. No longer worried about Bonnie at risk, a feeling of euphoria and lightheadedness overcame him. He began to laugh aloud. Passerby's smiled at him. *"God, we did it, we did it!"* He forced himself into a sober demeanor. He slid his right hand into his jacket pocket clutching the diamond. He was thinking, *"The three of us just pulled the greatest diamond theft ever... just a few more stages to go before the l'événement principal."* They were the words his father had always used just before delivering one of his finished pieces.

CHAPTER SEVEN

In Bergdorf Goodman, Fellows sat nervously in the customer's lounge tapping his foot in time to the music from the overhead hidden speakers; from his position he was able to see the phone booth in which he had hung plastic sign that read:

OUT OF ORDER

As he scanned the New York Times – the telephone suddenly rang: it was 11:40. Fellows dropped the paper, got up like a shot, took hold of his black physician's bag and reached the booth before the second ring. Once inside with the door closed, he allowed it ring twice more. He lifted the receiver. "Hello, Doctor's office, this Dr. Frank speaking."

"Oh, good," were the first words Fellows heard. "Dr. Frank, I am a police officer, my name is Dennis Flynn, sergeant Manhattan South."

"Yes. How can I help you Officer Flynn? Is it donation time already?"

"No sir. Not today. But I am speaking from the third floor at Vanlo and Eugêne, jewelers on Fifth Avenue. We have a lady here wearing one of those Medical Alert charms with the enameled red caduceus around her neck; it has your name as the physician along with your telephone number engraved on the back. This person has just had an accident, nothing serious, several small cuts on the left arm and hand. She seems to be all right; however, the human resources director and security head seem to think she might have had a heart attack or an attack of some kind. Anyway, she will not allow the rescue boys to touch her. Says her name is June Summers. Now we have ordered an ambulance, but she insists on only seeing you; says she can have terrible reactions to certain medications. Refuses to leave the store without speaking to you."

"Yes, yes, June Summers, an odd woman. I say, look here, tell you what officer. My nurses and I were just preparing to have our mid-day meal; I'll get them to hold off for a while. Rather than get involved with a telephone conversation eh, give me fifteen minutes and I'll get a lift there. And Sergeant Flynn, would you please have the ambulance wait for me, we might need it. She has had some heart problems in the past."

"Okay, Doc, I'11 do that. Not a problem."

"Many thanks, I'll be on my way in just a jiffy."

Harry, happy the way the conversation went with the policeman, removed the carefully folded blue smock from the black medical bag and slipped it over his jacket; he then hung the stethoscope into the oversized pocket, allowing the rubber tubes to casually hang out. With a small pair of wire cutters he snipped the phone cord in two and replaced the OUT OF ORDER sign. He then quickly departed the telephone booth, heading for the escalator. *"Bloody Superman, stepping out of a phone box,"* he mused.

Exiting the taxi, Harry was more than pleased to see the ambulance still parked out front by the main entrance - it meant that Bonnie was continuing to play out her role perfectly. *"Please dear God, let her be well."* He walked through the revolving door into Vanlo and Eugêne's main show room exactly at noon. He announced who he was to a security man and was quickly escorted to the third floor. "They've closed the third floor until they can get it cleaned up," the security man said as they stepped off the elevator. Bonnie was sitting in the office to the right of the private elevator; her eyes were covered by sunglasses; her wig perfectly in place. She had gauze bandages wrapped around her left arm from the elbow to her gloved hand. Two ambulance attendants stood by the open door chatting with two uniformed policemen.

"I am Dr. Frank," Fellows boldly announced, practically charging into the group. "Who is Sergeant Flynn?"

The policeman presented himself and Fellows shook his hand thanking him for his courtesy. The doctor then shook hands with the other police and security personnel and the two ambulance attendants who introduced themselves as Harvey and Michael.

Michael said, "The lady allowed us to take her blood pressure which was slightly high, a bit racy, but considering the damage ..." he never finished the sentence just pointed to the piles of broken glass that had been swept into three piles ready to be dumped into bins. Gormann then appeared on the scene. Speaking to no one in particular he said,

"Mr. Daisey has been notified. He'll be here momentarily. I want all cleaning activity to cease immediately. We will need pictures of the damage for the insurance company. Leave everything as it is." Gormann then singled out a security guard. "John, track down someone who has a digital camera as quick as you can or buy one if you have to. I cannot believe the damage!" He glared at the woman June Summers as he spoke.

Harry pulled on a pair of white vinyl examining gloves. Fellows said forcibly, "Gentlemen, I think we should get to the hospital straight away." He now focused his attention on Bonnie. He pulled an empty chair next to hers. "How are you doing Ms. Summers? What is all this business about chest pains?" His voice tones sounded all compassionate.

"Oh, Dr. Frank," Bonnie whined, "I am so embarrassed. Just look at the damage that I have caused. It could be millions of dollars."

"Now, now, I doubt if it comes to millions, but that's what insurance is all about. Everything will be taken care of in its proper order. Just tell me what happened?" As he spoke he removed the stethoscope, and after unbuttoning her blouse partially, he held it to her chest. He pressed his thumb and forefinger into her breast.

"I had this awful pain. It seemed just to come on. I think maybe that I blacked out."

"I am going to take you to St. Francis hospital right now. There, we'll be better equipped to determine what the problem was, and you can make whatever telephone calls you need to." Fellows nodded to the two attendants. Harvey had already opened the collapsible stretcher and helped the bespectacled woman lie down.

Michael said, "I'll need you to fill out this information sheet Doc."

"Yes of course. I'll finish doing that at the hospital. For now, please let's get underway."

Minutes later, Michael, driving the ambulance with blaring sirens, deftly moved through the noontime Manhattan traffic heading for St. Francis Hospital as ordered by Doctor Frank.

At the emergency entrance, Bonnie insisted on walking; she refused the wheelchair. Fellows nodded an okay to Harvey. The attendants shook their heads unhappy about ignoring hospital protocol - the four began their walk down a short corridor to the reception area.

The attendants moved ahead as Fellows and Bonnie slowed their pace. When Harvey and Michael reached the receiving desk, Fellows and Bonnie walked past the crowded waiting room through a set of double doors off to the right. The sign read:

"This way to the cafeteria ⊠"

Halfway along the corridor they came to an elevator. Fellows pushed the up button. As soon as the doors opened they entered, Fellows pulled the emergency stop button. He removed a light-weight woman's sweater from the black bag and helped Bonnie on with it. She removed her wig and sunglasses, put on a long sleeved sweater that covered her bandages, then quickly brushed back her hair. Then with a damp cloth, she wiped away the makeup and put on fresh lipstick and donned her own prescription glasses. Fellows was out of his smock, removed the wig, smoothed his hair with his hand then everything was shoved back into the black bag. It all took less than three minutes. Fellows released the stop button, pressed the fifth floor button - "Patient Rooms."

The two stepped out of the elevator, casually walked down a corridor leading to patient rooms, past a nurse's station onto another set of elevators. This elevator took them to the third floor. Down one floor and out, they changed elevators once again – walked half way down a corridor to another set of elevators, finally embarking onto the ground floor. A total of ten minutes had passed since walking out of the emergency waiting room. Now they were standing outside the hospital's main entrance. Fellows waved to a line of waiting taxis. The time was 1:30.

As instructed, the cab driver proceeded to take them to an address in the heart of a busy business district in Long Island. The two sat back and without saying a word held hands until reaching their destination thirty-five minutes later. Fellows paid the cabby; he and Bonnie walked several blocks to a restaurant bar called Waldman's Place.

It wasn't until after her first sip of wine, that the pent up tension was released. Bonnie began to laugh. Soon the laughter transposed itself into soft crying, finally deep sobs emanated from deep within; she removed her glasses, put her face protectively into her hands continuing to sob uncontrollably. Fellows watched silently from his side of the booth - seeing her slender back jerk with fitful heaves made him want to hold her and try to comfort her, but he knew better not to; Bonnie needed to get through this on her own. What she had done less than two hours before was a matchless performance of guts, undiminished nerve and expertise. Fellows could understand the emotion; there had been long days of tense planning; hours of discussions, expenses, then the actual execution of the crime. Then there was the sentiment of rekindling past loves, of falling in love once again with a stranger, and making love to him. The summation; the realization that it was all coming to a conclusion became unwrapped finally in her first moment of quietude.

Finally drained of emotion, she raised her head and looked at Fellows; her tear filled eyes were red and swollen.

She reached across the table and touched his face with her fingers; she began to laugh again only this time it was different. Fellows got up and sat next to her putting his arm around her shoulder; she shuttered as if cold. He lightly patted her in a comforting manner; he kissed her hair and eyes. He whispered, "The worst and the best of it are over. We did it. We really did it." She laughed; Fellows joined in the laughter. Soon they were laughing and excitedly sharing each event that took place over the past four hours.

"Hello, my darlings, am I allowed to join the party?"

Bonnie and Harry looked up to find Fritz standing over them; there was a wide grin cut across his face. He held Bonnie's suitcase along with Harry's two suit carry bag.

Then quickly, before anyone spoke, Barrow slid into the empty side of the booth. The three of them joined hands. "My God," said Fritz, "we were outrageously wonderful, were we not?" They answered by squeezing hard each other's hand. "And Bonnie, I heard your message loud and clear that you were fine; thanks for that."

Bonnie said, "Fritz, when I saw you leave Gormann's office, and yes, I know you were worried about me, yet you had a certain look, I thought I'd die with happiness … I just knew everything went well."

"I personally think you both are the greatest. Do I know how to pick conspirators or what?"

"I guess so said Harry, though I'm not so sure if it wasn't that we picked you."

Laughter by all followed.

"Even though the best has yet to come, the important thing now is that we have to conclude all of this properly, and that comes before we begin praising each other, though God knows we deserve praise in capital letters. But there is going to be plenty of time later to celebrate properly. For now, we need to check out certain details."

"Go," said Fellows.

"The only item left behind was Bonnie's Bahamas Air tote bag with the pocket books that she carried."

"Check," said Bonnie. "Probably still in the ambulance. Of no importance. All of them current titles, I selected them myself from different book stores. No fingerprints on the glossy covers, or anywhere. I guarantee it. A dead end investigation."

"Harry?"

"All my wares including Bonnie's electronic hair comb and disguises are in the doctor's bag." "

What about your business card, Fritz?" Bonnie inquired.

"As you know, the phone number on the business card I gave to Gormann originally is to a public telephone in Penn Station. I rigged the phone not to ring; in other words, although the phone is in working order, there is no ringing sound should someone dial the number, though I am certain that by now that Gormann has tried several times. Of course, the telephone at Bergdorf Goodman as of this morning is totally out of order as I cut the wires before going to the jewelry store."

"Fingerprints on the kunzite, Fritz?"

"Nil. I agitated Gormann by rubbing the stone with my fingers; something that is considered to be the height of bad manners. He wiped the stone clean himself when I handed it to him."

"Other possible fingerprints?"

"Just Gormann's on my brief case?"

"Bonnie?"

"My hand was a tight fist as we discussed so many times. No fingerprints."

"Then I would say, all has been covered," Fellows said.

"Well then if that is the case, I shall be on my way. God bless you both, I love you both dearly. We should be seeing each other within a week."

Fellows handed Fritz the black doctor's bag to take with him and dispose of.

A few minutes later, Bonnie walked out to begin her trip back to Washington, D.C.

Fellows paid the check, walked several blocks to a taxi stand, and drove to Kennedy Airport to catch the 5:00 P.M. flight to Heathrow.

*   *   *

It was 2:00 when Ernst Gormann returned from lunch and asked Patti Wells the receptionist, if there were any messages. Getting a "no sir" reply, he went to his other office on the fourth floor and removed Andrew Longmeyer's business card from a locked file labeled SINGHALESE DIAMOND. He sat at his desk and dialed Longmeyer's phone number – after two rings, the recorded message in a woman's voice repeated twice: "We're sorry; your call cannot be completed as dialed. For further information, please stay on the line." Gormann mumbled "huh, huh" figuring something or other had to be amiss with this weirdo guy. He was then informed by the operator, that the telephone number was a Penn Station public pay telephone. She tried connecting to the number only to discover it was out of order and that it would be probably out of service for at least three days. "Is there anything else I can help you with?" she asked.

Ernst Gormann's breathing had increased. His right eye began to rapidly tick, he rubbed it hoping the tic would cease - the rapid breathes through his nose caused a whistling sound. He next called the main number for the New York Fire Department; surely there had to be an obvious error writing the number - but now he was more than curious about the address on the card. It took less than three minutes to get a reply - the address printed on Andrew Longmeyer's business card did not exist the spokesperson from the fire department told him. Yes, she was quite certain.

Gormann felt unnaturally ill; nausea began to spread throughout his body. "Oh, my God," he thought and dropped his head in anguish.

His eye would not stop ticking. "Please, dear God, let it be there" he prayed and begged the good Lord. He removed the handkerchief from his breast pocket and wiped his brow. How could he tell that son of a bitch Charley Daisey that he had been fleeced … taken … FUCKED! Some con artist walked out of the store with the Singhalese diamond.

"Yes, Ernest, you've been fucked," he said softly aloud banging his hand on the desk. Then quickly he dialed the vault room attendant Morris Hopkins to tell him he would be coming there immediately. Hurrying as quickly as he could, once in the vault, Gormann and the attendant removed Box 85, Vanlo and Eugêne's private safety deposit boxes, Gormann lifted the cover; on top of everything else was the small white suede case. Gormann picked it up, opened the lid and removed the pink stone. He quickly examined it through his jeweler's glass; he felt his knees give way; he nearly fell. He wanted to throw up.

One hour later, assistant General Manager Charles Daisey, Ernst Gormann, and Vanlo and Eugêne's chief security advisor Dan Weiss sat in Charles Daisey's office staring at the synthetic pink kunzite stone that sat on top of Daisey's desk.

"Nestor is on his way here now. He left early to go to his daughter's birthday party. You are a dumb mother fucker!" Daisey shouted at Gormann. "You have been in this business over thirty years. How the fuck does some mooch switch a hundred twenty six carat, rare pink diamond for a two dollar piece of shit like this? All the fucking security we had in place … I just do not believe this happened; it has to be a bad dream. Tell me it's a bad dream Ernst? Tell me it's all a joke before I fucking kill you."

Gormann stayed painfully quiet.

"Was this guy checked out, and vetted properly? Ernst, do you think Lloyd's of London is going to say, 'gee, Charley, too bad, could happen to anyone. Here is our check for six and a half million dollars. And by the way, tell Ernst Gormann he's fucking dumber than a door mat, and Charley, no hard feelings?   And you tell me Ernst, how the fuck do I explain this tiny transgression of yours to the Board, Mauricio Vanlo and the de'Ortega family who own the stone and are expecting somewhere around ten million bucks? We are sorry, Señor de'Ortega but some fruitcake with a wig, bronze-colored glasses and a black attaché case stole it when a woman who looked like the spirit of Halloween past, fell across a show room table, sweeping away and destroying over one hundred thousand dollars worth of imported glass. No one knows where she is or where anybody is! The cops, the rescue people, the ambulance people, a doctor with a Scottish or English accent vanishes along *with* his entire office. No one knows a fucking thing! Except, we do know this, we got fucked out of the Singhalese diamond, isn't that right Ernst? You fucking little jerk off!" Spittle was dripping from the sides of Charles Daisey's mouth.

Dan Weiss began to speak in his usual controlled professional voice tone. "We have the perpetrator of the theft on video film as well as the woman accomplice. But the problem is this. As simple, as their disguises were, the effectiveness of the disguises leaves us with nothing really to go on. He is five, eleven, weighs about one seventy five. She is five, six ... my opinion is to begin giving lie detector tests to determine whether there was any inside assistance."

"For Christ's sake, Weiss," Daisey continued to shout, "Is everyone here a sub-mental retard? If this story gets out, you can bet your ass that our credibility will be history. Every damn estate-piece we have on consignment will be demanded back so fast our heads will spin, and that is a great deal of money for Vanlo and Eugêne to give up. No, no. We may be up to our assholes with trouble, but this we have to keep as quiet as possible as long as possible." Pausing for a moment, Daisey's gaze settled on Gormann. "We gave them a fucking blueprint on how to steal that diamond. If it wasn't for that fucking picture of the stone and that article, he," Daisey pointed his finger at Gormann, "insisted we put into Jewelers Keystone Circular, we would not be sitting in my office."

Gormann was inwardly enraged: "*Yes, everyone, I screwed up badly. Got conned out of my socks right up to my eyeballs. But I've had enough of this son of a bitch.*" He eyed the letter opener – Gormann wanted to grab it and thrust it into Daisey's throat. "*It's time I stopped taking insults from this piece of shit.*" He was just ready to lash out verbally when the telephone rang. Dan Weiss picked up.

"Yes, all right, send them in. Thank you." Dan Weiss looked at Daisey then at Gormann. "Two detectives and a police artist are on their way in."

"Okay," said Daisey, "I will explain the importance of keeping this from the press for as long as possible. And Ernst, I hope your eyes and memory are sharper than your intelligence."

Weiss looked at Gormann with pleading eyes not to say anything. But it didn't matter. Gormann was speaking to himself. *"I will get you for this, no matter what, you loathsome prick!"*

*   *   *

The following morning in the Manhattan South Police Precinct, Michael Anselt, Lloyd's of London's top east coast American claims man, sat with Detectives Joe Heywood and T. R. Trumball discussing the theft of the Singhalese diamond.

Trumball was saying we have the security films seven days prior to the robbery. One woman was definitely identified as being there the day before. Guess what? It was the same person who slammed dunked the three pointers on the glass table. We'll be questioning the sales lady who had direct contact with the woman, her name is… Agnes White. In the mean time, we are showing stills of this woman throughout all the departments. Maybe something will come of it. She basically was dressed the same way each of the two days. We now know for sure she wore a wig, her glasses hid her eyes, and the book bag she carried gave us nothing. What is most interesting, is what my partner Detective Heywood noticed on the security film while she was being attended to by the emergency response boys. She never held or touched anything with her hands; seemingly kept them away purposely… even the cup of water she drank from was held by a store employee. Man alive, what planning went into this heist."

*   *   *

LONDON – Three days following the diamond theft.

Harry was going through the London Times when he spotted a Reuters's article detailing the Milan Museum's robbery of a Greek antique. He got as far as "… heavily insured by Lloyd's of London, little progress has Occurred…"

It was then that Harry Fellows received the telephone call. He was just on his way out to imbibe a pint or two of lager and have a curry at a nearby pub called The Lamb's Ear.

"Harry hello to you dear man. I do hope I haven't disturbed you. It's me, Miles. Miles Jamison." Fellows kept silent, savoring the moment like no other he had ever had.

"Hello, hello, I say, is anyone there?"

"Yes Miles, I am here. This is a surprise indeed. Are you phoning to find out if I remarried?"

"How are you, Harry?"

"Actually quite well and fit. Now what is it you want Miles?" Fellows was intentionally curt. "I was just on my way to have a spicy chicken tikka and a Kingfisher beer or two at a new Indian restaurant that recently opened in the neighborhood."

"Harry, please, no bitterness now. Please try and be more cordial. For Christ sakes Harry, I'm an old man. A little courtesy is due the elderly, please."

"Skip the bull Miles. I'm repeating. What is it you want? Is that being cordial enough?"

I have a major problem. And to answer your question, what it is I want Harry, is to see you right away. I'm here in London, arrived just minutes ago."

Fellows said nothing, using his silence as a momentary advantage.

"Harry, are you there?"

Harry said, "I'm here. Is what you want to do Miles, is renew old friendships possibly? If so, forget it Miles. I don't want to be your friend.

"Lunch today at the Grenadier on Wilton Road? At about One? It'll beat the dickens out of Indian chicken tikka." said Jamison, his voice pitched slightly higher than usual.

"Why the Grenadier Miles; expensive, no?"

"It's a good thing I feel close to you Harry in spite of what you might think of me."

"Fine, Miles. I will see you in the Grill Room at about one."

"Harry, by the way, J. Edgar Davies will accompany me."

"Fellows put the phone down gingerly. He stood gazing at it. "Son of a bitch," he said aloud, "the human race is so predictable." His heartbeat quickened as his imagination began to construct the scene that would be taking place in about one hour.

As fast as his fingers would work, he punched out Fritz Barrow's number in New York.

"Guess what Fritz? Guess who I'm having lunch with in about one hour?"

Barrow's only comment was, "I told you so, mate. Those who know know. Jamison is no dummy. See you in the big apple soon."

Fellows laid out his best Saville Row three-piece suit, white starched shirt with French cuffs - gold and opal cufflinks, and the silk tie Bonnie Adele had brought him upon her arrival to London with Fritz Barrow. Harry hummed an old Noel Coward tune as he got dressed; "I'll See You Again."

It was Clive, the head waiter who enthusiastically greeted Harry Fellows as he emerged through the white-arched entrance into Grenadier's Grill Room. Harry Fellows who was a customer from his former days with Lloyd's shook hands and made small talk as Clive led the way downstairs to the table where Miles Jamison and J. Edgar Davies sat waiting. Davies was on his feet the moment he saw Harry and rushed over to clasp a handshake. "Harry it's so good to see you – and you looking so well. And Harry, thank you for coming."

Jamison looked as forlorn being no different then the way he had sounded earlier on the telephone. He and Fellows played at the role of being cordial; none of the three men speaking of the impending problem until they were well into their first cocktail.

As quickly as Miles Jamison could determine that the man across from him had settled down and showed a bit of being amiable, he said, "Harry, do you always dress so elegantly for an Indian curry lunch?"

"On with it Miles please."

"Harry old boy, we have had a bomb drop upon us. Devastating damage to be sure. Nuclear in nature. Vanlo and Eugêne jewelers in New York City had an important diamond switched on them. We had the blasted thing covered for six and a half million United States green currency dollars."

"Miles, please don't BS and old BS'er. Six million, even seven million is Lloyd's daily expense fund." Harry glanced at Davies to see his reaction.

"Michael Anselt," said Jamison, "has just this morning arrived from New York with the sordid details. It seems a faithful longtime employee by the name of Ernst Gormann was duped, the patsy, the mark or whatever it is you wish to call a fool who gets taken very badly. Been with the company thirty some years; hasn't as much as taken a paper clip or ball point pen. All the others associated with the store that might have been involved got A's on the lie detector machines. This heist, if I may call it that, came from the outside, flawless in planning, executed to perfection. A team. Three persons at least. So far as we know two men and a woman. Each of whom will receive an academy of award statue in California next March and definitely on judgment day. Each played separate roles, that when combined, conned the socks off of everyone. The timing and resources to pull this switch required money, an acute knowledge of gemstones, some electronic expertise plus disrupting the use of public telephones, a phony address, and Harry, knowledge of how the sale of the diamond was to take place. It was advertised to be an open bidding for the gem. Winner takes all."

Jamison then turned to J. Edgar Davies, who then reconstructed the events beginning with the magazine article; he then followed with each sequence as it might have occurred. Harry was astonished at Edgar's stunning accuracy.

Harry said, "Still, six plus million from your coffers isn't twenty million."

Miles said, "Funny you should say that Harry. The man in charge of the bidding has opened all the sealed bids. The high was twenty million. The bidder being a legitimate auction house in Paris. But no diamond, no reason to meet the bid. Fact is Harry, the auction house has presented Vanlo a bill for travel and hotel expenses; of seven thousand dollars."

"New York can be expensive. So I ask you Miles, where is all this going? Why am I here?"

"Don't be heartless Harry. Edgar please."

J. Edgar Davies said, "Harry, the owner of the diamond is a trust named The De'Ortega Family Trust. Venezuela people. As part of the consignment agreement with Vanlo and Eugêne, the trust receives a copy of each bid. The trust now says they are entitled to the high bid of twenty million."

Harry said, "And I suppose they are, according to what you tell me. But what has this to do with you. Lloyd's insured the stone for six five million dollars."

Miles said, "We insured the stone against loss Harry. The value has increased dramatically. A legal mish-mash to be sure. We've already gotten rid of the New York Underwriter who processed the policy. Our own man at Lloyd's who sanctioned the policy is looking for employment… somewhere in China I believe. This is going to require outside lawyers. Imagine the expense Harry? We will be sued for the full amount of that twenty mil bid. A legal duel that could go on even after I'm dead and buried. A black *X* will mark my grave stone. Michael Anselt is honest enough to tell me he doesn't know where to begin or who to recruit for help. He's met with the police, and the way he sees it, the police are viewing this as just a robbery. No one was hurt, property damaged insured, just a lot of hurt feelings. And I haven't anyone in the stables Harry who can take this on."

"Incidentally Miles, about being dead and buried. Needn't give it a second thought Miles, only the good die before their time. You have heard that expression? Haven't you?"

"When Harry… when Harry, will the bitterness you have for me subside?"

"Okay Miles, do you want me to loan you the money. Is that why you invited me for lunch?"

Jamison ignored the silliness. "Now, this is the way Edgar Davies and I see it Harry. To have this diamond recut or cut into smaller is foolhardy. The real value lies in its size. Plus its rich historical provenance. This theft took too much sophisticated planning to have it disposed of foolishly. I think this disgusting pack of thieves will want to deal directly with us. However, they may want to make us go chasing."

"How many were involved in this ... switch did you say?" Fellows asked.

"I reckon three; could be four. The overhead cam films seems to bear out three. The switcher, the crystal breaker, and the phony doctor." Fellows raised his hand, signaling for the waiter.

Jamison's accurate dialogue never faltered as he continued. "We already know the stone used for the decoy was made in Idar-Oberstein by a reputable house. The chap who took the order is the factory manager. He has given three conflicting descriptions of the culprit. Probably took a worthwhile bribe to remain quiet. Dealing with the Germans is like pulling teeth. Hard-hearted people. Still angry that they lost the war. Veins full of ice water. There was also a boy who delivered the stone to someone waiting in a nearby cafe, but the youth can only recall a very large tip he received from the culprit. Every damn detail necessary was carried out to perfection. It's is a though ...," Jamison stopped, his train of thought wandering; he stared at Fellows.

Fellows returned the stare with a smile. "Why are you telling me this story of deception and folly, Miles? Do you think I know the whereabouts of this diamond?"

Jamison blinked, without answering, and continued. "No dealer, private or otherwise would dare touch this stone, not even with a long stick. Interpol, the FBI, Scotland Yard, and our own boys have seen to that. Harry, what I am asking is for you to take charge of this entire mess."

Fellows said, "You have some damn good investigators in your employ Miles; why ask me? Michael Anselt knows plenty of New Yorkers qualified to get results, don't you think so Miles? What about you Edgar?"

Both Miles and Edgar ignored the question not wanting to get into the fact that Harry Fellows was the very best investigator that Lloyd's ever had.

"Look Harry, even my right arm by the name of J. Edgar Davies says to me, Miles don't waste your time putting a team together. Call Harry Fellows. And I agreed. So Harry, go to New York, carte blanche of course. Put out your bloodhounds, find the diamond. Negotiate. If we are lucky the thieves will ask three, four million dollars. A goodly amount for their efforts." Jamison paused. "And Harry, let me be completely honest."

"Does that mean you have other than honest with me, Miles?"

"Edgar please explain to this stubborn man." said Jamison.

Edgar Davies said, "Harry, the consortium that insured the Singhalese diamond is another new money group. They are young, rich, spoiled, and used to getting their own way. This was their first large venture."

Harry said, "The big print giveth, the small print taketh away."

Nodding agreement, Davies turned to the waiter who had materialized to take their order.

Fellows selected the Aylesbury duckling with rhubarb sauce and mashed potatoes. Jamison ordered the filet of beef Wellington with a small side salad. J. Edgar Davies ordered a Ploughman's platter with Stilton cheese. Another round of fresh drinks was brought.

"Unfortunately, there is a larger problem," said Jamison. "We might have a problem with these new boys paying up past the six point five million; this blasted business of switching stones always creates legal entanglements. Which could leave us the burden of dipping into our own resources for the difference? The whole bloody business is going to come down on my old brittle shoulders, Harry. Please Harry, go to America, the land of the brave and the free. Get that damn diamond back for me Harry."

"It's like I always say, there's nothing like a good old fashion stickup, eh Miles? So what's in it for me?"

"A fair question indeed. All I ask Harry is that you be fair," Jamison asked, his eyes had briefly diverted away from Fellows toward Davies.

Fellows sipped his drink - then deliberately stretched his arms backwards, the gesture of someone tired; he made a short powerful burst of air through his mouth. "Well, Miles, I am flattered by your confidence."

Jamison forced a rare smile; his yellowing teeth barely showing.

Harry said, "Before we get into the monetary side of things Miles, I'd like to tell you a personal story. Fact is it just came to mind."

"Please do Harry."

"As you know, I lost my father before my teen years."

"A tragedy dear boy," said Miles.

Harry said, "Every morning before heading off to school, my dad, would always hug me and tell me that he loved me, then would add, be careful of those who you trust in life. On one particular evening after dinner, we always helped mom with the dishes, I suppose I was about age seven, my dad says to me, I always tell you to be careful in whom you trust. He then takes me by the hand into our small living room. This how it went Miles: "Harry," he says, "my little warning about trust has advanced to *trust no one*. Do you understand me son? At the time I really didn't know what to say, bit I obviously shook my head that I understood. Over our fireplace was a mantle. Top of the mantle was neatly covered with several odds and ends… a collection of memorabilia they were. My father removed each piece; carefully placing them on a nearby table.

He pointed to the mantle; I held my arms stiff, he

lifted me up by the elbows as he often did, and stood me on top of the mantle. My boy he says, I want you to jump off and I'll catch you. Don't worry, I'll catch you. Miles, I bent my knees slightly and jumped – at that instant, my dad back away and I hit the floor … hard … I scrapped my knees and wanted to cry but I didn't. Dad was full of apologies, and swore it would never happen again, then again, he pointed to the mantle. He lifted me up, told me to jump, which I did, and once more he backed away - and again I hit the floor. I held out my arms for him to pick me up … he didn't move from where he stood; he just stared for a few moments; I'm fighting back tears, he finally said, Harry, if you can't trust your own father, then you can trust?"

"No one," says I, "No one"

Then he says, let's try it again. I got up, and ran to my room. I trusted you once Miles and you let me hit the floor. Hard!"

Jamison looked at Edgar Davies – neither man said anything

Harry said, "I should think three hundred thousand pounds would be a fair figure win or lose. Plus a hefty extra bonus if I'm able to retrieve the diamond. What do you think?"

Fellows looked Jamison squarely in his shrewd eyes; eyes that similarly were scrutinizing the man he had chosen to rescue him.

"Harry, I need the best for this one. The money will be yours. You have my word."

"Like your word concerning my promotion, the new section Miles?"

"Harry for Christ sakes, we must let bygones, be bygones."

"Okay, Miles, it's a deal."

The two men shook hands. Jamison downed his drink, Davies then handed Fellows a large brown envelope that he removed from his briefcase.

*　　　*　　　*

Desiring to wash his hands, Jamison excused himself, and as he walked towards the Gents Room, Harry began to think about the proposal.

Harry knew Jamison was pleased with himself. Capturing Harry Fellows for this situation was no easy chore. Fellows smiled. Somehow, with the passage of time, like an aging sage, Jamison ably used his appearance and intellect to gain countless advantages. By now though, Jamison might have realized that it was without too much effort that he had altered a rock-hard antagonist to comply to such a wild goose chase.

Miles Jamison fully understood that these professional thieves who pulled off the Singhalese diamond switch would be no easy group to deal with. *"Had I not been one of the renegades, I would have opted out of Jamison's proposal for sure,"* he thought.

Regardless, for Miles Jamison, Lloyd's came first no matter the cost. Some said Lloyd's replaced Jamison's own family. Miles Jamison had been the ill-suited issue of solid traditional British upbringing; he had also been influenced by an army of indifferent nannies. Truthfully, Harry figured, Miles by choice or otherwise, did not make himself a likeable person.

Miles' father had been a career officer in the British Foreign Service, who under a veil of secrecy seemed constantly to be called away from home. A most crushing experience for young Miles was his father's absence from graduation ceremonies at Eaton. His mother was a successful shopkeeper of a prestigious china-and-silver business in Marble Arch, who also was away much of the time either buying or catering to the well-to-do of London. All of this parental absence resulted in producing an aloof man, singularly content who adopted the tenacious attitude of 'I call all the shots'- towards anything he looked to accomplish - the one exception whom Jamison depended upon was his assistant, J. Edgar Davies.

CHAPTER EIGHT

"Mr. Gormann, Mr. Daisey would like a word with you."

"Thank you Maggie," Gormann answered pleasantly, though hearing the name Daisey turned his stomach.

Gormann often wondered why a fine, talented woman like Maggie Blair would work so many years for such an obnoxious, vulgar human being. Then ironically, hadn't he been loyal to the same obnoxious, vulgar man for most of his adult life.

"Yes, Charley," Gormann said dispiritly into the telephone.

"Ernst, listen carefully. I just finished speaking to Nestor Brunnell. He informed me that we have a visitor from our insurer in England; a Lloyd's man. His name is Harry Fellows; peculiar name isn't it? He'll be in my office in a matter of minutes. Brunnell says he wants to interview you. But first, he wants a few words with me and Dan Weiss. Naturally, Weiss and I can only tell him what happened in the aftermath of things. After our talk, I'll have Weiss take the Englishman to Maggie's office. He told Nestor he wants to speak to you privately. Lloyd's wants a firsthand account of what took place. Just stick to the facts, Ernst, and for Christ's sake don't deviate. Be certain this limey is a shrewdy; they wouldn't just send anyone to settle a major claim like this. Just tell him what he wants to hear Ernst. We don't want this to be the beginning of a long drawn out problem. So let's try and get this goddamn situation wrapped up as quickly as possible. And Ernst, call me as soon as the limey leaves your office. I want to know what you both said."

Daisey put his phone down before Gormann could respond. Gormann muttered aloud, "I hope you burn in hell," then angrily slammed the phone.

Twenty minutes later, Maggie rapped lightly and opened the door to Gormann's office and quietly said, Mr. Gormann this is Mr. Harry Fellows from Lloyd's of London.

Silently, Gormann stood looking at the Englishman as Maggie closed the door behind her. "May I come in?" Fellows cheerfully said, smiling. "I am a bit weary and would love an invitation to sit down."

Returning the smile, Gormann extended his hand in the direction of a two-seat sofa. "Kindly sit there and please do forgive me, one always expects the worst under these circumstances, and I must admit, I had an image more befitting the grim reaper carrying his sickle."

"That is more encouraging then you think; actually a complements of sorts when compared to what others think of me and have called me." Fellow's voice was gentle and friendly. Gormann later described it as 'offering clemency'.

"Regardless of what you may heard from your supervisor, I am not here Mr. Gormann to interrogate or to make judgments. I am not even requesting that you go over the unfortunate events that led to the Singhalese diamond's disappearance. I am quite sure that you have suffered enough embarrassment over this bizarre theft. Remember, in a theft of this magnitude, the perpetrators always have the upper hand. They have it all figured to the last detail. Sometimes things go wrong, but in this case, everything went according to their plan. Perhaps in hind sight, you might chastise yourself for missing a revealing moment that might have turned, shall I say, them dropping the ball."

Gormann nodded, oddly, he felt relaxed; he was relieved he would not have to repeat again the details of what took place over that horrible ten minutes. But he was somewhat confused - he said, "I am obliged to you for that Mr. Fellows, and I thank you. So if that be the case, would you please tell me what is it you want from me?"

"Ah, an excellent question sir. What I do want to know is this, Mr. Gormann. I am interested in the man that sat in your office ... the person that called himself Andrew Longmeyer and your observations of him. Anything at all. Post game feelings. I am as interested in subtleties as well as the obvious. I am told that you have been in the business many, many years and are truly an expert at what you do. So I need you to look beneath the thief's disguise, beneath the wig, and whatever else he successfully used to fool everyone involved... I need you to look through the surface of the murky water, so to speak. Tell me anything that you can recall about this imposter, as slight as it might have been. Physical mannerisms, speech, your own impressions before the showroom disruption of breaking glass. I think you know what it is that I'm after." Fellows intertwined his fingers and leaned forward; a motion that elicited confidentiality. He said, "Almost two years ago, we had a similar occurrence, the same bloody pattern. There could be a connection. If so, I want the dirty bastards caught." Fellows got up from the sofa. "Not even necessary we go over it now. Perhaps we can have a get together later in the day. Mr. Gormann, make notes, write whatever comes to mind. Writing does inspire memory... white matter that exists in the brain... you would be surprised what one can remember when the brain's white matter is exploited." Giving Gormann no time to reply, Fellows added, "I say, Mr. Gormann, if it sits right with you, would you mind being my guest for dinner? We could discuss this nasty episode over a good meal in more ... more congenial surroundings. Nothing for you to be overly concerned about. New York City is your town." Fellows smiled warmly.

"Well ... yes, I suppose that would be very nice." Gormann was caught off guard by Fellows' sensibility, and responded by saying, "What type of food do you enjoy?"

"The truth of the matter is, Mr. Gormann, English cooking is for the best part atrocious and I unfortunately take most of my meals out."

Laughing, Gormann said, "Yes, I know. I visited the UK two summers ago." "Truthfully, I would love something Italian," said Fellows.

Gormann replied with enthusiasm. "I frequent a wonderful little place on Madison Avenue and eighteenth – the restaurant is called Giovanni's."

"Jolly good. Sounds wonderful. What would be a convenient time for me to meet you Mr. Gormann.?"

"How does eight o'clock sound?"

"Perfect. I'll find it and shall be there promptly at eight."

The men shook hands cordially, and Fellows left.

For whatever the reason, the short meeting Gormann had with Harry Fellows had left him with a sense of relief. "*Like he says,*" thought Gormann, "*con-artists work their scams throughout the world. It could have happened to anyone put in my position.*"

Returning to his desk, he pressed the digits, zero and seven on his desk phone. This time Charles Daisey's voice was casual in contrast to his former attitude. "Well now, Ernst, that was quick. What did you and the gentleman talk about?"

"Surprisingly little," Gormann said guardedly. "He wanted me to try and recall certain mannerisms of the guy calling himself Andrew Longmeyer, and wants to meet with me later to discuss it."

"Uh, yes ... he mentioned the same thing to me." Gormann wondered momentarily why Daisey lied. "Look Ernst, try and feel him out as to when the claim might be settled. I have a sales meeting with the giftware manager and his staff, after which I must leave the store. We will speak about it first thing in the morning."

Once again, Daisey dropped the telephone before Gormann could reply.

*　　　　　*　　　　　*

Fellows understood clearly that the evening's get together with Gormann was crucial. He needed to know something about each of the players involved with the sale of the Singhalese diamond, how Gormann figured in, and how Gormann felt about each of the others. Fellows' intuition was such that he felt Gormann would be the perfect central figure to lay complete the plan that he Fritz Barrow and Bonnie Adele had worked out. Fellows also knew this might be his only opportunity to sound him out.

Ernst Gormann and Harry Fellows arrived at Giovanni's Restaurant within minutes of each other. The maitre d' greeted Gormann by name, and as requested, escorted the men to a table somewhat more private then the others.

After being seated, Gormann took the initiative and spoke first. "*Why not,*" he thought. "*I haven't murdered anyone.*"

"Mr. Fellows, I'm curious to how one chooses a vocation of being an insurance investigator for a global insurer. I hope I'm not intruding on anything personal."

"Not personal at all. Most often, those that I interview are so uptight about their own hidden misgivings they loose sight of the central reason for the interview to begin with.

In your case Mr. Gormann, you got duped by a gang of con men – there was nothing that you could have done to prevent it. If your friend Mr. Charles Daisey had been in your shoes behind the desk, sitting with two hundred thousand dollars at his side, and wanting to end the bid-off, believe me, the sad outcome would have been the same.

"Oh yes, and to answer your question, I was recruited for my job. I had been working for the British Government in a second-tier security position – the team I headed got lucky and we broke up a small organized group of outside contract workers trying to do harm to the government. It's all I can actually reveal, but I was contacted by Lloyd's and with the blessing of my own Chief, I took on the open position of investigator. A finger from the fickle hand of fate pointed me out."

Gormann said, "Too bad it wasn't Charles Daisey behind the desk last Friday."

Picking up on the antagonistic tone of Gormann referring to Charles Daisey, Fellows said, "Though I only just met Mr. Charles Daisey and spent just a few minutes with him, he comes across as somewhat ... let me choose the correct words ... rather thorny, yes, thorny might express him best. Though I dare say that that type is far more predictable than the quiet, mischievous kind."

"*He is an inhuman son of a bitch,*" Gormann thought but thought it best to refrain from saying anything negative about his senior boss.

Fellows was pleased to see Gormann's facial express acquiesce to his statement regarding Vanlo and Eugêne's store's assistant general manager.

"Not too long ago," continued Fellows, "I worked for a similar type chap at Lloyd's, except he covered his special brand of nastiness with a soft tone and a smooth articulate manner of speech."

"*There is nothing about Charles Daisey that is soft, except his brain,*" Gormann thought.

Switching subjects, Fellows said, "Ernst, in a day or two, as a matter of form, I'll be interviewing the store's general manager Nestor Brunnell. Any background you'd like to share on Brunnell? Anything you tell me; you can trust me to be discrete."

Gormann said, "Harry, Nestor Brunnell is the salt of the earth... a fine gentleman. Liked and respected by all. Once a month he addresses our store-wide sales meeting. He's an inspiration. I only wish he took a more active role in the daily workings of the store. At our last meeting he tells the story of a summer job, his father had arranged for him at a bank. May I tell you the story?"

Harry said, "Please do."

"Nestor was a teenager. One of Nestor's duties at three o'clock, when the bank closed, he was to carry a sealed envelope to the Federal Reserve Bank a few blocks away and before three fifteen, deposit the envelope in the brass receptacle at the Reserve's entrance. In the morning at nine a.m., he would go to the Federal Reserve Bank, enter, pick the same envelope up, and take it back to his bank where he would hand it over to the bank manager.

"Each day, every day, the same routine; back and forth. On one particular afternoon, it was sunny, he decided to buy a hot dog from a street vendor, sit on a bench and eat it. He says he closed his eyes and kind of drifted into a nap. When he awoke, he realized it was three thirty; he looked at the envelope that by now after having been transported, who knew, maybe for years, had become limp and soiled. So he decided to go home. The following morning, ten minutes past nine, he entered the bank to find the bank manager, the bank's president and head teller waiting for him. What had occurred was this. The envelope contained a check for one million dollars which was to be deposited, payable to the Federal Reserve – the check was a daily overnight transaction; a deposit of one million dollars. Because the check was not dropped off, the interest due on the errant million dollar loan for the one day was several thousand dollars. Everyone at the meeting understood the story's message. It's important to be reliable and do what one is expected to do regardless of its logic."

Harry said, "Rather a good story. When a man makes a confession to making a mistake, it tells quite a bit about him, don't you think?"

"Positively."

"I'm curious Ernst; you looked rather dismayed when I mentioned the name of Charles Daisey. Is there a reason?"

Unable to control his motion, Gormann blurted out, "He's a conniving son of a bitch, and no one likes him."

Fellows said, "Was there an incident that perhaps made Charles Daisey develop into a conniver and an unlikable person?"

Gormann undoubtedly unhappy with his outburst gathered together his runaway emotion saying, "About fifteen years ago, someone kidnapped, or dog-napped Daisey's prize dachshund. A door man at his building was walking the dog; suddenly he was knocked down by two assailants. One of the attackers snatched the dog. A car pulled up, and gone was the dog and the attackers. The next day, Daisey received a note demanding ten thousand dollars if he ever wanted to pet his dog again. If he paid up, they would drop the dog off at a police station with a note stating who the dog belonged to. Charles adored that dog. As I recall, his name was Hanz.. What ever the arrangement, Daisey delivered the money."

"And the dog?" Harry asked.

"The criminals, as Daisey called them, did drop the dog off in front of a police station in Brooklyn. The dog was dead; strangled. He always felt that certain people at Vanlo were behind it. I must admit, the likelihood of it was a distinct possibility. Daisey is brutally egotistical. He believes that his brilliance is unmatched, that he can intimidate you until he gets what he wants. From then on, he eyed everyone in the company with suspicion. Made life difficult for many of us. A paranoid man for sure."

Harry said, "People get strangled, dogs get strangled and die." With no more commentary concerning the dog, Fellows now immediately switched subjects again. "Well now Mr. Gormann, since this is the restaurant is of your choosing, and I might add very classy indeed, what would you recommend to a limey italianphile?"

Gormann retorted, "Initially, two items that need to be cleared up. First is, I would like dinner to be my treat; secondly, please call me Ernst."

Fellows nodded that he understood, and replied, "It is quite impossible to go along with your first request, sir, as it was I who invited you to be my guest. Aside from that, it is absolutely against company rules to accept such a generous offer as dinner; you can understand that. Therefore, this is my treat. However, the second item I would agree to with pleasure. I will call you Ernst, you call me Harry." Harry then signaled the waiter and asked for the wine list.

Gormann said, "Harry, may I tell you one particular story about Charles Daisey, though it has nothing to do with Vanlo and Eugêne"

"Yes, please do."

Gormann said, "About fifteen years ago, Charles purchased a large parcel of land in southern Florida. He made no secret about it and told everyone he was going to parcel it out in small pieces. Half acre sites to be exact - so much money down, and a low payment each month for fifteen years. He explained it was a great opportunity for store employees to own a piece of land in Florida. Who know what it would be worth in the future? Word got around and all of a sudden, Daisey had a land rush going on. Apparently, he had divided the original property into fifty parcels all of which he sold in a matter of weeks. Each buyer got a contract and a legal description. He then put out the word that he had purchased additional land. But that was a lie which was revealed later on. What he did do though was to begin selling the same parcels not once but two or three times to different buyers."

Fellows let out a hoot, as the waiter poured the wine – Ernst signaling his approval. Harry said, "Daisey probably figured nobody would stay in for the long haul."

Gormann said, "Exactly. Except for one chap, Moe Stillwel, who paid the whole thing off and wanted a deed to the property. Which Daisey did deliver. Unbeknownst to Daisey, Stillwell went to Florida and found his way to the property, which he discovered was under water ten months out of the year – plus the parcel he bought also had a cloud over it as to ownership. Daisey had sold it twice. Land fraud in Florida is no misdemeanor. To avoid going to jail for land fraud, Daisey got himself a high priced Florida Real Estate Lawyer; the courts allowed Charles to pay everyone back with interest and was forbidden to ever deal in land sales again."

Fellows simply shook his head, and raised his wine glass – the two men touched glasses, Fellows said, "Caveat Emptor when it comes to Charles Daisey. Now Ernst, let us forget about Mr. Daisey and his shenanigans for the time being and talk about Mr. Andrew Longmeyer.

*   *   *

Typical of Harry Fellows' scrupulous planning and remarkable trade craft technique, Gormann scarcely stopped speaking of the errant Andrew Longmeyer.

"... in retrospect, I now see clearly that he intentionally tried to annoy me, and damn him, he succeeded. He began his charade by placing his briefcase on top of an exquisitely finished mahogany desk. The desk is in the third floor office that we use to show important jewelry pieces to wealthy customers, as in the case of the pink diamond. With that particular instance of Longmeyer's inconsideration, one is inclined to think that only an asshole drops a briefcase on polished wood. Additionally, during my prepared presentation concerning the Singhalese stone, which is, even if I have to say so myself, quite excellent, he just sat there like a bump on a log totally devoid of any expression, which also annoyed me."

"That too can be disconcerting to one's exuberance," Fellows piped in.

"Indeed. It was quite upsetting not to get any kind of positive response. Maybe I am just losing tolerance in my old age. Or shouldn't I confess to that."

'Go on, Ernst, nothing you say will be used against you."

"Just before all the tumult in the showroom, he introduced an inane commentary on the Queen Elizabeth diamond, which once again, I found aggravating. So to end his distracting conversation, I opened the case containing the Singhalese diamond and started to hand it to him. It was at that precise instant that ... that terrifying scream filled the show room along with the breaking sound of glass. God, I still shudder at being so stupid; I should have known. Nevertheless, I looked away for an instant."

"No lies coming from this chap," thought Fellows. *"His account jells exactly with what Fritz witnessed."*

Fellows said, "Ernst, you must believe me that you are being too hard on yourself. This Longmeyer character knows just as much about stimulus response as you know about diamonds. When you come to cross a street, you look both ways, correct? An involuntary response. No one can control not being attracted to screams and sounds of breaking glass. There is nothing more unnerving. I have this feeling Ernst, that much of your being upset is from Charley Daisey coming down on you like a claw hammer."

Gormann in his agitation of recalling insults barbs from Daisey, gulped at his wine. "Harry," he said, "you cannot imagine how that man humiliated me. Today, this morning, he had the balls to ask me, to ask you, when the claim might be settled."

Fellows ignored the statement. "Ernst, answer me this. Besides the beautifully polished mahogany desk, why did Vanlo and Eugène elect to use that office?"

"Security, atmosphere, plus fifty thousand dollars worth of special lighting. The lighting is state-of-the-art. The person behind the desk, selling, can manipulate the lights to enhance the liveliness and color of most any precious stone being shown. Rubies can be made more red, sapphires bluer, emeralds a few shades greener. Plus, the liveliness of diamonds can be enhanced. We brought in a lighting expert from Geneva, Switzerland."

Fellows whistled.

"And, Harry," Ernst added, "the other two offices on the third floor have identical lighting." Both men became silent as a waiter once again refilled the wine glasses.

"Ernst, listen to what I have to tell you. As you have become aware first-hand, we know as well that the doctor was a masquerading phony, and even the telephone booth he used in Bergdorf Goodman's Department Store he was able to put out of work. That phone booth had the same phone number as the number engraved on the Medical Alert charm that Longmeyer's female accomplice wore, plus the address was a nonexistent Manhattan address. Ernst we also know where, by whom, and how the stone replicating the diamond was made. Ernst, all of these elements is a repeat of what happened in Beverly Hills, California, two years ago. There, they switched a huge parcel of top Columbian Muzo Emeralds which you know are the most expensive emeralds in the world. Based on other information from Interpol and the FBI, it is now our opinion that the thieves will contact someone here soon."

"Here, did you say here Harry? Here as in Vanlo and Eugène?"

It was now time for Harry to follow his intuition concerning Ernst Gormann. "Yes. And to be perfectly honest, there is another reason why I wanted to see you alone tonight. Ernst, you are the only person in this entire scenario I feel can be trusted."

Leaning forward, Gormann said quietly, "Honestly, Harry, as suspicious as it may look to some, do you actually think I had no part of it?"

"I absolutely think you had nothing to do with it. I have already been in communication with Lloyd's. And that is why I have been instructed to reveal to you the following." Fellows leaned slightly forward. "We think the persons who perpetrated this crime are going to contact the head man, most likely Charles Daisey and attempt to deal with him directly - the main reason why I have questioned you concerning him. I have surmised from being with him this morning that he has not yet been contacted."

Gormann shook his head in disbelief. "I don't understand. Why Charles Daisey?"

"More often than one might believe, big money thefts committed by professionals try and deal with insurance companies directly."

"Yes, I am aware of that Harry."

"The modus operandi of the modern big time thief is to move quickly; contact the insurance agent, make a deal and wave bye, bye. It saves the Insuring company, Lloyd's being no exception, lots of money, so there is a tendency not to pursue the thieves with due diligence. Everybody is basically happy. But since we have not been contacted, we think that this particular trio of crooks is going to work the same way they did in the Beverly Hills heist two years ago." Fellows lowered his voice almost to whisper. "What I am asking you, Ernst, is to tell me more about the ... the unprincipled side of Mr. Charley Daisey. You have known him for many, many years."

Gormann said, "Too many, Harry."

"You can only have my word that anything you divulge to me will be held completely confidential. No notes, no tape recorders."

"Harry, please forgive me for asking, but why Charles Daisey. Why not Nestor Brunnell?"

Fellows now leaned back in his chair and stared directly into Gormann's eyes. Gormann picked up his wine glass and studied it for several moments.

Fellows said, "I've been involved with people like Charles Daisey, and Nestor Brunnell most of my working life as an insurance investigator of fraud. I don't like Daisey. I don't trust Charles Daisey. Call it instinct, call it intuition, but that's the way it is. As far as Nestor Brunnell is concerned, he's the type if contacted by the thieves, wouldn't hesitate to call the police, notify your security man Dan Weiss and Charles Daisey. I have no way of knowing if any of this will materialize Ernst. But what I do know is that our think-tank boys and girls have reliable data base information to back up their theories, but most of all, are expert in psychological behavior."

"Jesus Christ Harry."

"Charles Daisey if contacted will try and come out ahead somehow in any negotiation by dealing on the quiet."

Gormann went quiet. He stared at Fellows. Harry knew that this was the moment of truth for the scheme's success.

What Gormann was contemplating wasn't Harry Fellows' sanity. He was thinking that after all these years this dirty son of a bitch Charles Daisey would somehow, deservingly, get it up his ass, all the way. Gormann's face looked grim. "Harry, tell you what. The time has come for me to have my pound of flesh. I will tell you what I know about Charley Daisey. But first we order, we eat, and go to my place to split a fantastic bottle of thirty-year old port I have been saving it for some special occasion. And Harry, just in case you're wondering; I'm not gay."

*   *   *

It was ten o'clock, when the taxi dropped them off at Gormann's Park Avenue Apartment. Gormann prepared a cheese tray and after pouring the vintage port wine, he brought out two Cuban cigars. "Been saving these too Harry."

After the initial pleasure of sipping the port and lighting the cigars, Gormann began: "Harry, Charley Daisey uses his position to satisfy his insatiable hunger for making a fast buck. You have to realize that Daisey is very well to do, but is so greedy, it makes you ill. I know for certain that he has a friend who has post-bid certain estate transactions that involve important articles of jewelry. His friend, a Sheik, pays Daisey a commission in cash under the table when the buy is complete."

"How does it work, Ernst?" Harry asked.

"Charles Daisey is privy to the final price that our company and a select group of other bidders has decided to offer on a certain collection of jewelry left with us to sell, often by estates where the last parent dies and the off-springs want cash. Our offers preempt a public sale. Daisey tells his Arab pal what the top offer is, his pal ups the offer minutes before the sale closes. Vanlo advises the sellers of the top bid, and more often than not, the sellers agree to the price. Hence, the Arab buys the collection. Our own appraisers have done all the work figuring weights, provenance, and values. No one is the wiser, but Vanlo and Eugêne are out the potential profit they would have legitimately made by purchasing it themselves through a separate division, and reselling those pieces at a public sale. It makes me sick to my stomach to think what a fucking scoundrel Daisey is."

"Does the GM wear blinders when it comes to Daisy?"

"Harry, Vanlo and Eugêne are third generation jewelers. Mauricio Vanlo, a direct descendant of the founder, a fine man, I have met him personally, puts his complete trust in our general manager Nestor Brunnell. Brunnell is a savvy money man. Although he works closely with the company CFO, Brunnell deals with funding, credit, the banks. But what works for Mauricio Vanlo are the numbers which translates into profit. And that is where Nestor Brunnell's energies abound. There are three major departments; each having an entire floor to sell their goods. First floor, watches, second floor is jewelry, third floor gift ware, and the fourth floor is where he accounting, human resources, credit and customer service are located. Part of that floor has a section where estate jewelry, second-hand consigned jewelry is sold. Nestor allows Daisey to do his job unfettered and Daisey gets away with murder."

Fellows asked, "Any theft or inventory problems?"

"None. Harry, except for gift ware, sales people are trained never to show more than two pieces at a time. Security cameras and a security people keep everyone honest. Even at closing, every piece of merchandise is physically counted, the counts are then entered into the computer and the numbers must jell with the company's inventory. If it doesn't, then that section is recounted."

"How did Daisey and the Sheik become acquainted?"

"Mauricio Vanlo, who lives in Paris, came to New York and held a black tie affair. The occasion was for a sale of jewelry that belonged to the late King Farouk."

Harry said, "Ernst, Farouk died in the sixties I believe."

"Yes. There was a story that accompanied the sale. As I recall, it goes like this: before the revolution and the overthrow of Farouk's regime, someone in the family put together many of the King's pieces, smuggled them out of Egypt and all of which eventually ended in the hands of a friend of Farouk's son Prince Ahmed Fouad. I'm certain there's more to the story, but none of which that I know. Any way it was at this affair put on by Mauricio Vanlo that Daisey met the Sheik."

"Ernst, tell me a bit about Mauricio Vanlo if you don't mind."

"Vanlo is the major owner of the company. He receives reports weekly from Nestor Brunnell. He wants bad news first, then the good news. He is very generous at Christmas, doesn't have any problems with maternity leave, we have the best health care program available. I suppose one couldn't have a better employer. However, he is pretty upset about the missing diamond; he did personally call me and wanted to hear first-hand what had occurred, which I told him of course."

More important than Brunnell and Vanlo, before the evening ended, Gormann had related to Fellows all that he knew about Charles Daisey and his under-handed dealings. As Fellows approached the door to leave, Gormann said in parting, his words slurred slightly, "This Singhalese diamond incident has made me realize it's time to throw in the towel. Harry believe me, it was not that long ago when I would have told that cocksucker Andrew Longmeyer to take a long walk off a short pier. I would have spotted that scam a mile away. It's age Harry. It changes us in strange ways. Nevertheless, with my Vanlo and Eugêne pension and what I have managed to save, I can get by, provided I live close to that proverbial bone."

"I too have been bloody lucky Ernst," Fellows responded patiently. "I cannot deny it. I have tripped over a few dead bodies in my day, but with God's help, have avoided personal injury. It is also time for me to quit too Ernst. Quit while I'm ahead. Incidentally, I am at the Hilton, the one closest to your store should you feel the need to get in touch with me."

The evening ended amiably. They had become friends. Fellows had even invited Gormann to come to England for his next holiday to be his guest at his Ebury Lane Flat.

-All's well that ends well, so it is said.

CHAPTER NINE

Ernst Gormann said good-by to Harry Fellows and closed the door; as he walked to his bedroom the effects of wine caused him to stumble slightly. He felt good about being drunk; the last time had been years before. Gormann also felt good about meeting Harry Fellows; for the feeling that now surrounded him was one of elation. Elated that he was able to reveal to Fellows what a conniving rat Charley Daisey really was.

It was rare for Gormann to sleep soundly through the night, but this night he had. He rose early without any affects of a hangover, made himself a large pot of coffee and sat on his terrace watching the news on television.

The telephone rang at 7:30; he had just gotten up from his chair to take his shower and get dressed.

He answered, "Hello?"

"Please pay close attention. What I have to say will be said just once." It was the voice of a woman; she spoke softly but with authority. "I have in my possession the Singhalese diamond."

Gormann's heartbeat quickened; he felt dizzy. "Who ... who is this?" He stammered.

"Do not waste time with stupid questions. I told you to pay close attention to what I have to say. I am prepared to offer you the diamond for the mere sum of three million American dollars. I repeat. Three million United States dollars."

Gormann, who had been standing, flopped back into a chair.

"At Grand Central Station, downstairs, close to the Clam Bar entrance, there is a series of public telephones on each side of the walkway. At precisely three p.m. today, one of the phones facing the clam bar that is not being used will ring. You need to stand by - get to it promptly. I will then give you additional instructions if you are interested. Please, no shenanigans. If you don't show, then I'll know Vanlo and Eugêne do not want to play ball, or they have called the authorities. We are professionals, as you have already discovered for yourself. There are no traps that we will fall into. There is no reason why this should not be a clean exchange. Tell your bosses that you are only person we will deal with. Should you not show, then there will be no further contact. And the diamond will be disposed of accordingly." The woman promptly hung up.

Gormann was confused. Harry Fellows had told him that in all likelihood, the thieves would contact Charles Daisey. As quick as he could, Gormann got pen and paper and wrote down the conversation as he recalled it. He then phoned the New York Hilton, and asked to speak to Harry Fellows.

After informing Fellows of the call and what was said by the woman, Fellows asked, "Would you be able to recognize the voice if you heard it again?"

"Probably not. But why do you ask?

"If you receive another call with a different voice, it might help to indicate how many persons we're actually dealing with."

"Yes, I see."

"Ernst, it would be best if we met. Please come here to the Hilton, we'll meet in the coffee shop."

*   *   *

"These people mistakenly think you are the one person at Vanlo and Eugêne to negotiate with," were Fellows' first words after shaking hands with Gormann. "I rang London immediately after your call, and we agree the thing to do is tell Charles Daisey about the woman's call and what she said. You must leave me completely out of the picture. And Ernst, that Mr. Daisey of yours is surely going to inquire as to our meeting yesterday. Tell him I said nothing of any importance, though I did mention that I would be leaving New York for London in a day or two."

"Fine, fine, Harry, but why all the cloak and dagger now that I've been contacted. Why not call the police or the FBI and set up a force of men to make an arrest?"

"Ernst, as I explained at the restaurant, the only thing we at Lloyd's are interested in is retrieving the Singhalese diamond. Lloyd's will be thrilled to pay the ransom in exchange for the diamond that somehow you, me, and Daisey will arrange. Two or three million is like a pound of birdseed in a case like this. Vanlo and Eugêne will return the diamond to its proper owner, bring any potential lawsuits from the trust to an end. At which point your company can decide if they want to involve the police or FBI. And for the record, Ernst, as of this morning at my bequest, Lloyd's of London has agreed that you are entitled to a substantial reward, if and when we successfully recover the diamond. And of course, all of that will be held completely confidential."

Laughing nervously, Gormann was unsure of what to say.

"Ernst at this point, you happen to be Lloyd's only hope in getting that damn diamond back from this group of scoundrels … who knows, they might decide to take it to Europe and sell it there. Three million is a hell of a lot less than eleven million or more."

Gormann frowned. "I see what you mean. What is it they want me to do, Harry?" he said wearily.

"Tell Charley Daisey the entire conversation you had with this woman caller, except for the amount of money. I repeat. Be certain you make no mention of money. Then tell Daisey you want an early pension, and four hundred thousand dollars severance up front. Be firm. Tell him you have had it, and want out. You're sick and tired of his abuse and you want no part in dealing with the thieves. At that point Ernst, say nothing more. Do not explain anything; it would be a sign of weakness. He will be the one to break the silence, and although he won't know immediately what it is that you are actually talking about, he will in all probability agree, or at least invent some sort of a stall. Trust me on this, Ernst. I know about greed and the criminal mind. Stay calm, and let Mr. Charley Daisey take charge. If he tells you to fuck off, then we let London handle it; but he won't. Now go to your store and tell him about the call. I will be in touch with you tonight. Incidentally, I have a meeting with your friend Charles Daisey later in the morning to discuss the posture of the claim."

"Harry, are you absolutely certain he won't decide to tell you my story about the phone call and want to contact the police?"

Fellows gave Gormann a special look, and smiled.

Gormann pursed his lips. "Okay, Harry, you're the boss."

*   *   *

Two days later in the coffee shop of the Mayflower Hotel in Washington, D.C., Bonnie Adele, Fritz Barrow and Harry Fellows ordered roast beef sandwiches on sour dough bread with thick slices of red onion, three draft beers in frosted mugs. Bonnie related what had happened the previous day, and her encounter with Charles Daisey at Grand Central Station.

"I knew Daisey was a shrewd scoundrel," said Fellows. "After hearing Gormann's explaining the phone call from the mysterious caller, Daisey being the SOB he is, decided to deal with the caller by himself. He's not going to tell Gormann anything that's going on."

"Little wonder he wouldn't allow Gormann to get a promotion and move up the power ladder; he would be too close to all the privy data that has been making Daisey rich at the expense of Vanlo and Eugêne."

Bonnie said, "He is shrewd, Harry, and just as you figured it, he wanted to be certain he wasn't being set up. I had a clear view of him from the mezzanine. He was standing super-casual as if waiting for someone to meet him. And you're right, there was no sign of Gormann."

Fritz said, "Great. He's playing right into our hands."

Bonnie said, "I dialed from our new pay-as-you-go mobile phone; Daisey moved quickly to the ringing and answered. - I told him where to look for me. He then put a folded piece of fabric over the receiver, to camouflage his voice I suppose. He wanted to know if I was the female who destroyed one hundred thousand dollars worth of imported glass; he then asked some questions that only I could answer. He said the saleslady from the previous day recognized me, what was her name? I told him Agnes White."

Fritz said, "He was attempting to make sure he was dealing with one of the crooks and not a cop or insurance investigator."

"When he felt reasonably certain that all was well, he asked if I had the diamond. I told him yes. I then removed the chamois sack from my pocket, and waved it. I told him if he moved one step from where he stood, or if anyone came near to me, there was someone that would blow his brains all over the tracks. It was then he took notice of Fritz in his black trench coat and sunglasses.

"Jesus Christ, talk about a thin-cover,' said Fritz shaking his head.

Fellows said, "We're talking about a guy who sees a giant profit for himself. He wants the diamond and will do nothing that will screw the deal."

"He asked me how much we wanted for the stone," Bonnie continued, "I told him three million in cash. All used one hundred dollar bills. He said okay, and didn't bargain. Then, he asked me to repeat the amount of money - which I did. He then said it would take two days to put it together. He needed to contact a particular party."

"More than likely the Arab sheik Gormann told me about," Fellows said.

"I asked him what he was going to do with the diamond; contact Lloyd's of London and make a separate deal? He didn't answer the question. But then said the only way he would deal was to see the diamond prior to making any arrangements. He wanted to be sure we had the Singhalese diamond and not just another two dollar piece of crap – "after all," he said, "you're just a bunch of thieves. You had already made one phony stone, why not two?" His procedure would be, he would examine the diamond with his loupe, weigh it on a portable scale, seal it, which was customary. Then he said, "Figure out the logistics of the exchange and let me know. But not a word of it to Ernst Gormann. Understood?"

"Yes," I said, "understood."

Fellows interrupted saying, "Yesterday, as my meeting with Charles Daisey began to conclude, I mentioned there were no leads to go on, that I would be returning to London and that Lloyd's would be in touch, but before leaving New York, I inquired of Daisey as to whom should I contact regarding any inquiries that required clarifying."

Daisey was plainly irritated by this question. "Inquiries? Why me of course, I'm in charge of this damn fiasco. I'll see that our lawyers and legal department are notified promptly of any pending settlement. See here Fellows, you've had a first hand glimpse of the damage, you now have in your possession copies of letters from Mr. De Ortega's lawyers, and you have I'm certain, what you are required legally to have to pay out. Let's not make what should be a routine settlement into such a big deal. You're in a risky business; are you not?"

I said, "Lawyers deal with big deals, do they not Mr. Daisey?"

"I have no idea what you are talking about Mr. Fellows. However, I must now conclude our meeting. Have a nice trip home."

Fellows then nodded to Bonnie saying, "Let's review what went on the next day."

"Okay," Bonnie said. "It was like a scene out of a good British mystery. Fritz chose the Elyses Hotel for the initial meeting. We only told Daisey the approximate location we would meet not which hotel. He agreed. We called him on his cell and told him to meet us in the lobby of the Carlton. We stationed ourselves to watch - a few minutes later we saw Daisey enter. No one followed him – nothing suspicious happening to send us running. We called him again and told him to meet us at the Elyses Hotel between Park and Madison. Quite a long walk for everyone, but Fritz knows New York; and says the Elyses Hotel is the perfect layout for our purpose. We again watched Daisey go in. I followed a few minutes later. Fritz had possession of the diamond. Upon entering, I took an envelope from a writing desk in the lobby and walked directly into the bar; which according to Fritz's expert experience, is practically empty at this time of day. There was Daisey sitting at the bar. As soon as he saw me, I nodded, he nodded, he then followed me to a table in the rear - Fritz came in and positioned himself at the bar, his hand always in his pocket pretending there was a gun. Daisey also took notice of him right away."

"Mystery writers everywhere please forgive us," groaned Barrow.

Bonnie said, "I told him before he could see the diamond, he had to remove his jacket and roll up his shirt sleeves. After all, it was he who now had the synthetic pink kunzite, not us. "Wouldn't want another switch, would we," I said to him. He must have found this very funny because he let out a hearty laugh."

Barrow put down his mug of beer, he wasn't laughing.

Bonnie continued, "I walked over to Fritz, he handed me he stone; we both walked back to the table. Standing, I placed the diamond into Daisey's open hand. Fritz is now standing directly behind him."

Fritz said to Harry, "The knuckle of my thumb is pressed into his back. To him it felt like the tip of a barrel."

"Daisey looks at the diamond through his jeweler's loupe for no more than five seconds and breaks into a wide smile. "This is it," he says. "I don't need to weigh it. I give you people a lot of credit; you are good. Maybe we can do some business in the future."

"Why not," I say, than I grab the stone from his hand and put it in the envelope and seal the flap. He takes a marker pen from his shirt pocket, motions for the envelope, than carefully makes certain scribble designs across the gummed flap on the back."

"Yes. That assures him the sealed envelope remains undisturbed," Fritz said.

"I now tell him the exchange can only take place Saturday at three p.m. - it was a matter of logistics, rental cars, plane schedules and the lot. We would let him know where. If that's not okay, then it's adios. He says okay, writes down a telephone number on a napkin - this is the number you need to call when you're ready finalize. He gets up, while he's gathering his jacket to leave, Fritz and I are out of there through a rear entrance in less than one minute. No one is following us."

Fellows beamed a huge smile, leaned over and kissed Bonnie on the cheek..

"Here is your check folks," the waitress said. "Is there something wrong with the sandwiches, you haven't touched them. Shall I prepare them to go?"

*   *   *

The following morning at 7:00 a.m. Ernst Gormann's telephone rang. He was in his kitchen preparing his usual morning pot of coffee; he answered cheerfully expecting Harry's voice. "Good morning," he said.

It was the same woman's voice. "Mr. Gormann, everything is set for the exchange Saturday at three. Same place, Grand Central Station. There can be no changes. Promptness is essential. Again, do nothing foolish." The woman hung up. Gormann stood there staring unfocused out of his window.

Once again, the telephone rang; it had an ominous sound to it; Gormann now picked it up hesitantly, his voice kept low, almost in a whisper.

"Hello,"

"Good morning Ernst, it's me Harry. Did I wake you? Are you ill? You sound… I'm not sure. Is everything alright?"

"Harry. Good morning. No I am fine. But just seconds ago that damned woman called again. I recognized her voice. Spoke of an exchange Saturday … at Grand Central Station. What the hell is going on Harry?" He questioned in a demanding tone. "I know nothing about an exchange"

"That damn Daisey," said Fellows. "He did not even bother to tell the crooks who he was. What do you think of that," Harry asked rhetorically. "They must think that you are him … let me think this through for a moment. Fellows paused momentarily. "Ernst, the crooks must think that they are actually dealing with Charles Daisey. There must be some confusion about telephone numbers – I'll explain later," Fellows said. "It appears that the SOB decided to deal with the woman caller himself. He's not going to tell you anything that's going on. Please Ernst get ready and come to my hotel. We'll meet in the coffee shop. All of this must be discussed now. It sounds like the big break for all of us. Apparently not only have the crooks contacted Charley Daisey and made a deal, but are all set to deliver the Singhalese diamond!"

Fellows greeted a nervous Gormann with his usual warmth and friendliness. They took a booth and Fellows ordered double shots of sweetened espresso.

"Ernst, forgive my inquiring again, just indulge me on this one matter, please. Tell me what you told Daisey at your morning meeting the other day."

"I told him about the woman caller, just as you told me to, never mentioning money. When I told him I wanted out, four hundred thousand in cash along with my full pension, he merely stared at me. I kept silent as you suggested; he then asked me if I had anything else in mind. I indicated *no* with a simple hand gesture. Daisey then began to nod as if he had silently understood something and he said, and I quote, 'A reasonable request under the circumstances Ernst, though I am surprised you have the balls to ask. Let's see what happens in the next couple of days.' That was it Harry, I turned away and walked out of his office."

"Ernst, I'll get right to the point," said Fellows. "I spoke to London whilst you were on your way here. The think-tank chaps posed this question. What does one do to secure a diamond worth millions of dollars late on a Saturday afternoon?"

Gormann paused momentarily. "I suppose," he replied smiling, "one tries to locate a suitable safe hiding place."

Fellows returned the smile. "That is correct, Ernst. A suitable safe hiding place. Now according to the woman's message, the exchange is to take place at three p.m. Saturday afternoon. Practically all banks are closed on Saturday, no? So what would you do with an expensive rare diamond?"

"If it were me," said Gormann, "I would take it to the safety of our store and stow it away."

"Where would that be?" Fellows asked.

Gormann paused again. "I would put it in the underground vault; there is a safety deposit box that we use for certain company business; we call it box eighty-five. It's where extremely valuable merchandise is temporarily placed that has not been logged into the computer; access is absolutely limited. I have used it myself for personal belongings, and I know Charles has used it also. Still I can think of no better place under these circumstances."

"Suppose you were certain that under the circumstances of what is going on, no one is suspicious about exchanging the diamond for money?" said Fellows.

Gormann said, "The truth is, there is no safer place. Only four people have access to box eighty-five. The store's general manager Nestor Brunnell, me, Charles Daisey, and the vault room manager Morris Hopkins, but Hopkins must accompany one of us. Naturally, there is a secured company plan to open it, should the three of us be incapacitated at the same time."

"When does Morris Hopkins call it quits? Leave for home."

Gormann said, "Usually when the store closes."

Fellows asked, "So where else might one put a diamond worth millions on a late Saturday afternoon for safe keeping until Monday morning when the stone can be retrieved?"

Gormann thought about it. Nowhere in the store that I can think of. He downed half of the espresso and winced. "There is Harry, no where else as safe than box eighty-five."

Fellows sipped the overly sweetened black liquid.

"But, Harry, if you know Charles is going to buy the diamond from the crooks, why not simply call the police and let them make the arrests."

"Ernst, forgive my French, but fuck the police. If the exchange goes sour, we will never, ever, see the Singhalese diamond again. There is nothing to charge Daisey with. Lloyd's pays the claim money eventually, I am out a handsome bonus, and you are out your reward. Suppose the police do move in successfully, Daisey can always say he did the transaction on his own, with all the intentions of returning the diamond. Ernst, my boy, we must give Charley Daisey all the rope he needs to hang himself and let this entire episode all play itself out."

"Okay, Harry, tell me what it is I have to do now."

"Call Daisy, tell him about the phone call you received this morning."

*　　　　*　　　　*

At 3:10 Saturday, amongst a multitude of scurrying people in Grand Central Station, Charley Daisey waited. He was hot; sweat ran off him. Though the case was sitting on a luggage cart with oversized wheels, he clutched tightly the leather handles of a fifty-five pound, twenty-six inch Pullman suitcase that contained three million dollars in cash, all used one hundred dollars bills as requested.

Out of no where, a woman in a white linen dress and a large brimmed hat approached him. She was heavily made-up and wore large sunglasses which practically concealed the upper part of her face. She casually handed Daisey, who had been fighting a relentless battle to stay calm, the sealed Elyses white envelope. "If the money is short, you will be killed," she said matter-of-factly. "So now is the time for true confession. We can start all over."

"It is all there," said Daisey, uneasily letting go of the handles. After checking his markings he proceeded to carefully tear open the white envelope, admonishing himself silently not to be careless and drop the diamond. His hand shook as he examined it. When satisfied, he put the diamond back into the envelope.

"If you move a single step, a bullet will shatter your spine. Now it's time for my peek. Please open the bag very carefully."

Daisey bent down, snapped the fasteners open and opened the case just enough to reveal the piles of cash. She nodded and he snapped the fasteners closed. They stared at each other briefly. "Go. Go now!" she ordered. Daisey quickly walked away, shoving the envelope into his jacket pocket; he was trembling; so was Bonnie.

It was 3:50 when Charley Daisey entered Vanlo and Eugêne. Looking straight ahead, purposely taking no notice of floor activities, he proceeded to the rear of the store. A small group of elderly woman shoppers standing in the main aisle turned their heads at the rude man who brushed past them; he had not the courtesy to even say "excuse me."

As he approached the rear staircase, he ignored the two armed uniformed security guards who smiled their greetings and stepped aside permitting him to pass through. Daisey punched a coded series of numbers then pushed open a bullet proof glass door. Quickly, he descended the steps to the entrance of the store's walk-in vault. The attendant greeted Charles Daisey by name and from his desk position, buzzed open the outer gate; he waited for Daisey who now stood in the entrance way to pull close the outer gate. The attendant then buzzed the inner gate open for Daisey to enter the vault room.

"Don't bother getting up Morris," Daisey said, "I need to open eighty-five."

After Daisey signed the log in sheet, Morris handed him the master key to be used along with Daisey's own box key. Daisey walked to the rear of the all steel room that contained various capacity sized lock boxes; he opened and removed Box 85 - lifting the top open. he placed the white Elyses Hotel envelope containing the diamond into another large manila envelope, writing across the front:

CHARLEY DAISEY, PERSONAL

On his way out, Daisey handed the master key back to Morris Hopkins.

Now sitting in his office, nervously gloating over his good fortune, he was surprised to receive a phone call from Harry Fellows, who began a lengthy discussion with respect to the six million dollar claim.

"Mr. Daisey, although we had desperately hoped the thieves would contact your jewelry store or Lloyd's, it bloody-well appears they have taken their booty elsewhere. Therefore, I have sadly decided to cut my stay short and return to London this evening. There's a Delta flight that leaves about eleven. From my view of the situation, I should say your lawyers will be contacted by us within the next ten days."

"Yes?"

"For the record, Mr. Daisey, is there any documentation, information, or anything that might have been left out, that you would have me add to my written report and presentation. I can come to your office now, and, oh yes, I also need your home address."

"What report? What presentation? My home address why?" His voice was demanding.

"Do you actually think that Lloyd's will accept my verbal explanation? Please, don't be naïve Mr. Daisey. Again I ask, do you want to add anything to the report that I will be presenting to our claims committee at Lloyd's headquarters at Windsor? The more complete it is, the faster things move."

"There is nothing that I can add. You have Ernst Gormann's statement of how the switch went down. You have everything Mr. Fellows, including the copy of the letter we sent to our South American client explaining the robbery. I just hope that the family will not pressure me on a quick settlement. We are talking about a great deal of money. But that is matter for your company attorneys, is it not, Mr. Fellows?" Daisey now felt in control.

"Indeed, Mr. Daisey," said Fellows, wanting to carry on the conversation as long as possible - keeping Charles Daisey at his desk talking, supplying a safety bridge element for Ernst Gormann. "Excuse me one moment," Harry said. Daisey listened patiently as Fellows seemed to be rifling through papers as if looking for something specific. "Ah, yes, do you happen to have Mauricio Vanlo's fax number?"

"Please, no more of this. Mr. Fellows, don't you have a plane to catch." With that said, Charles Daisey hung up.

While the previous conversation between the two men had scarcely reached mid-point, Morris Hopkins buzzed Ernst Gormann through the inner gate.

"Everything fine with you, and your family, Morris?" Gormann asked in his usual friendly way. "I need to put something into Box eighty-five."

While Hopkins was speaking of his family, Gormann signed his name on the log in sheet - just seeing Charles Daisey's signature above his, caused a slight heart tremor – he took a deep breath. Knowing time was not a moment to be wasted; he walked quickly to the rear of the vault, slid the master key and his own into the Box 85, pulled it out and lifted the lid. He immediately tore open the envelope marked Charles Daisey, Personal. Inside Gormann discovered a white envelope from the Elyses Hotel. The envelope containing the Singhalese diamond. "Mother fucker, cock sucker, piece of shit," he muttered silently as he removed the diamond from the white envelope and dropped it into his inside jacket pocket. He then replaced the empty white Elyses envelope.

"Damn it all," Gormann said as he reached Hopkins' desk and handed him the master key. "I meant to lock my keys away. No need taking them with me, I'm to take a few days off beginning Monday. Safer here in the vault than with me. Would you mind securing them in the key cabinet?" Gormann then dropped the key ring containing several special made Medeco keys into Hopkins' open hand. "See you next week, Morris," he said, sadly knowing he might never see the aging man again.

Back on the main floor, Gormann picked up a store phone and punched Daisey's office exchange.

"Maggie, put me through to Charley, it is extremely important, urgent actually."

Gormann tapped his fingers nervously as he waited.

"Yes, Ernst, what is it? What is extremely important?" growled Daisey. "It's late and I've had to hang up on this Fellows character.

A pain in the ass if you ask me. I couldn't get him off the fucking phone."

"What we spoke about, Charley. The money, my early pension."

"Truthfully, the phone call you got Ernst from the woman was a hoax; just a goddamn hoax. I have no idea who it could have been. I waited what seemed forever. No one called. Look these things happen Ernst. Scammed again, wouldn't you say? The diamond is a lost cause. Plus I am a little upset that you tried to back me into a wall ... but I am willing to let bygones be bygones. Is there anything else Ernst? I really need to get back to work."

"No, Charley, that was all," Gormann said quietly, and hung up.

*   *   *

"Miles, it's me, Harry. Can you hear me clearly?"

"Yes Harry," Miles Jamison said, his voice sounding like sandpaper, "I hear you just fine. Any important developments concerning our pink diamond?"

"I say, Miles, I have done it, old boy. I can deal for the merchandise."

"Good Lord, Harry, are you absolutely certain? Have you seen the stone, Harry? Is it the genuine article?"

"I have indeed. And yes Miles, it definitely is the Singhalese diamond. I have held it, examined it, weighed and measured it against a copy of the appraisal."

"Harry, you have my old heart racing. Even Edgar is smiling. Cuanto amigo, and do not give me a coronary," Jamison said, his voice not quite as raspy as it had been.

"Three and a half."

"Three and a half bloody what Harry? For Christ sakes what? Pounds? Dollars, Yen?"

"Dollars Miles. American green backs. Old bills. And Miles, Mr. Andrew Longmeyer is standing next to me." Fellows could detect shortness in the breath of Jamison. "He says, they will leave for Europe tomorrow with the diamond if we do not make the deal by tomorrow. Mr. Longmeyer trusts me, so he says. If I say we have a deal, I will then inform him as to the details you set forth."

"Where are you Harry?" asked Jamison. "I am going to have to ring you back." "When will that be, Miles?"

"One hour, Harry. In one hour."

"Can't tell you where I am Miles. Longmeyer says we will call you at this same number in exactly one hour. And Miles, these people are all business. Any screw-ups, I am d-e-a-d." Fellows spelled out the word.

"Fear not, dear boy, today, you're like a son to me."

Fellows replaced the telephone into its cradle gingerly. He turned to Bonnie and Fritz and nodded.

The following day, Sunday at 5:00 P.M., Miles Jamison arrived at New York's JFK Airport. He was accompanied by J. Edgar Davies and three men, one of whom was wheeling a military duffel bag.

At 5:30, Fellows slowly approached the four men who sat waiting for him in the British Airways arrivals. Without a word, Fellows placed the loose pink diamond into Jamison's empty palm. Fellows whispered that they were being watched by tense, armed thieves. "Don't have your boys do anything stupid Miles. When they shoot, they might miss me and put a bullet through your scrawny neck."

Jamison struggled to his feet, and without looking at the diamond, but keeping a steady gaze on Fellows, handed the stone to the slightly-built man who stood beside him. J. Edgar Davies, a gemologist himself, acknowledged Fellows' presence with a friendly nod. He then kneeled, and on the floor opened an undersized aluminum briefcase. He removed an electronic carat balance and digital millimeter gauge. Davies weighed the diamond and checked the measurements; he studied the pink stone through a jeweler's glass. He looked up at Jamison. "This is the Singhalese diamond, Miles."

Following the J. Edgar Davies announcement, Fellows and Jamison stopped staring at each other. Jamison turned; he and Davies began walking away signaling the others to follow. The wheels and duffel bag containing three point five million dollars was left at Fellows' feet.

*   *   *

The following day at precisely 9:45 a.m. when Charley Daisey entered Vanlo and Eugêne through the employee's entrance, the senior security guard greeted him and repeated a message from his secretary Maggie Blair that he was to go directly to his office.

The first person Daisey recognized was the store's security chief Dan Weiss. Weiss was speaking to a pale, sickly looking man who was to be shortly introduced as Miles Jamison of Lloyd's of London. Also present were Joe Heywood and T. R. Trumball, the two detectives assigned to the case of the stolen Singhalese diamond, plus there were three other men. Everyone appeared to be in good humor as he approached.

After shaking hands all around, Miles Jamison pointed to the man who had examined the Singhalese diamond in the airport.

"Mr. Daisey, this is J. Edgar Davies, not only a remarkable person, but Lloyd's resident gemstone and diamond expert. He is a certified gemologist, has more degrees than the Carter Company has liver pills." Only Miles laughed. "Yes, well, Edgar, kindly inform Mr. Daisey here what has happened in the past eighteen hours or so."

"Mr. Daisey," said Davies quite loudly, "I am very pleased to announce that the purloined Singhalese diamond has been successfully retrieved," Davies spoke in a perfect, clipped, formal British accent.

Daisey began to shake beneath his tailored suit; he could feel cold sweat seep out of the pores on his forehead; trickles of perspiration wet his underarms. His expensive silk shirt was not absorbing the sweat as it dripped downward.

"It is absolutely, fantastic, isn't it?" Dan Weiss said to apparently no one, looking around.

"Well, of course... that is, uh wonderful ... uh, how?" Daisey knew he was stammering. "I mean ... do you actually have the diamond in your possession?"

"Yes sir, Mr. Daisey, right in here," Davies said, patting the side of a briefcase. "Would you like to see it?" he asked beaming a wide smile.

Daisey said, "Please, let us all go into my office," his legs were shaking and he needed to sit.

Inside, with everyone circling Daisey's desk, Davies produced the Singhalese diamond along with copies of the original appraisal papers substantiating its weight and dimensions and the original declaration papers of the insurance. He also placed in front of Charles Daisey several documents. "These documents also require your signature. They rescind any and all present and future claims pertaining to the disappearance of the diamond." Daisey saw that Nestor Brunnell had already put his signature to the documents.

Davies spoke again. "Lloyd's of London is also withdrawing any further insurance protection for the diamond as of twelve noon today." Edgar looked at his watch. He said, although there is a thirty-day grace period and should you want that thirty day protection, Lloyd's will have to take possession of the diamond. At the end of the grace period, the diamond will be returned only to its rightful owner and not Vanlo and Eugêne in light of the security breakdown and the robbery that followed. You will be billed for all expenses that are incurred during this time."

"*Fuck you, you skinny faggot,*" Daisey thought picking up the stone. He carefully inspected it. Finally he said, "I am speechless." He felt every one's eyes on him waiting for a favorable comment.

Maggie Blair, said, "It's a pity Mr. Gormann couldn't be present, he would have been so thrilled."

Sixty minutes later, after the signatures were notarized and his office was cleared of everyone, the confused Daisey with his head in hands stared at the diamond.

Maggie Blair knocked softly and entered Daisey's office. "I tried buzzing you Mr. Daisey. Are you all right?" Should we have the diamond taken to the vault room?"

"Yes, yes, Maggie, I'm fine. What is it you were buzzing me about?? Where is Gormann? I asked you to have him call me. Did I not?"

"Yes Mr. Daisey, you did. I called Human Resources; they report that Mr. Gormann has combined all his accumulated sick days and vacation time saying he'll be sending in a letter of resignation. Also, Mr. de Ortega's principle lawyer called from Sao Palo, he sounded as if he was ready to go through the ceiling with happiness when I gave him the good news that we recovered the diamond. Sheik Arami has been on hold - demanding in an ugly voice that he speak to you."

As soon as Maggie departed, Daisey picked up his phone; he tried to keep his voice steady, but it pitched too high.

"Arami, hello there. How are you today? ... yes, yes, everything is just fine ... I was going to call you but quite frankly, I got very busy ... Yes I know three million is a great sum ... see here Arami, I do not like that kind of talk. I have run into a small problem. I will have to call you back. Calm down for Christ sakes. The situation regarding the diamond requires a long explanation. Good bye."

Ten minutes later, Charley Daisey entered the vault. Seeing Ernst Gormann's signature below his own merely stunned his thought waves. His hand was shaking as he lifted the lid to Box 85. "*Of course ... that German fuck stole my diamond ... I'll find him and-*"

One of Daisey's two cell phones vibrated in his pocket, it was the Motorola RAZR V3 – the one that only three people knew the number to: his daughter in Canada, his stock broker, and Maggie Blair his secretary.

"Hello," he said sheepishly

"You think you can fuck with me, you're wrong."

"Arami, how did you get this number?"

"Your secretary Miss Blaire was kind enough to give it to me. I suppose I frightened her."

"*That bitch. Probably in cahoots with Ernst.*" Look Arami, the deal went south, caput. It's a risky business, don't cry over spilt milk. The Singhalese diamond was stolen; chalk it up to a bad investment..."

"Where's my money you lying prick?"

Daisey's face was wet with perspiration He was trying not to shout – he saw Morris Hopkins get up from his chair and look in his direction. Daisey softly said, "The money is gone Arami – we got scammed The deal went sour. Don't you understand you ass hole?"

"I want my money. I want my three million."

"It's gone. Forget it. You made plenty of money with my deals and what you gave back to me amounted to a pile of crap compared to what you made ... so stop your fucking crying."

"Keep talking you moron, I'm taping this conversation."

"Fuck you, you Arab piece of shit." and with that said Daisey flipped closed his cell phone.

Returning to his office, Daisey found a private memo on his desk from the Nestor Brunnell. Gingerly he lifted the top half of the folded memo bearing Vanlo and Eugêne's logo – Daisey's eyes rested on the brief handwritten message

"Charles, two Board members have received some very discouraging information concerning some alleged activities of yours. I'm certain this information is an ill-timed hoax. However, the caller says he can substantiate his charges. Regardless it needs to be addressed. Let's you and I have a private meeting as quickly as possible. Mauricio Vanlo is flying in tonight."

Signed,
Nestor Brunnell,
General Manager

AFTERWARDS

In the weeks following his departure, Ernst Gormann had written a letter of resignation to Vanlo and Eugêne's Board of Directors stating that his eyes had reached the stage where he sadly felt he could no longer be an asset to the company, particularly in the light of the Singhalese diamond incident. He also acquired a Labor Attorney to bring harassment charges against the assistant GM of Vanlo and Eugêne that person being Charley Daisey. Gormann cited that Daisey illegally blocked him from receiving his retirement pension. Gormann was asking one million dollars in damages.

Harry Fellows, on behalf of Lloyd's of London, awarded Ernst Gormann a substantial reward for his role in recovering the Singhalese diamond - Lloyd's and Ernst Gormann signed mutual pledges of silence. In addition, the unholy alliance of Bonnie Adele, Fritz Barrow and Harry Fellows deposited an additional five hundred thousand dollars in the name of Ernst Gormann into a numbered Swiss Account – Harry Fellows and Ernst Gormann also signed mutual pledges of silence.

In retaliation for his lost money, Sheik Arami exposed Charles Daisey and his outside underhanded dealings to the Vanlo and Eugêne's Board. The records he provided were evidence enough to allow the corporation to bring criminal charges against the assistant GM.

To Charles Daisey's greater embarrassment, two weeks before his lengthy and costly trial would begin, a steady stream of Process Servers for the District Court for the Southern District of New York served him with a variety of Summons and Subpoenas all within eye sight of employees (the majority of whom gloated at the spectacle of Daisey trying to avoid service; these same good citizens hesitated not in pointing out the man's whereabouts - the subject of the service).

And so it was, prior to the jury's decision dealing with monetary and criminal consequences, Charles Daisey saw the handwriting on the wall - a prison wall. With his passport, illegal cash salted away for that proverbial rainy day, he transferred all accessible funds from his bank to the Central Bank of Iceland. He then fled the United States and is currently fighting extradition in Reykjavík, Iceland. (*Daisey lives in the same apartment building as did Bobby Fischer, the former World Chess Champion) Both law firms that represented Charles Daisey and Vanlo and Eugêne are seeking damages in excess of twelve million dollars. Internal Revenue has attached whatever is left of Daisey's USA holdings including his Park Avenue apartment. Agents have finalized his unpaid tax bill that is estimated to be in excess of three million dollars, which steadily grows each day with penalty and interest – the Government has also issued international arrest warrants.

Ernst Gormann was awarded six hundred thousand dollars in his law suit against Daisey - he too awaits payment.

Harry Fellows received a bonus payment of three hundred thousand dollars from Lloyd's which he shared with his partners. Bonnie added her two hundred thousand whereby the members of the unholy alliance, after expenses, each pocketed almost two million dollars.

Bonnie Adele returned to Washington, resigned her position with the FBI, seeking a career change moved to New York City. Fritz Barrow resumed his normal business activities and thought it a good idea for Bonnie to try her hand in his business – Bonnie who wanted nothing more to do with law and order, accepted with the understanding that although she and Harry had mutually agreed to put their romance on hold for one year, each taking the opportunity to make a sensible decision; however, should they later decide to become soul mates, she would return to England. In the meantime, Harry Fellows returned to his Private Eye business considering only select situations.

-...and the song goes on and on.

PART II

CHAPTER TEN

Several days after the Singhalese Diamond Switch.

Diadem defined:
An often decorated golden garland fitted around the head, used as a symbol of royal dignity.

The diadem became symbolic in the beginning of the fourth century among rulers in the Greek world especially during religious ceremonies. For example, Dionysius I and Dionysius II are known to wear these crowns of gold. The gold diadems suggest that the rulers claimed a superhuman status and demanded the same respect that was shown to the gods.

In the richness and odor of old oiled leather in Lloyd's Windsor conference room, two men sat at opposite sides of a large oval mahogany conference table. In heavy silence, J. Edgar Davies and Miles Jamison stared at each other. In the center of the high polished wood that separated them was an exquisite crystal tumbler containing several newly-sharpened pencils imprinted in gold leaf: "LLOYD'S." In front of each man was a green leather binding that contained an eight-page report documenting a three-million-pound insurance claim from the Milan museum in Italy.

The younger man spoke first. "I hate to say I told you so, Miles, but I did say at the time I appraised the diadem, that I felt it was much too high a price to insure against loss. We simply can no longer insure provenance and historical value at foolish values."

"Yes, Edgar, dear boy, I do agree. I also agree that Lloyd's is supposed to collect large premiums and avoid paying large claims," the older man said. "Yes, in the case of this diadem, we were greedy for the high premium money. The underwriter used poor judgment in thinking that bloody Italian security was any more than amateurish. But who in his bloody mind, other than the thieves could foresee the Milan museum to be such an easy target? We must begin in secret of having all of our underwriters given tests to determine if their logic begins under the cap of a gin bottle?"

Edgar Davies merely smiled at his mentor's sarcastic remark. He said, "I say, though, fortunately for us, Miles, the perpetrators have really not a great many places to go to sell such a well-known Greek-style diadem. Interested audiences would be limited to Greek historians; mostly universities and other museums who would already be informed as to its theft. Plus, we know from experience they will not break up such a desirable item and sell it by bits and pieces. I'm certain they must realize the quandary they put themselves in."

Miles said, "Edgar, my boy, we are only interested in the payout and avoiding irritating publicity. Everyone hates insurance companies, though I dare say who could bloody-well live without us."

Davies said, "Sir, I reviewed the original appraisal this morning and I calculate that the weight of the pure gold leaves plus the size and quality of the uncut rubies should on today's market bring at the very best cash-wise, fifty thousand pounds. Maybe."

"A pittance to be sure," said Miles. Miles Jamison looked pale and drawn as usual. However, with the passage of time, like an aging sage, he ably used his appearance to gain considerable benefits, and as many times without too much effort altered the rock-hard antagonist to be his very own disciple; but always, only on behalf of the Lloyd's firm.

For Miles Jamison, Lloyd's would always come first. His eyes were closed as he spoke. "Edgar, you are aware more than most, that even though I am a good Catholic, I also am a religious scholar, and according to ancient verse, Jesus Christ said the ruby was the most precious of the twelve stones God created when he created all things. Christ also sermonized something to the effect of, to use rubies sacrilegiously was to incur the Lord's wrath. Let us hope, dear Edgar, though I doubt it strongly, that these thieves are God-fearing Christians, certainly not Catholic, and as well-versed in religion as I."

Davies chuckled admiringly at Jamison's dry wit; it was moments like this that his liking for Miles Jamison was at its peak.

"Nevertheless," said Miles, "This misdeed of theirs has already translated into a direct ransom which brings along the possibility of a lot of terrible publicity."

Davies said, "I agree. The theft was a highly-skilled one. The team of thieves cleverly bypassed the museum's alarm system by installing their own duplicate set-up. They did it in such a way, that when the museum alarm did go off, it actually terminated into a barrel filled with water."

Miles raised his eyebrows in response to the information though he had previously known of the water barrel. He said, "The Italian Police report that the crooks made access keys at each of the three entrance doors they needed to enter. They used a high-tech portable key-making machine – laser beams inserted into the lock themselves gave a reading of whatever it is they required. One would think that the Milan Museum, like so many of their sisters and brother museums would have their own advanced electronics to ward off such potential thievery. Naturally, they didn't leave their tools and equipment behind except for the old water-filled pickle barrel. These monsters even terrorized an elderly guard by threatening to kill his grandchildren if he didn't cooperate plus they jolly-well gave him a good bash aside his head. My guess is it required a team of at least four. Italian police and Interpol admit to no leads or suspects. As such we can realistically forget about any prospect of recovery from those law enforcement channels. So! I quite agree with you Miles, it appears to have the stamp of a direct ransom. And yes, the negative publicity might have been something they figured into their equation of this particular theft. "

After another long session of silence, Miles Jamison asked,

"Then whom Edgar, dear boy, do we have to manage this large transaction when the pirates rear their hideous faces and contact us or the likely possibility that the Milan Museum will contact us first."

Davies chose a pencil from the crystal holder and began to jot names on a pad.

"We can recall Edwin Flowers. He's on a golfing holiday in Scotland. There is Solomon Ross, a Jew as tough as nails, though I must say he does not like Italians; so if these crooks are Italian, that could hamper us horribly. Peter Hazelstone just finished settling a claim against Harrods; he is definitely available –"

Miles held up five fingers of his right hand; a signal for Davies to stop. He wrinkled his already heavily-creased brow. "Yes, yes, let's talk about dear Peter Hazelstone's settlement. The open top of a concert grand piano fell on the arm of a so-called child prodigy. The Board seems to feel our young Hazelstone was a bit lenient in recommending an out-of-court settlement of half-million pounds for a tike ... who might no longer be able to play Swaying Silver Birches. I understand the child is not even good looking."

Davies smiled at Mile's misshapen wit. Miles continued, "Needn't go on Edgar, none of them will do for this unpleasant museum crime ... fact is, there's only one person that I can think of who is able to negotiate with this type of criminal. Unfortunately, he'll turn me down flat. Damn him! He could be imparting his extraordinary knowledge to some of our young minds. I'm certain he still hates me even though the Singhalese affair brought him a tidy sum."

"You did do him out of what was promised to him."

"Let us not get into that discussion again Edgar, dear God, it was a tactical decision made at the time, based on what was best for the company, not Harry Fellows. But we do have a great deal at stake here, and cannot allow a deflated ego to interfere. My decision is made. "I'll be damned if I'll okay a three million pound payout. Edgar, call Harry Fellows. Ask him on my behalf if he'll oversee this case. He likes you and won't hang up."

"Miles, I hate to put it this way, but Harry did tell you with certainty that he would refuse to take on any additional investigations."

Tell him on my word that this will be the final request I will ever make of him. I know what you say is true Edgar, but pay no mind to that. Harry will save Lloyd's a ton of money"

Jamison then got to his feet with effort. "So there it is Edgar, do what you have to get Harry to agree. Now then, Board members will be arriving shortly for a special briefing session. It appears that another rate increase is imminent. These are hard times and the cost of living dear boy abounds. Stealing is not quite the way to counteract financial dilemma; is it not?

Davies nodded agreement.

"I have quite a lot to do," Miles said. "I'll pass on to committee what we discussed here, and Edgar, call me as soon as you have finished speaking with Harry. Damn him!"

*   *   *

Later that same morning, as Fellows casually made his way through the final room of the National Portrait Gallery's membership self-tour; he concentrated on the display of the last batch of Dutch masters brought in by the Gallery for a special exhibition. Fellows particularly liked sixteenth century portrait work. Especially the first half of the century when portraits were formal and stiff in composition. Paintings portrayed groups often seated around a table, each person appearing as if he was looking at the observer. Much attention was paid to fine details in clothing, and furniture and other signs of a person's position in society.

During his final walk through, and for whatever unknown reason, Fellows had also the overall impression that he'd finally arrived at a point in life when he was able to counter-punch into ignoring that which caused him problems and pain and able to get in touch with his true nature. So with that invisible armor, one hour later, Fellows walked out of the museum and hailed a taxi, instructing the driver to take him to a pub on Fleet Street called the "Lamb's Ear."

From years of having stalked the city streets of London, from one end to the other, his connection with the better eateries had come by various incidents: a sudden downpour or freezing rain, a heavy thunderstorm laced with lightening, or simply by ducking-out to avoid someone he'd rather not encounter. His appreciation for such opportune shelter was getting acquainted with many menu specials.

In his memory, these places were like part of his being. Often unexplainable to even himself; he sometimes felt the need to revisit these places, and the establishment he had today chosen for lunch fit into this part that had wrestled him successfully away from any earlier dismal thoughts.

Inside the well-appointed hundred-year-old establishment, Fellows ordered a lager and lime - stood at the bar and chatted politely with an American doctor and his wife who lived in Florida and were just returning from a holiday in South Africa – the doctor's love for everything Victorian gave them reason for the stopover before returning to the *grind* as the wife had put it. She said, "A few days in the shops of your London museums will arm the Doctor with plenty of books and picture postcards to happily take him deep into the wee hours illuminating Queen Victoria's reign. Who knows, maybe he'll find some time for me." She then turned and gave Fellows' elbow a slight squeeze.

The Doctor gave half a laugh. Fellows slowly pulled his arm away.

Whether all was done in jest or otherwise - and as friendly and poised as two total strangers could be, most likely due to Fellows' past distasteful professions, there was a part of him that survived a Gothic instinct to always be suspicious.

Harry indeed had a marvelous flair for seeking out interesting people, as in the case of this American couple. He also admitted that strangers provided him with other human behavior alien to that which he was exposed to in his particular line of PI work, and, often more honest than that, of his contemporary work partners. Still, he remained cautious. Thinking about the novel "The Eye of The Needle," Harry thought to himself, "*Jesus, German spies are a thing of the past.*"

Later in the dining room, he ate leisurely, glanced through a travel magazine, finished his third lager, and ended his noon meal with a selection of English cheeses and a glass of Spanish port. Fellows couldn't recall when he felt so quite content. He gestured for his bill only to be informed that it had been taken care of by the American doctor. Fellows felt like shouting his appreciation across the restaurant, but merely nodded to the smiling waiter and gestured a *thanks* to the doctor and his wife who sat with wide smiles at the far end of the room.

Outside on the sidewalk, slightly inebriated, Fellows clearly showed a level of heightened spirits as he joined the selection of shoppers that chose to stroll along Fleet Street admiring the elite shops that displayed their wares for the upper class.

Harry spotted her about thirty feet ahead coming his way. As she approached, he caught her eye and smiled lecherously, his face full of fun – and why not? The four lagers and the glass of port gave him a happy edge. She was striking, almost middle-aged with rich auburn hair pulled back. A saucer-thin red hat was neatly pinned at a rakish tilt. Her suit, tailored herringbone, and a smart black-skin handbag, made her a standout. She slowed as she came alongside the man with full gray hair brushed straight back, save one forelock that bounced on his brow. She returned a half smile. His friendly smile set above a determined chin, and the sound humor in his eyes must have made Harry special. Fellows slowed and turned as she passed. He kept pace as her own pace slowed. He gently slipped his arm through hers.

"Dear me," he said to the stranger familiarly. "I'm about to make a horse's ass of myself and end up in the Old Bailey for sexual harassment."

She answered him with a French accent. "Not really. My name is Winifred, and who would wish to walk alone on such a grand day."

Fellows squeezed her arm. "Oui, Winifred, who would wish to be alone on a wonderful day like this."

*　　　*　　　*

If there were such a thing as perfect sex in Fellows' life, the afternoon interval between Winifred and him left no need for anything like it to happen ever again.

They had walked arm in arm several blocks before Fellows dare hail a cab and ordered the driver to his Ebury Lane residence; as quick as possible, a ten pound note for a tip if he did it in less than fifteen minutes. They both giggled like children as the cabbie raced along.

Now the sound of bleeps from the telephone shoved him into awakeness. The effects of the earlier drinking loomed heavily within his forehead. He slid his hand in a circular pattern. There was no blanket on the bed; he lay on his cover sheet totally naked. Where was Winifred? He dreamily thought of her. She had aroused him twice - he needed his secret lover called Winifred. He called her name - the phone continued to bleep. She gave no answer to his call. Maybe it was her ringing. What time was it? He'd only slept one hour – though he felt drugged, he thought happily about Winifred. "God, what a woman" he said aloud reaching for the telephone receiver, praying it was her.

"Hello, is that you Winifred he asked?"

"Hello, Harry. J. Edgar Davies here."

"Edgar, Jesus, Edgar...I mean hello. What in ... is everything all right?"

"Yes, Harry, everything is fine, that is..."

"Speak up for Christ sakes, Edgar. Wait for my fog to lift." Fellows was slowly becoming fully aware of Davies on the phone, the missing blanket and the missing Winifred."

"I say, Harry, I am sorry to disturb you, but I need to see you about a matter of great importance. Do you think we could meet this afternoon for a chat?"

"For a bloody chat Edgar?" Fellows stuck the phone between his shoulder and chin, and rubbed his eyes with both hands.

"Hang on, Edgar,' he declared loudly and dropped the receiver on the bed. Fellows got up and walked rapidly through each room of the flat looking for the blanket and Winifred – both were definitely gone.

"I am sorry, Edgar for my rudeness, but I was looking for my blanket. It seems to have vanished. Now what about this chat, dear boy?"

Davies quickly decided not to pursue any discussions concerning the blanket. "I say, Harry, can we meet sometime today?"

"Edgar, I say, old sock, do I detect a certain British rigidness in your tone. Good Lord, have I done something to offend you? You don't sound very bloody friendly at all."

"Sorry, Harry, but to be perfectly honest, Miles asked that I ring you for this get-together."

"Jamison, that sly old yellow dog. What's the bloody field general being so modest about?" asked Fellows sarcastically.

Fellows knew Jamison was a figure who struggled constantly over right and wrong: a man who thought and acted in absolute terms without patience or compromise. There would be no sense searching for an explanation over the telephone.

"Harry, I need to speak to you."

"Why me, Edgar dear boy?"

"A theft that most likely will be a direct ransom."

"Go on then Edgar."

"It has to do with a stolen fourth-century Greek-style garland diadem. Heavy gold and uncut gem quality rubies. It was burglarized from the Milan Museum. We insured this Greek crown for three million pounds Harry. It would break-up to no more than, I would say, a quarter-million pounds."

"Tch, tch. You cannot insure history, Edgar. Surely your able Board Director knows that by now."

"We are always aware of that, Harry, but thank you anyway for the advice. Please, Harry, meet with me. I have my original appraisal of the diadem, complete with breakdown of weights, assay report, dimensions and actual size photographs. Look it over. We would like you to-"

Fellows interrupted, he didn't feel like carrying out the conversation any longer. He wanted to think about Winifred and the missing blanket. "Tell you what, Edgar. I'm in no mood to discuss the meeting you've requested. Nor do I want to hang up on you. So meet me at seven-thirty this evening - we'll have dinner. The Chanterelle on Old Brompton Road. My treat. We'll share a saddle of hare and a decent bottle of claret."

"Thank you Harry, that is good of you. And Harry, it would be best if you checked the papers concerning this particular robbery from the Milan Museum of an antique diadem." Davies then hung up his telephone.

*   *   *

Twice that same day, Fellows had been caught off guard. The first was the shocking disappearance of his blanket by someone called Winifred - but he flashed a forgiving smile thinking about her many unprompted sexual virtues.

The next was the present shock: the usual uncomfortable sense of bitterness settled over Fellows seeing Miles Jamison seated next to J. Edgar Davies. They were in arm chairs quietly chatting at the back of the lounge. Fellows walked over. Davies nervously sat up straight when he spotted him.

"Well, Miles," said Fellows, his voice cutting a firm edge, "to see you actually out of the Store again is somewhat of an event, I must say. The last time was right here at the Grenadier when you asked me to find a missing pink diamond. Now I understand you're searching for a missing Greek antique. I say Miles have you ever considered changing careers. Perhaps a less risky business, like a home bookkeeping service or maybe teaching basic arithmetic to special needs children?"

"Hello, Harry. It's always nice to see you," Miles said. Neither man extended his hand.

Fellows winked at Davies, but got no response. Davies looked anxious; there was a bead of perspiration above his top lip. A waiter appeared and Fellows ordered a brandy and soda.

Jamison was a hard man who liked to act weak; he had no interest in image, only results. The voice he now spoke with was the one he used when cornered. "Speaking of teaching Harry, I understand from the education section we have some prospects bright enough to replace aging masters." Jamison smiled, his yellowing teeth an artistic contrast to his pasty complexion.

Fellows thoughtfully pressed his right index finger against his lips. He took a moment he needed; he wanted his answer cocky and brassy. In the old days he would have sent back a suitable reply, standing tall trying to foster appreciation for his old-world Englishness. Today he simply said, "Pity I chose a lifetime involvement with Lloyd's only to be double-crossed."

"Let me tell you a damn odd thing, Harry," Jamison said, neither ruffled nor perturbed. "That is precisely why we are here. You are the best, and it is for that very reason, I left the Store, as you so aptly put it."

Jamison then nodded sharply to Davies.In a clear crisp voice, J. Edgar Davies said, "Here, Harry, have a look at this." He handed Fellows a copy of the claims report bound in a green leather folder.

Fellows sat back and slowly read the four page report. Another waiter came by and placed the brandy and soda on a small side table. Fellows left the drink untouched as he read. Then if struck by an interesting thought, he looked up, intense, but his face a picture of humor. He stared at Jamison for a second, then said, "To steal this, these boys are what I call daring to say the least. And I dare say, bloody damn clever. Yes, yes I agree. It has to be a direct ransom; they appear to be too smart to break up this particular treasure if in fact it is a treasure, nor are they in any particular hurry."

"The peculiar thing is, Harry,' Davies went on to say, 'that during the theft of the diadem, they did not take anything else of value."

Jamison and Fellows exchanged the first friendly glances of the evening.

"You see, Edgar," said Fellows, "smart thieves are not necessarily gluttons - they don't get entangled in headlines. I can tell you that not too many people can get bloody excited or give a damn about a stolen Greek diadem except for the insurance company. But steal a bloody good impressionistic painting, a Rembrandt, or a well-known marble sculptor, and the entire bloody art world wants to come down on you and see you lynched upon capture."

"Makes sense Harry," said Davies, nodding his head

"Miles, before we go any further, I'm here because my friend Edgar Davies asked me. Your presence is a surprise, and I won't hold it against Edgar."

"Big of you Harry," Jamison whispered.

"Miles, I am bowing out of any more investigative work. The missing diadem is not my problem."

"Harry please listen-"

"No Miles, you listen to what I have to say. It seems as you take on more aging, each of the risks that Lloyd's takes on that go sour you go after with vengeance, a vendetta like the underworld. It's neither my diadem they stole nor yours. So get over it!"

Miles said, "Harry, I understand you have a well-stocked flat with many interesting curios and such. Of course never have being invited I can only imagine how carefully everything is displayed. But just suppose Harry, someone broke in to your flat, stealing from your collection, one of your most precious pieces. Would you not attempt to find the culprit and the stolen article? Would you not say in a loud voice, I'll get that thieving bastard no matter what and cut his heart out. Harry sometimes there is a cause for vengeance. My Store is my home, fire and other disasters that cause claims are one thing-" Miles showed signs of coughing – his face turned red - but managed to mention a sizeable bonus for Harry before the coughing began. Edgar moved quickly to assist the half-choking man, but Miles waved him off. An attentive waiter filled a small glass with water. Miles drank it slowly. His eyes fixed on Harry.

CHAPTER ELEVEN

After acquiring another blanket for his guest room from the hall closet, he left a note on the front table reminding himself to acquire a replacement as soon as possible.

Harry couldn't recall what time it was when he finally fell into sleep. It had been after midnight when he arrived back at his flat, and he had stayed up a long time working untiringly on a plan. He didn't even mind admitting to himself that his brain feasted on this daring exploit that had been committed by a group of professional thieves. As for Miles and J. Edgar Davies wanting him to set in motion the inquiry, the two couldn't disguise their verbose and elation when he finally agreed to accept the investigation of the diadem's disappearance. What was not known was why he had actually accepted Jamison's pleadings to undertake the job - for as Jamison coughed, feigned illness, spoke of causes for vengeance, allegiance and bonus money, Fellows was mentally devising a scheme that might possibly equal Fritz Barrow's diamond switch; if not in money value then in planning and intrigue

Late that same morning, following a restless dream-filled five hours of slumber, Harry telephoned Fritz Barrow in New York City.

* * *

"Hello dear boy and how are things in the land of diamonds and Daisey's?"

"Harry it must be magic," Fritz shouted. "I just now returned from driving Bonnie home to her apartment. Her car is in for servicing. She said if I happen to speak to you, to please send her love. She'd like to call you, but is honoring the agreement."

"And how is the woman I adore?" Guilty thoughts of cheating popping into his mind about his tryst with the female stranger Winifred. *"Did that woman steal my blanket for some insane reason?"*

"Bonnie is just superb Harry. Plenty smart. She has caught on the subtleties of the business amazingly quick, knows the inventory, can figure estimates with uncanny accuracy, and what's more, my customers have confidence in her and like her. But never mind that. How is everything with you?"

"Fritz, I'm thrilled to hear such good news about Bonnie. Thanks for passing it along. I do miss her you know ... but for now, the reason for my call. You are taking up ninety percent of the nasty part of my brain. Fritz, tomorrow I'm flying to Milan, Italy. I expect to be there two days and I should be back no later than Tuesday. Fritz, I need you here in London no later than Wednesday morning."

"Bonnie too?"

"Not just yet."

*   *   *

It was 1:00 p.m. that same day. After dropping off his newly purchased blanket from Marks and Spencer back at his flat, Harry headed out to the nearby cluster of royal parks – it was time for a long walk.

As he hurried across the busy traffic circle in front of Buckingham Palace to the safety of St. James' Park, Harry slowly strolled along Bird Cage Walk admiring, as he had done so many times, the formal French-style gardens. Yellow, red and pink colored roses were still in full bloom with little indication that leaves on the giant trees would ever be changing to mellow tones if indeed an early autumn struck the thousands of trees as so predicted by weather experts. For the moment however; his thoughts wandered away from the nature's beauty – he was objectively going over in his mind each point that might be required in recovering the stolen diadem and at the same time create a tidy profit. He wasn't sure why, but his heart raced with excitement.

*   *   *

Fritz Barrow's taxi delivered him to Harry's building in the morning hours; as he departed the taxi and paid the driver, Fritz paused on the sidewalk. He looked up and down Ebury Lane surveying whatever his eye could take in. The residents of Ebury Lane as Fritz had come to know, rarely paint their wrought iron railings or mend torn awnings. They boast of little, and get nervous when sidewalk and street repairs are made. Ebury Lane where Harry chose to live is one of those rare and peculiar places that are uncommonly scattered about certain parts of enlightened cities where inhabitants wage an implacable war against reformation.

Well-tended plants in teak and cypress wood boxes fertilized with expensive emulsions hang from fronts of what appears to be uncared-for façades which purposely obscure from sight cared for exclusive flats over smart shops below - luxurious guest houses, and expensive co-op dwellings such as that which belongs to Barrow's friend.

Fritz smiled, happy to be in England, as he made his way to the front entrance.

*   *   *

After a late morning meal of smoked herring, pan fried bacon and green tomatoes at the Ebury Grill and Tea Room, the two men walked to St. James' Park, selected an out-of-the-way bench by the big pond and sat. Harry held a legal size zipper case.

Following a lengthily discussion of the Singhalese diamond affair and what each of them had been doing since then, did Harry Fellows begin to talk about details of the museum theft as told to him – he then retold the story of Miles Jamison and J. Edgar's Davies' overture to have him take charge of recovering the missing diadem and negotiating at a fair price – that caused both Fritz and Harry to have a good laugh.

"So to go on," Harry said, "have a look at this." He unzipped the case Davies had left with him; his voice now employing a more serious tone. As soon as I saw the pictures of the crown, I thought about you. Fritz, this piece hardly approaches some of your more intricate finished pieces of work."

"Okay my friend, compliment well-taken. Go on, I'll thoroughly study all of it in a few moments."

Harry said, "According to J. Edgar Davies' appraisal, the diadem is made up of thirteen different size sections. Each section is fashioned in a circle of twelve miniature-shaped laurel leaves each touching one another. The leaves are also of various sizes. Each circle is centered-set with an uncut red ruby crystal; blood red in color. The whole shebang is made with twenty-two karat gold. Have a look for yourself."

Fritz snapped open the green folder and removed Lloyd's appraisal for the ancient Greek crown. He studied J. Edgar Davies ten photographs before reading the descriptions.

Harry said, "Davies photographs are actual size, showing different angles. Trust me Fritz; you can be sure they represent perfect renditions of the crown." Harry grabbed hold of Fritz's wrist giving it a hearty squeeze. "When we do present your finished diadem and it's compared to Davies' appraisal and photographs, I needn't say it but it must match up exactly."

Barrow managed a tight-lipped smile through an intense expression; he began to read the description. Fritz skipped the first two pages that detailed the non-readable nor understandable small print that Insurance Companies delight in using to employ non-payment tactics. Page three began with Davies describing the insured Greek style diadem. It read in part: *... a historically decorated crown placed on the head as a symbol of royal dignity though often a wreath or ribbon was used, but this particular gold and jeweled diadem was used during religious ceremonies ....*

As Fritz continued to read, Harry got up and walked away from the bench. He observed the daily strollers many of whom were totally unaware of the natural beauty surrounding them – he vicariously felt the boredom of their lives. He threw a few pebbles from the gravel path into the pond watching the ripples wane away. He threw a few more then walked back to the bench, sat down, closed his eyes. For the first time since they arrived, he became of aware of soft music coming from a nearby radio – he felt at peace amongst nature and the strains of what he thought was Beethoven. Suddenly Harry jumped – his heart skipped a beat. Barrow had roared," WE CAN DO IT!" Fritz then got up and began pacing back and forth in front of the bench, his left index finger pressed against his lips – a thinking pose.

"Harry, listen and stop me if I figured wrong. Thirteen sections. Each section, beginning at the front, then tapers down in size to the back. So we'll need, let me see, thirteen times twelve ..." As Fritz did his calculations, Harry withdrew a piece of paper from his pocket containing his own figures. Fritz said, "Harry, we're going to require thirteen rubber molds to make one hundred fifty-six finished waxes of laurel leaves and thirteen settings for mounting the uncut ruby crystals."

Fellows handed Barrow the paper he held. "Exactly dear fellow, the same number results I got."

"Fritz, I'm going to attempt and push the thieves into action. Here's my plan –"

Fritz began pacing again. Fellows could sense Fritz's brain wrestling with some particular detail. After a few moments Fritz took Harry by the arm and led him away.

"A drink, is what we need right now. Show me the way to a decent bar with atmosphere and fifteen year old scotch. This is my kind of fun, profitable, and a cause for continued vengeance."

$$-(A1_2 0_3)$$

CHAPTER TWELVE

After exiting the park, Harry hailed a taxi and directed him to the Haymarket Hotel in Trafalgar square. After a small wait, they were seated at a table at the rear of the lounge.

Harry had remained particularly quiet during the cab ride and in the bar likewise while Fritz devoured the tiny shell fish in vinegar and drank his scotch neat.

Barrow hungrily finished off two jars of cockles and drained a double Green Label Johnny Walker. "Another double please," Fritz asked the waitress, "and another large Sherry for my friend here."

"Okay, this is how we do it Harry. And it's all very simple, though unlike the Singhalese diamond switch, we're now counting on several outside resources. Today, we make copies of Davies photographs which I'll take back to New York."

Harry said, "You're sounding a bit nasal Fritz."

"I know. I might be coming down with a cold and I'm very tired, so tonight I'll have a good rest. Sweat it out with tea and brandy and tomorrow, Thursday, I'll leave for New York on an early flight. Friday, I'll see a chap named Bill Chao. He's a top-notch model maker. From the photographs, he'll make a model from green wax of each of the different size laurel leaves – as you say, we can assume that the photos are actual size."

"I guarantee it."

Barrow said, "Good. On Monday, which is the seventeenth, I'll give the finished waxes to the man who does my special-order casting. I'll have him cast each one of the laurel leaves in silver. Next, individual rubber molds will be made from the silver castings."

Harry said, "Does the wax model maker still allow for fifteen percent shrinkage."

"Yes, Some things never change Harry."

"We then have a gal named Mamie, she has hands and a touch unequaled to anyone in the four corners of the earth. She'll pull as many laurel leaf waxes as we need from the rubber molds. The leaves then go through the procedure of preparing them for casting, touchup work mostly. Then casting the pieces in twenty-two karat gold. Another shop will do that."

Harry said, "And each of your experts unaware of what we're looking to end up with."

"Exactly. Aside from using as many different people as I am, the actual method for making my own cane handles and other jewelry items is just about the same. "

"How many days more we'll we need?" asked Harry

"Three, four maybe should do it."

"Partially assembling the pieces to finish the diadem will carry over into the fourth day."

Harry said, "That leaves the ruby crystals."

"As soon as we get back to your flat, I'll call my old friend Herr Adalfredo Leder in Idar- Oberstein, and have him overnight me a few synthetic ruby boules – he'll know where to find them. Synthetic ruby boules are made by at least a dozen houses. I'll tell him my appreciation will far out weigh the cost of the boules and mail costs. A thousand marks will be in overnight international mail as soon as I receive them. He'll believe me. And once I have the boules, a lapidary trade shop I use, will slice and cut the rubies to the identical shape of the rubies in Davies' photographs.

"You know Fritz, you never really explained to me how synthetic rubies are made and I'd really would like to know."

"Okay my son. But bear in mind synthetic rubies and sapphires are used in huge markets around the world; industry, military and jewelry. We're just expanding it into a new questionable business."

Harry laughed aloud.

"The source for our synthetic rubies begins with the Verneuil oven or the chalumeau as the French prefer to call it. The chalumeau is essentially a stationary oxyhydrogen blowpipe that melts finely powdered purified aluminum oxide as it falls through the flame. To maintain the flow of the powder, the container holding the powder is tapped at regular intervals from above. The powder falls on a heat resistant clay rod in the furnace chamber and forms a pyramid of alumina. The powder continues to melt and flow forming a solid red crystal. Hence the ruby boule."

"What do they weigh Fritz?"

"My guess is anywhere from five hundred carats to a thousand carats. The ones I've seen are about one inch thick."

Harry said, "Very interesting. So how does one determine the real from the synthetic?"

"Only by magnification. Other then natural inclusions, genuine stones have straight internal growth lines. Synthetic growth lines are slightly curved. Often the curving is so slight, they appear to be straight. A trained gemologist has no problems detecting curved growth lines. When I receive the boules and after they're cut, I'll quench-crackle them myself just to be safe."

Harry let out a roar of laughter. "You are kidding, no? Quench-crackle wasn't that a ruse they used in Europe years ago?"

"You know the game Harry. I'm proud of you. Unscrupulous dealers trying to make a synthetic ruby or sapphire look like a real one would heat the stone with a jeweler's torch to a certain temperature, then plunge the stone into a saturated liquid solution. And as a result of going from hot to cold, the stone would crack internally and the solution would crystallize into the cracks. Forgetting growth lines, the stone would then appear to have natural inclusions and fractures. In our case, it would be the perfect procedure. After all, quench-crackle stones have misled many a jeweler, especially the greedy and careless ones."

Harry said, "And what about those wretched suckers on the street who bought synthetic gems for genuine? But I must say, in this case the beauty of the scheme is in its simplicity although there are many parts that need to come together."

"True what you say Harry. But after I have the particular sections finished and assembled, set the rubies, and connect everything, I defy anyone to call it a phony."

Harry asked, "Using Edgar's photographs as your guide, what does the final phase consists of?"

Fritz pointed to the green leather binder sitting in front of Harry. "In the photographs, it's obvious that the ancient goldsmiths made each section flexible because high-karat gold is uniquely soft so if the crown were made stiff, it would bend not flex, and would eventually break apart. What they did was to make it flexible, was put two heavy gold wire links between each section and bend them closed – no soldering I'll do the same with heavy wire. The rubies of course, are held in place by simple wire prongs, and don't forget, even though the original is several hundred years old, and making it might sound complicated to the layman, it's still a relatively easy thing to make."

"Right Fritz and a thorough knowledge of jewelry making don't hurt either," Fellows said with sarcasm. Then he asked, "What do you figure our final cost will be from beginning to end including gold, material, labor and your flights back and forth?"

Barrow thought for few moments, then said, "Twenty to thirty grand at the most."

Harry said, "Okay. There are three problems to be dealt with. One: The diadem was stolen months ago. My experience of the brand of thief I think we're involved with will give police, maybe, several months to work the case. I've seen this time after time. Whether it be stolen art, jewelry, There comes a tome when the case goes cold. A formula always comes into play. On top of it, several months of being jerked around, the museum people will begin to get more than a bit jumpy and begin a full court press to see what Lloyd's has in mind for paying up. The crooks know this just as well as I do and there's always the possibility they might make contact directly with the museum, though I don't think they'll deal directly with the thieves since the piece is covered by insurance.

"Now for the number two problem: Normally, the crooks come to Lloyd's. On the surface, this is simple heist. No third parties to deal with. Lloyd's approved the museum's security plus the diadem is clearly the museum's property. And Lloyd's has the payoff money. But I'm pushing them into action with my personal columns in the Milan newspapers. Negotiations normally can last a few days especially if we're dealing with a lunatic fringe wanting to buy guns and bombs. Hopefully these crooks are old-fashion robbers and know what they're doing. They know not to stall too long after we've contacted them; I'll tell them to go fence it to some wealthy collector, though it will bring them a lot less money. Which is to our advantage. They either move on it, or they can shove the diadem were the sun don't shine."

Barrow said, "So you and I have until the twenty-third if the formula still holds true; we finish then present our diadem to Lloyd's, make a deal with Jamison, and collect the ransom money. If the thieves want to move before then, we've had it."

Harry said, "Then there is problem number three. We must keep our ersatz home-made diadem out of the hands of J. Edgar Davies"

Fritz Barrow then said, "Harry, now for my sixty-four thousand dollar question. Please explain to me why in the devil must we go to so much trouble and expense in re-inventing the diadem, when we can deal our own imitable way with the crooks, repossess the crown, make a nice tidy amount via the crooks and a commission from Lloyd's just by handing over the original diadem? After all, Jamison chose his celebrated ex- investigator to deal with the thieves."

Harry said, "A sensible question Fritz, a question that I knew would be coming. What I intend to do Fritz, once having been contacted, is to tell this group of bandits they're late in coming. That I've already been contacted and have actually seen the diadem, yours of course, and am in the process of negotiating a price for it – so take your little scam and shove it!"

*   *   *

It is one of the less subtle signals of being past middle age – it is called quick fatigue. In spite of an energetic mind and a drive to work, in spite of Harry wrestling with his brain's white matter, he could no longer keep in check his wanting to nap. A nap, even fifteen minutes could cleanse his tiredness away. He closed his eyes, placed his head in the crook of his arm and quickly dozed.

After ten minutes Fritz, shook gently Harry's arm. "We really must be going old boy. I need to make that call to Herr Leder. *Fugit irreparabile tempus.*"

Harry opened his eyes; blinked several times. He then clumsily slid his chair back, still half asleep. Fritz took hold of his arm to steady him. Harry said, "Let us be on our way Fritz, what the devil are you waiting for? And please release my arm." Harry smiled, totally aware that he awoke groggy. Shortly hereafter the men walked briskly out of the hotel, the doorman hailed a cab, and the pair headed for Harry's Ebury Lane Flat.

CHAPTER THIRTEEN

From the moment he left Harry's flat and boarded the Delta flight to back to New York City, Fritz Barrow had put together all the savvy and composure he could draw upon to make certain the diadem project would move along expeditiously and quietly until completion.

As each step of completion was achieved, each person that contributed was given credit to his particular craft by a sizable cash bonus. *"How else can one show one's appreciation,"* he thought sitting behind his shop desk.

Barrow now anxiously waited for the final section of the crown to be delivered to his shop. He looked at the wall clock for the hundredth time. A buzzer sounded. He looked at the closed circuit monitor. "It's me Albie," the voice said.

It was Albie Soler looking straight into the overhead camera. Relieved, Fritz let out a large puff of air and buzzed the door open. He then hurriedly passed through the door of his shop, locking it behind him. Once inside the receiving foyer Fritz said, "Albie, I can't tell you how much I appreciate you putting in the extra time and bringing it to me."

"My pleasure Barrow, glad I could do it. It happened to be an interesting job. I can't remember when I worked from a photograph with almost pure gold. Probably never." He then handed Fritz a large wrapped package. "Plenty of bubble inside Fritz." Fritz put his arm around Albie's shoulder and apologized for being in such a hurry. From his pocket he handed Albie a white envelope stuffed with hundred dollar bills. "Five grand and thanks Albie. Go on and count it."

"Not necessary Fritz. I've known you too long."

With that said Fritz pulled the door open, said goodbye and hurried back into the shop. Then slowly, ritualistically, opened the box. It was now in his hands; the main piece, the frontispiece, the final part. He went to his workbench and deftly set the last and largest ruby crystal into the center of the diadem. All thirteen sections were complete and ready to be assembled into one bogus Greek crown. He checked each part carefully making certain there were would be nothing to give him trouble when he completed the final task of putting it all together in London. He would have loved to have completed it in his own shop, but to chance carrying an ancient Greek Crown made of twenty-two karat gold and uncut rubies through British Customs, and not be questioned by airport police would top all definitions of insanity.

After a thorough inspection, Fritz began packing the pieces by size sequence in two different boxes – each piece, bright and shiny, was wrapped in bubble - each box marked "Reproduction Jewelry Samples" his business card carefully attached. With the packing chore complete, he studied his watch then phoned Bonnie Adele. She was on her way; about ten minutes away from his shop.

The plan was uncomplicated: Bonnie would take one of the boxes, fly out of Kennedy, and land at London' Gatwick Airport - Fritz would leave from LaGuardia, and land at London's Heathrow. Later, they would meet at the Heathrow Bus Terminal. Bonnie would then taxi to Heathrow, not Gatwick; fly back to New York. Harry might be upset that he couldn't see her, but an agreement was an agreement and though at times its logic seemed questionable, it had to be kept - at least that's the way Bonnie felt.

After Bonnie left the huge bus terminal, Fritz called Harry on his cell aware that Harry's home phone telephone now bore an extension to his temporary Windsor office. Moments later he relayed the good news avoiding any language that might be questionable to an errant listener. Fritz adding he would be leaving the bus terminal for London and Ebury Lane by taxi and was looking forward to a good bottle of champagne.

*   *   *

At Harry's request, Miles Jamison had moved Harry into a small second-floor office close to the front stairs in the old management building. Though tiny, the office contained the few essentials Harry had requested; the most expensive being a telephone line that would ring simultaneously in the new office and his own Ebury flat.

There was an outdated Rand McNally atlas and an Oxford dictionary stood side-by-side on an old badly treated large Chippendale side table. "*God knows where that came from?*" he thought with a smile. There was a hot plate and an old tea kettle. A calendar hanging crooked depicted a large Russian-blue cat sleeping in a huge pink blossomed begonia plant.

He wanted a surge protector for his laptop, a comfortable leather chair with an adjustable foot rest. Alhough it was uncertain that the thieves would contact Lloyd's, Jamison was thrilled that Harry wanted to be close by.

Harry stood in the doorway staring into the dismal room realizing dispassionately that the British truly only admired the high-born – they were unmoved by the ordinary man. "*Keep the bloody buggers in place,*" he once heard a well-to-do land owner tell his wife concerning people living in the nearby village. The same chap generously offered his estate's day old bread to the outdoor staff.

Harry tried the chair; he pushed the foot rest out and closed his eyes. "Great," he said. He had heard from his friend Stanley Need that the leather chair had come from Grant Merlyn's office.

Grant Merlyn was Lloyd's man in charge of rates for insuring museum and large gallery exhibitions of provenance merit – apparently, Jamison was letting Merlyn know that he was being punished by removing his chair; a punishment of sorts for not spotting the over-insured value for the Milan Museum's diadem. Merlyn had let on to Stanley Need, also a Lloyd's appraiser, that the premium, though maybe a bit excessive, was received with smiles by the review board before the theft. Harry smiled at the shenanigans that still existed in large corporate institutions.

Harry suspected that Miles figured he'd be using the office for no more than one week - Fellows figured the same amount of time. Suddenly, events were on the move. On the side table was a folder labeled 'Diadem'. Davies had brought Harry the massage; Fellows clipped it to the front of the folder. It was a handwritten message undoubtedly from the crooks that read: "Are you ready to deal for the gold crown. If so, place a personal column in two Milan newspapers." The message was left at Lloyd's London office.

Also clipped to the folder was the hand written copy of Fellow's own personal ad he had placed in the evening's personal columns of two Milan newspapers. It read: "Odd, *I have possession - la corona de oro. Take a hike.*"
Signed
Harry F. Lloyd's Windsor Office

Making sure the door was locked, Harry was about to cut wires and remove any electronic activity from the phone line – when the ringing caught him by surprise. He hadn't anticipated such a hurried response … there was an unexplainable tenseness with each ring tone.

"This is Harry F," he answered.

"Listen my friend" the caller said with a trace of an eastern European accent, "About the Greek diadem -"

Harry interrupted quickly, "Sorry to cut in friend, but I need you to call me at another number in five minutes. A matter of privacy. The number is …."

Five minutes after Harry had dismantled the Lloyd's extension line, Harry's new cell phone vibrated. Harry immediately pressed the answer button.

"Who is this?" Harry asked.

"The man who is looking at a Greek diadem belonging to the Milan Museo."

The moment had arrived. Harry felt good that his plan was beginning. Harry said, "Really. That must make two. Though the circumstances weren't to my liking, I've already seen and held the diadem and am negotiating the ransom money. Fact is when you rang, I thought it was them. So if this is attempted scam forget it. I wasn't born yesterday."

The caller paused. Fellows also remained silent aware that of the two, it was himself coming from the best position of strength – at least for the time being."

The caller said, "I do not know what is going on, but I do know one thing for sure, you weren't born yesterday. The original diadem when compared to that piece of shit you say you have will raise many questions that will need to be answered."

"Such as?" Harry asked trying not to lose control of his voice.

"Like who verified its genuineness. What bull shit! Perhaps we can avoid the embarrassment to your company and to you."

"You're forgetting one thing Mr. Camel Jockey."

"Which is what, you English faggot?"

"You will be confessing to robbery, extortion, assault and battery, destruction of private property, and god knows what else those garlic eating Guineas will come up with. So let us get to the point. I should believe you and assume the crooks who showed me the diadem are double crooks. What is it you want Mr. -"

"Dimitri. The name is Dimitri."

"I repeat, what is it you want Mr. Dimitri.?"

"Let us meet face-to-face."

"Why is that Mr. Dimitri? "

"You're negotiating for a knock-off, a reproduction if you prefer a different word, of a valuable antique from some con-artist. That is not going to sit well with your superiors, especially when the museum slaps all of you with a major lawsuit for being party to a fraud should you bring this phony diadem to them to shake off the insurance payout. You think they will be so excited to have it back; they will simply take you at your word that it's the real McCoy."

"Possibly."

"Go to your boss Harry F, tell him the problem that has developed. Make me an offer to buy the original back; and you can be sure Mr. Harry F, my only interest is the money. If you try and fuck me, I will anonymously mail, and carefully explain in a letter along with new photographs what they see in their possession is a phony. My name will be excluded, there will be no confession. I'll simply do it for vindication, vengeance if you like. Then there's always the chance they might want to meet my charges and make arrangements to see it, and then make an offer – by then the price will be more than the insured value. All else can be done without the police."

"It would be foolish for me to meet with you and show you the diadem. It has been compared to the original appraisal papers and has passed inspection with high marks. I could also deploy the police to jump you before you can say sausage pizza."

"Believe me Harry F, you are leaving yourself and Lloyd's open for many future problems and questionable business practices, that is, if you decided to rat me out for one reason or another. I don't think you would. You're too smart. Also the word is you can be trusted."

Harry said, "Two questions. How is it you know so many English words and phrases Mr. Dimitri?"

Harry F. do you recall many years ago there was an antique shop on Bond Street called Dimitri's."

"Yes, of course I do. Is that you? Your shop was known in the trade and in tabloids as the crying Dimitri's. If a customer couldn't be sold, the salesperson would begin to cry and tell absurd ridiculous stories about illness, blindness, and cancer in the family, and if certain sales numbers were not made they could be fired as the consequence."

The caller said, "The whole Dimitri family were professional criers and it worked well for many years."

Harry laughed aloud. "Then there was the story about the deaf uncle."

Now the man on the telephone laughed.

Harry said, "Yes, dear Uncle Anastas. I remember the name. A customer would ask the price of a certain article. The salesman would say it just went into inventory. He would then shout to someone in the back and ask the price of the item. The person in the back, your Uncle Anastas, would answer by saying sixteen hundred pounds. 'What? The salesman would say, I still can't hear you.' They would go through this routine about twice; Uncle Anastas would always holler sixteen hundred pounds. The salesman would then apologize for being hard of hearing and tell the customer the price was six hundred pounds. The customer, thinking about a thousand pound mistake and a huge discount, would jump on the piece immediately - most likely it had a real selling price of much less then six hundred pounds.

Dimitri said, "You have the persons reversed. It was my uncle who pretended to be deaf. Makes no difference now. Then we had that tragic fire. It wiped us out. There wasn't enough insurance money to stay in the glamour district of Bond Street, so we opened in Soho. But that was short lived. My uncle died. Irony was such he lost his hearing in his later years. The cousin in the back went to jail for smuggling guns into Wales and selling them to the Irish, another crying Dimitri cousin converted to orthodox Christianity which left me figuring out a way to support me and my family. So I began stealing antiques, found more cousins to help me, and was able to locate buyers through my Albania connections. The diadem was just waiting to be stolen. It was housed out of the main building in a secluded wing near to a store room which was close to a delivery door. The rest, the authorities have figured out."

Harry spoke slowly, "Dimitri. If Lloyd's and I should happen to agree after examining your crown that what you say is true, and I tell these other scammers to take a long walk off a short pier, and Lloyd's decides to offer a settlement, obviously neither of us would want a dragged-out negotiation, what would be the amount of money you have in mind?"

Dimitri responded, "I have my cousins to pay, other expenses. Five hundred thousand pounds would be an acceptable figure."

"Half a million pounds? Impossible and utterly ridiculous," Harry blurted into the phone. "And how in bloody hell do I know what you're telling me isn't another Dimitri scam?"

Harry now eagerly waited for Dimitri's response thinking, "*What in bloody hell did J. Edgar Davies miss? His description was flawless. The photographs didn't lie. Fritz's crown matched Davies photographs exactly.*"

Dimitri said, "Inside the original, barely to be seen are Greek engravings. Unless you know they're there, they remain concealed and can only be seen under certain lighting. Dionysius is mentioned somehow."

"*Fuck!*" Harry thought, and remained silent for a long moment. The cat stared out at him from its position on the wall calendar. Harry then said quietly, "My office is in Windsor. I'll leave for London by train. In about two hours, I will walk the perimeter of St. James Park. I'll be carrying an umbrella that will have a blue ribbon tied to the handle."

Dimitri said, "Even though I have nothing to fear, please understand Harry F., it would prove to be unhealthy for you if the police are involved. Now for the second question, yes?"

Harry asked, "Why have you waited so long to come forth?"

Dimitri said, "What are a few lousy months when lots of money is involved? When it comes to kidnapped art, desperation can push things to a best conclusion."

As soon as the conversation ended, he called Fritz and explained what he had to do.

Harry had walked for about twenty minutes and felt somewhat light headed. He was worried: there wasn't enough time to plan an escape route. A neighbor from his building approached with a warm greeting. Harry never slowed his pace, simply nodded and kept walking. It was few minutes later he heard the familiar voice of Dimitri from behind. It was businesslike and pleasant.

"Keep walking Mr. Harry F.," he said. Please don't turn around. Take the path to your right and walk to the sidewalk. There is a green Jaguar parked next to a lamp post. Seat yourself in the rear. You will be going for a short ride. I will be right here when you return."

Harry did not like the idea of getting into a strange automobile. But figuring there was no way of Dimitri knowing if he had an accomplice watching and taking down the license plate number, Harry decided to chance it.

Fifteen minutes later, after a complex circuit of turns and running through red lights, the Jaguar slowed and came to a stop in front of a small group of attached shops in the Marleyborne district. A short chap with oversized sunglasses and wearing a yellow stocking cap opened the rear door and sat next to Harry. He then placed the box he carried onto Harry's lap. He then proceeded to remove its top. "This is the real diadem," the short man said. The driver then started the car and began to drive slowly.

"*Good Lord*," Harry thought. "*That damn Fritz Barrow is positively a genius.*" Lifting and studying the crown, Harry came to the quick conclusion that the one Fritz had put together looked better then the one he held. He felt giddy and wanted to laugh. The driver then passed to Harry a black flashlight and a readers magnifying glass. "This has a 4000 LED light wave. Shine it in the diadem, and use the magnifying glass, and you'll see the markings that Dimitri told you about."

There was no question about it. There were scores of words and symbols that ran along the inside base of the crown. So faint were they, that Harry figured it would take hundreds of hours to decipher each letter and symbol. If Davies appraised the crown under normal lighting conditions, there was no way he could have observed such intricate details.

One hour later, Harry was sitting next to Dimitri on a park bench. After Harry properly introduced himself, as did Nicky Dimitri, Dimitri said, "I was born in a village outside of Tirana where we lived for many years. My father, once a carpenter, was paralyzed from the waist down; a shooting accident; he had no proper wheelchair. Bicycle wheels, without rubber tires attached to a chair gave him some mobility. Otherwise, my mother, a very pretty woman, spent the entire day attending his needs if you follow. At night she went into Tirana and sold herself. I would lie on my mattress and pretend to sneak across the border into Greece and steal money and treasures from the homes of wealthy people. These were elaborate, complicated plans coming from the mind of an unhappy child with a father who was a cripple and a mother who was a whore. Now, here we sit discussing payment of a half million pounds for a stolen piece of gold. My dream of stealing treasures is a reality. Laughable is it not? Irony is it not?"

Harry said, "I jolly well understand old chap, that to you this strictly a business transaction. Yet you are still taking risk by trusting me not to involve you.

"I trust you because I know that you are a smart private detective, ready to retire, not a dumb policeman. Chances are we will never have an encounter again, plus I'm going to give you a share of the money."

"A bribe! Dear me Nicky, I say, that's not cricket you know."

"Go then," said Dimitri getting to his feet. "Tell your superiors the story. Have your reply in place by tomorrow noon. I'll call at noon time. If the answer is no, the diadem will be in the hands of some thieving collector two or three days from now. Thank you and goodbye."

"Dimitri. Listen to me. Before I do anything, I'm going to ask the would-be scammers to show me the crown one more time. I will not mention the ancient markings – I'll make my judgment when and if I return alive."

Fifteen minutes later, before going to his flat, Harry stood alone at the bar of the Goring Excelsior Hotel drinking a double whiskey, neat."

*   *   *

"Trust me old boy. The original diadem stolen from the museum compared to yours is the fake, not taking into consideration the mysterious markings that an untrained eye could not detect without a high intensity light and magnifier plus knowing where to even look."

Fritz said, "I do trust your eye Harry. But that's what makes the original so fantastic. The ancients didn't have the lost wax method of centrifugal casting or controls for melting gold at a precise temperature. There were no vulcanizers, vacuums or burning ovens. They did it all by hand; piece by piece with tools fashioned from hard wood. It was pure art Harry."

"You too are an artist Fritz."

"Please Harry, I appreciate the compliment, but more important than all of this, it's your friendship and the friendship of Bonnie Adele that I value most. Now what about this character Nicky Dimitri?"

"He's a genuine whack job. Damaged from childhood. Definitely not all there, but what crook isn't crazy to some degree. Personally I don't like him. But he is serious about his intentions. If we don't pay up, the real diadem goes to some unknown person. Not a good idea. I feel we give him the half, we keep the other half."

Fritz said, "I agree as long as he thinks the money is coming from Lloyd's, we're safe. But from what you told me, I'm bothered about the comment that he knew you were a PI and ready to retire. You don't talk about retirement except to annoy Miles Jamison. Someone told Dimitri, and he used the information just to be a smart ass."

"Rossini," Harry blurted out. The night we all had dinner at Rossini's restaurant; Bonnie was telling us about the virtues of Chianti. She said to me, 'I hope you remember that Harry when you retire.'"

Fritz said, "It was your friend Rossini who overheard us when he meandered near to our table."

Harry snapped his fingers. "Of course! That's it. They're two bloody thieves. Dimitri probably uses Rossini to fence some of his stolen goods. He might have asked Rossini if he knew a Harry F. that possibly worked for Lloyd's."

Fritz said, "Rossini says sure. I know the guy, he put me in jail. He's now a PI ready to retire. You're right Harry, that's the connection. But Harry, one more thing. We cannot allow Dimitri to set up the meet for this exchange. Tell him only you can set up the meeting. If Dimitri says no way, then we can speculate he's looking to take you out."

Fellows now had a worried look on his face.

The next day, Barrow and Fellows were sitting just staring at each other when Harry's new cell began to vibrate.

"Hello, this Harry."

"It's me, Nicky Dimitri. What's the story Harry?"

Harry replied, "It comes down to this Nicky. Though I was insulted by your offer to take a bribe, the exchange can take place. The other diadem is definitely a fake. Five hundred thousand pounds, all cash for you, I get the original diadem. No police, no problems."

"When?"

"The money is ready."

"You remember where the Jaguar waited -"

Harry jumped in, "Not a chance Nicky. I make the call where the exchange takes place."

Fellows waited for the long silence to end.

"Where and when?" asked Dimitri, his voice showing irritation.

"In two hours. Kew Gardens. In front of the Dutch House. A man will be sitting on a park bench close to the House. He'll be wearing a blue French beret and sunglasses. There will be a sports bag next to him. The money is in the bag. He'll allow you to take a peek. Then look around; I'll be close by. Approach, hand me the box with the diadem. I'll signal the man and he'll walk away from the bench. The bag is all yours. Nicky, there is a third unobserved person. If anything happens that shouldn't, that third person will put a bullet into your spine and you can look forward to living in a wheel chair for the rest of your life like your old man. Irony no?"

"You are a very clever PI. Mr. Fellows. Two hours, Kew Gardens."

CHAPTER FOURTEEN

Harry sat back in Grant Merlyn's borrowed chair and speculated the best way to proceed. He scowled. The door opened suddenly without a knock. It was J. Edgar Davies.

"Oh, sorry Harry. I was going to leave this note. Miles has had an indigestion attack of sorts… nothing serious so I'm told; however, my opinion is lately Mile's has been drinking too much, probably using medications that irritate the stomach lining, being overworked, and having ongoing stress can also cause indigestion. He's is the Princess Margaret Hospital right here in Windsor. He asks that I take up his duties until he returns. He referred to the missing crown as one of his major concerns. You know Harry; it might be a good idea if I had your new cell phone number."

*   *   *

Sunday

Harry awakened early, no alarm clock necessary – he hastily got ready for the day ahead, put on his Vicuna overcoat, and managed to catch the 6:30 at Sloane Square Tube Station for the forty minute journey to Lloyd's Windsor Offices.

Harry climbed the outside steps, walked a short distance to where his office was and paused before opening the door. It took a moment for his eye to locate a tiny bit of paper he had carefully wedged into the door jamb. Once inside, after hanging up his Vicuna coat and turning on the overhead light, he again checked to see if anyone had entered. Satisfied, nothing had been disturbed, he left the office, went back down the steps, walked across the deserted quadrangle to the employee's cafeteria to have a buttered scone and a hot cup of Earl Grey. Little more than that was served on a Sunday morning

Alan G. Davis

It was 8:00 when J. Edgar Davies approached Harry's table. He pulled out a chair and sat down looking suspiciously around the room.

"What's going on Edgar?" Harry joined in looking around.

"Harry, Lord, I'm glad I found you. We were contacted earlier this morning. A muffled voice, that of a woman possibly. We think she might be Eastern European. She left a message on the switchboard recorder for Harry F. Part of it is all of it in English. Davies handed the transcribed note to Fellows.

"Harry F. *We're ready to negotiate.*"

Harry motioned for Edgar's pen and wrote on a paper napkin his reply. He handed it to Edgar. "Have this personal ad phoned in for the next available editions of the Milan newspapers. To be run only one time. And Edgar please call me when you have verification when it will appear." *Be quick. Tempus fugit.*"

Edgar said, "Harry, I must be honest. I thought the idea of personal columns would be a waste of time. I bow to your expertise and sharpened instincts one more time. I'm sure this good news will get Miles out of the Princess Margaret and back into the fold pronto."

Harry said, "One of the unexplainables of life Edgar, is there are no logical clarifications when it comes to one's instinct. And don't cut yourself short Edgar. Your instincts happen to be exemplary." *God only knows,*" Harry pondered as he watched Davies walk away, "*how all this is going to play out. Poor Edgar is going to have to deliver the ransom money to Fritz.*" Harry shrugged and shook his head. "*At least we're not spies or murderers – are we Lord?*"

Monday

It was 5:00 p.m. when Edgar Davies knocked on Harry's office door and walked in. Davies handed a sealed envelope to Fellows. It was addressed: "Harry F c/o Lloyd's, Windsor.

"Harry, this was delivered by hand; given to one of our maintenance people as he was walking away from his car. How can it not be from the thieves?"

"Let's open it and find out together," Harry said politely handing the envelope back to Edgar."

Using the blade from a tiny red Swiss Army knife attached to his key ring, Edgar slit the top of the envelope open and carefully removed the folded page along with two Polaroid pictures. Both showed the fake diadem. One was sitting on the previous days' front page of the London Times. The second displayed the diadem next to an electric melting pot used by refiners to melt precious metals – usually scrap gold or silver. Davies studied the photographs for several minutes. "This is the diadem Harry, no question about it."

Harry silently took a deep breath – he wasn't sure if it was relief, or he was avoiding a surge of heartburn."

The contents of the letter read that one million British pounds was the nonnegotiable price for the safe return of the Greek crown. It went on to read that they would contact Harry F according to his instructions; instruction that were to appear in the same Milam newspaper's paper personal column.

*   *   *

Miles Jamison lay quietly in his hospital bed studying the pictures while Harry told him about his initial meeting with the Milan Museum thieves the evening before.

Miles said in raspy voice, "If this wasn't so bloody costly and dangerous, one could actually extract a bit of humor from all of this."

Standing next to Harry, Edgar Davies was rigid and tight lipped. Harry admired Jamison's cleverness, acumen or whatever one wanted to call it. Miles patted the edge of the edge of the mattress and signaled for Edgar to sit.

"So is there danger attached to this Harry?" Miles asked staring at the ceiling.

"I'd say their not the violent type, but then you never really know. They did put a pretty big knot on the head of a security man. But you know what Miles? I think they did it to try and create the impression that they are tough guys. I also think they're strictly educated amateurs reckless enough to steal and brilliant enough to pull it off successfully. Though, as I told Edgar before coming here, when they did turn down my counter offer for a half million pounds refusing to budge, and even though their faces were covered with ridiculous party masks, I did sense some relief in their apparent leader that at least there was an offer on the table. And let us not forget, they did have a Mauser automatic pistol aimed at my temple. You just never know just how crazy people like this can be." Harry then went silent.

"The crown Harry. The bloody crown. You are certain it's the one stolen from the museum?" Miles asked. This band of robbers sounds like something from an American silent movie."

Harry controlled his wanting to laugh. "Miles, I'm certain. I have studied Edgar's pictures and appraisal description for hours before meeting them in that deserted building by the docks."

"How could they have been so sure that you wouldn't bring the police?"

"Because as I told them, the chances are with police presence that someone was going to get shot or hurt at best. My only interest in the entire affair was getting back the diadem, returning it to the museum in one piece, saving my company money, getting my bonus, and walking away with all my limbs and senses intact."

Miles looked at Davies. "What's your opinion of all this Edgar?"

"The photographs I took which are an integral part of the appraisal will show the diadem exactly as I remembered it. Harry actually physically held the piece when he met with the thieves. You and I both have the utmost confidence in Harry. Miles I say let Harry work out the exchange details."

"There it is then," Miles rasped. "I'll make arrangements to get the cash. As soon as the diadem is in our hands, the three of us will fly to Milan and bring the damn thing back to the museum. Harry set up the exchange. Don't dawdle. Edgar, you get the papers ready for the museum people to sign – Lloyd's will no longer be insuring the bloody thing. Cite any reason the legal department can come up with. You might even talk to Grant Merlyn; he's full of nasty excuses. Now the both of you out of here while I convince my doctor to set me free from this wicked place.

*   *   *

The following morning at 10:00, Harry arrived at Windsor's front entrance. He went directly to the conference room - the duffle bag filled with the ransom money sat on the floor next to Edgar. A trolley with fresh coffee and scones had already been gone into by the security guard who had delivered the cash. Harry dismissed him from the room for the time being, having to explain to Edgar what the thieves had outlined for the exchange – he had received the ominous call at his flat late the evening before.

CHAPTER FIFTEEN

It was close to 1:00 a.m. when a nervous J. Edgar Davies sat behind the wheel of a company Ford Cortina parked on Mart Lane, a side street near to the Millwall Docks. Seated next to him was a calm Harry Fellows. A white linen handkerchief folded several times to make a narrow strip was tightly tied around the outside of the door's rear view mirror. Harry explained to Edgar that the handkerchief would make the vehicle easy to spot for the crooks. Both men had their windows open as per Harry's instructions.

Davies said in a whisper, "Bloody damn cold sitting like this. Do you think they will kill us Harry? Take the money and scram with the booty as they say in the movies. In the hospital you implied there was always a possibility of –"

"Edgar, just do what they tell us. Follow their instructions." Harry turned away lest Edgar see him smile.

"Harry, I hate to say this, but Miles had no right insisting that I come -"

"Edgar, it's you who Miles wants to make the determination that it be..."

"Everyone stay as you are," the voice from the outside said. At that instant, J. Edgar Davies felt cold metal the size of a shilling coin at the back of his left ear. "Don't move one fucking millimeter, look straight ahead," were the words that followed. "You, put you're your hands where I can see them." Edgar saw Harry quickly place his arms on the dash board. Davies could feel his heart pounding along with the pulse in his neck – thump, thump. He took a deep breath. *My God, don't get sick now.*

A box was dropped on Davies lap. A flashlight from outside the window shone onto the box – "lift the top off," the voice said. Davies looked down into the open box; it was the diadem, he had originally appraised - bright and shiny in the beam of light. The same voice said

– a disguised American accent to be sure Davies thought. "Now for the money!" the voice demanded.

Harry said, "The rear seat."

"Get it! Drop it out your window." Harry reached behind him, retrieved the suitcase and did what he was told – he dropped it out the window.

Edgar closed his eyes, ready to be shot. Harry's voice brought him back to his senses. "Is it the crown Edgar?"

"Jesus, I think so Harry. Yes."

*   *   *

It was 7:00 a.m. the same morning when Harry noisily entered his flat. Fritz was stretched out on the sofa.

"Did Davies die of a heart attack?" Fritz asked as he got to his feet and ran to Harry. They clasped hands.

Harry said, "He didn't die, but I nearly broke up when he asked if we were going to be killed. Then afterwards, when I drove away, he was lying prone on the back seat and he bloody-well never stopped taking about the danger he was exposed to, like it was okay for me to get murdered but not him. By the way, you were absolutely convincing Fritz.

"I told Edgar I'd drive. His nerves were unbalanced. It was the least I could do. As we were changing seats, I switched the two crowns. As soon as we met Miles back at our hotel, Davies was so delighted to hand over the box with the Diadem; he never mentioned the frightening misadventure, except to tell him in detail all that occurred. As Edgar went on with his story, I watched Jamison particularly close when he remove the lid and peered into the box. I could see no question marks in the old man's eyes, thank God. His trust in Edgar is such, that he never questioned him further."

Fritz said, "He was thrilled to have him back alive and well and with the damn crown."

Harry said, "You bet, and Bonnie will be thrilled getting her share of the loot. After all, she did deliver half the crown."

Fritz laughed.

Fellows raised his hand. "Fritz, this is important. Miles is sending a car with two armed security men at one o'clock tomorrow. The guards, Miles, Edgar and me are taking a three o'clock flight to Milan to return the diadem. It's about a five hour flight, so I figure we should have everything concluded before ten tomorrow night. The museum director has been contacted, and is thrilled. Jamison thinks they're going to have a small ceremony. The person in charge of antiquities will probably verify its authenticity.

"Anyway, the abbreviated story of the crown's recovery should appear in tomorrow's newspapers. Then the fun begins."

Fritz said, "I don't reckon the thieves will contact us again."

"Miles wants to return to England straight away and check himself back into the hospital – a deal he made with his physician. And as soon as we return to London, I'll hightail it back to Windsor and settle down in my office. My guess is they have a contact in Milan who will go to the museum, who will report back to the crooks that sure enough the crown is safely back in its glass covered home."

*　　　*　　　*

Excitement was high when Giuseppe Ponce de Leon carefully placed the diadem on its blue satin pad with the now impregnable see-through cover securely atop it. Security precautions were then immediately put into place amongst applause from those imbibing vintage Chianti. As in the movies, unseen beams protected the area surrounding the pedestal which once again supported the once lost treasure. That same evening as the five Englishmen were flying homeward, the Western European wire services were given the story regarding the successfully retrieved and safe return of an ancient Greek diadem.

The story in the Corriere della Sera, the daily newspaper of Milan, provided the following news report:

"... though no details were available from the Milan Museo sourcess at press time, the historical value of the diadem was described as gigantic at a small celebration led by Professor Stefan Tasso of the Greek Historical Society:

Antonio Jonivicinelli, assistant to the Museo's Director, commented, "The return of this ancient Greek treasure, in another singular achievement for the museum."

In the morning, hundreds waited for the museum to open to see the popular piece of ancient Greek history.

*   *   *

Lloyd's entourage arrived at London's Heathrow Airport Thursday morning as scheduled. Jamison, ignoring his doctor's advice, had suffered a severe gastronomic relapse after having an evening meal in the Airport that consisted of pasta and red anchovy sauce. While waiting in a wheelchair outside Customs for a chauffeured company car, Jamison dismissed the two security men with thanks and told them to take the rest of the week off - Friday and the weekend. Both Edgar and Harry couldn't help but turn away and smile at Jamison's generosity.

While waiting for the limousine, off to the side, out of ear shot of Harry, Jamison chatted with Customs Agent Bobby Teaneck who on several occasions had been privately employed by Lloyd's as an expert witness – Teaneck's testimony exclusively dealt with the unlawful entry of certain "art objects" into Britain.

Harry had known for years, that Lloyd's had taken advantage of this illegality by taking measures unethical and unscrupulous to find ways and means of avoiding some payments of claims. By exhibiting evidence that certain "art objects" entered the country without proper payment of duty, (possible smuggling charges imminent) it meant that many claimants, wanting to avoid the possibility of nasty inquiries, often dropped legitimate claims where there had been a hint that Lloyd's cooperating with the Office of Duty Collections and British tax by revealing signed clauses in policies to the effect that proper duty and taxes had been paid. Proud of it, it was one of the many connivance Miles Jamison adopted for the sake of his global company.

Shortly the chauffeur driven limo arrived and Miles cheerfully bid adieu to his friend Agent Bobby Teaneck

"I have something to tell you Miles," Harry said, walking along side the wheelchair as the limo-driver guided Jamison towards the car.

"I most likely will be moving away from London shortly. What, with the generous bonus promised me in this case and the bonus money from the Singhalese diamond fiasco, I think maybe it's high time for me to quit London, go somewhere and search for the meaning of life and maybe do a bit of salmon fishing in Scotland."

Miles held up his hand, signaling the chauffer to halt; he then began to cough and speak at the same time. "Harry you are daft! ... How can you think like this? Tomorrow I was going to make you an offer... it's bloody expensive paying out these bonuses... I want to put you on the payroll with a handsome salary ... we'll talk-"

"Careful sir," the driver piped in, "you're close to choking."

Upset by the man's interference, Miles began to cough – his face turned a light crimson. He was livid. He tried to speak but couldn't. Unobserved, Fellows placed a note in the driver's hand, turned away, quickly disappearing from sight.

Harry chose to forgo the limo ride back to Lloyd's. Instead, he boarded a bus outside the terminal building and settled in a seat for what now Miles Jamison and J. Edgar Davies would easily surmise would be his final trip to the Windsor offices. Harry figured that Miles small relapse would keep him in the Princess Margaret Hospital for a few more days which would keep Davies unusually busy dealing with unexpected routine matters. Harry smiled, closed his eyes, and fell asleep.

The note Harry that had pressed into the chauffeurs hand simply read: "Please give this to J. Edgar Davies -

Dear Edgar, beginning tomorrow, I need to be by myself after these hectic three days... not in the mood to listen to Jamison's whittling about my leaving. Speak to you soon."

Harry.

That same evening, while Miles was convalescing under starched white sheets, Harry sat comfortably in Miles office reading the first draft by Davies describing the events leading to the ransom payment. As was Davies' usual work, the report, which was to be presented to the Board, read sensibly and tidy with all the details void of drama. The Board would accept it with no questions asked.

Harry said, "Good job Edgar as usual."

"Thank you Harry, and Harry, after taking Miles back to Princess Margaret, he did mention that he will see that you get your money and bonus within the next few days."

*   *   *

The next day, Fritz and Harry sat staring at the Greek crown and money. They knew how to handle the money, what they didn't know, was what to do with Fritz Barrow's Greek crown.

Fritz said, "We could peddle it to someone in the Greek mafia; no?"

Harry said emphatically, "MALAKAS, NO!"

CHAPTER SIXTEEN

The inspection came just as Big Ben struck 4:00 p.m. Before the fourth 'dong' disappeared into space, four official cars and a score of Inspectors from the Westminster Fire Brigade including a large red fire truck, City of Westminster Code Enforcement, and Westminster City Council's Food Inspection Service, all converged into Rossini's Restaurant. Red side walk police cones and yellow tape created a "no trespassing" warning. Inside, ten inspectors spent two hours going from front to rear writing up fifty-seven violations all of which having enough cause to close down the restaurant. The restaurant owner, Angelo Rossini stood on the sidewalk telling customers as they approached for their early bird specials why the restaurant had been closed by the police – claiming he was the target of misplaced vengeance by jealous competitors.

Harry and Fritz sat in a waiting taxi across the street from Rossini's watching the nasty scene that was taking place. Harry dialed a private phone number on his regular cell phone – it was call to Miles Jamison: Harry's message was left on an answering machine: "I say Miles thank you. I consider what you've managed to do for me a huge favor and please give my best regards to J. Edgar Davies." He then turned to Fritz. "Do you think Nicky Dimitri will be popping by for dinner?"

THE END